The Prince Kidnaps A Bride

CHRISTINA DODD

An Imprint of HarperCollins*Publishers*

HarperCollins books may be purchased for educational, business, or sales
promotional use. For information, please write: Special Markets Depart-
ment, HarperCollins Publishers, 10 East 53rd Street, New York, NY
10022.

FIRST EDITION

ISBN: 978-0-06-134090-1
ISBN-10: 0-06-134090-1

Printed in the U.S.A

10 9 8 7 6 5 4 3 2 1

To Bernadette and Roberto—
Thank you for being so patient with me
through six years of learning to write.
I'd be lying if I said
that I enjoyed every minute,
but I'll never forget you
or what you taught me.

The Prince
Kidnaps A Bride

Prologue

From the time Crown Princess Sorcha was three, she prayed for a baby brother. A baby brother would be a prince and the heir to the throne of Beaumontagne, leaving Sorcha free to be like other children.

Well, not like other children, but at least like her sisters, who were mere princesses.

Unfortunately, to the little family's deep distress, when she was six, her queen-mother died bearing a third daughter.

So Grandmamma came to live with them.

Sorcha never forgot that day.

The opulent traveling coach drew up to the great door of the castle, and Grandmamma stepped out—ancient, tall, skinny, with regal bearing, a thick, carved cane, white hair, and cold blue eyes that froze Sorcha down to her bones. From that moment, Sorcha grew up under the direct glare of Grandmamma's critical gaze. Of course, Grandmamma also made sure that Princess Clarice and Princess Amy were supervised to within an inch of their lives—no one could accuse Grandmamma of shirking her duties—but it was Sorcha who occupied most of her time and attention.

Grandmamma approved Sorcha's tutors and made sure that Sorcha was taught everything a crown princess should know—language, mathematics, logic, history, music, sketching, philosophy, and dance.

She made sure that the elderly archbishop of the church of Beaumontagne visited every Sunday, rain, snow, or shine, to teach the princesses their religion, and when he left, Grandmamma personally drilled Sorcha on her catechism.

She instructed her in geography, showing her maps and demanding she know rivers, mountains, and seas. Somehow, Grandmamma managed to make tiny Beaumontagne, perched on the spine of the Pyrenees between Spain and France, sound like a center of culture and learning—in fact, the most important country in Europe.

In a private weekly session, Grandmamma taught Sorcha the art of governing, posing intricate crises that would face a queen and demanding Sorcha unravel the problem. Grandmamma made Sorcha argue law, taking either side as Grandmamma required and with Grandmamma as her opponent. And Grandmamma never let an occasion pass without reminding Sorcha that the crown princess and the crown princess alone was responsible for the continuation of the Beaumontagnian royal line.

From Sorcha, Grandmamma demanded perfection.

Which was why, at the age of twenty-five, Sorcha found living in a convent on a tiny, rocky, barren island off the isolated coast of Scotland a freedom she cherished. Her duties there were simple. She prayed. She read. She gardened. She wore a brown habit. To differentiate her from a novice, she wore no headdress, and because she was a princess of Beaumontagne, the silver cross of her church hung on a chain around her neck.

She kept the plants alive in the greenhouse in the winter and in the garden in the summer. She ate with the nuns and slept in her bare little room. And after so many years of listening to Grandmamma's voice nagging on and on, she cherished the silence.

Yet one night almost three years ago, she had had a dream.

A dream? No, it had been more than a dream. It had been a vision of unremitting darkness...and empty years.

The air was foul. The indifferent stones closed in around her. No voice disturbed the silence. No hand reached out to bind her wounds or cure her pain. The bones of rats were her bed and the long drape of cobwebs her blanket.

She was buried alive.

And she didn't care. Somewhere close, water seeped into a pool, and the slow drip which had once driven her mad now contributed to her indifference. Her world was sorrow and loneliness. She was dying, and she welcomed the end of desolation, of grief, of anguish.

Her fingertips touched the skeletal hand of Death....

Sorcha woke with a start and a horrified gasp.

The cross she wore around her neck seared her chest. She wrenched it from beneath her nightgown and in the darkness of her cell the silver gleamed like a blue coal. It blistered the palm of her hand, but she grasped it as tightly as she could, desperately needing its comfort. Sitting up in her bed, she trembled, gasping for air, wanting nothing so much as to breathe, to escape, to live!

And the first light of dawn shone in her cell, and the first seabird called its high, sweet call outside her window.

She ran to the window, wrapped her hands around the cold bars, and looked out at the ocean, trying to clear the remnants of that awful dream from her mind.

Yet she couldn't, and in all the time since, never had she regained her serenity. Day after day she found herself donning her brown wool cloak and wandering over the island as if seeking something.

Or as if something were seeking her.

Chapter 1

**On an island off the northwestern coast
of Scotland**

1810

Sorcha didn't really know what she was watching
for; she'd watched all summer and seen nothing
except for the passing of the bright, brief warmth. She
had seen the full moon at the end of October and then
a fortnight later she'd observed Mr. MacLaren's arrival
in the shallow harbor where, twice a year, he came from
the mainland to off-load supplies of meat, wine, and
cloth. She'd viewed the clouds of the first winter storm
that had roiled on the horizon, then roared over the
island like a greedy giant, thrashing at the sea, turning
it green and wild.

All of those events had been nothing more than the normal cycle of life on the island.

Today she walked along the rocky beach and picked up driftwood cast up from the storm. The waves still raked the shore and the clouds raced across the thin blue of the sky. Ice settled in hollows that never saw the sun. The wind whistled in her ears and caught at her clothes. Her red hair escaped her scarf and tossed around her face, and she blew it out of her mouth in disgust. She ought to go back, but the convent needed fuel for their meager fires, and besides, she felt as wild and restless as the sea.

She combed the length of the beach and piled bare, salty branches on the ragged old length of cloth. Then she stood still. If she looked in one direction, she saw only the thin line of the horizon where the ocean met the sky, but if she looked the other direction, she saw the Scottish mainland, a hump of brown and green. She hadn't set foot on the mainland in seven years, yet she couldn't shake the sense that something needed to be done.

The annoying logic Grandmamma had insisted Sorcha learn poked at her conscience like a hot embroidery needle.

Poppa was dead. He'd died in battle regaining his kingdom from the revolutionaries.

According to the newspaper Mr. MacLaren had brought, Grandmamma was in charge of the government of Beaumontagne and governing wisely.

Therefore, Grandmamma's trusted servant should have appeared to demand the return of their crown princess.

So where was Godfrey? Why hadn't the big, bald, muscle-bound messenger yet come?

In the ten years of her exile in England, Sorcha had seen Godfrey one time, when he came in the middle of the night to secretly remove her from the home of the exiled Beaumontagnian loyalists who sheltered her. On her desperate, hurried trip north, he'd warned her over and over that the war was going badly and that assassins sought to kill her. He insisted she must stay at the abbey until he came to tell her it was safe.

Now she had to wonder—was Godfrey dead? Was that why he hadn't come for her? Should she take matters into her own hands and go to Beaumontagne?

As she stared out at the whitecapped waves and contemplated going out into the world, she shivered in fear.

Grandmamma had given Sorcha the best education, but she had never been able to teach her courage.

A patch of sunshine moved across the water, turning it to blue, and as Sorcha watched, a movement caught her attention. She shaded her eyes with her hand and looked. A small unmanned fishing vessel drifted along, bobbing on the waves, and she clambered over the rocks, keeping it in sight, wondering if someone had been caught on the ocean during the recent storm and needed help.

That was one of their primary objectives at the convent, to render help to the hapless, stranded sailors who washed up on the shore—and pray for and bury the dead.

A current caught the boat and tossed it toward shore.

She looked around for a long stick, anything to use as a hook, but found nothing. "Come on," she urged the little vessel. "Come closer." For she didn't want to plunge into the icy waves to retrieve it, and duty, her ubiquitous duty, would require the sacrifice.

The skiff seemed to hear her, coming closer and closer. She climbed higher on the rocks, trying to peer inside, to see if a body lay sprawled on the boards... then, like an unruly child, the boat stopped and hovered just beyond the breaking waves.

"Don't stop now!" she shouted.

The boat bobbed a few feet farther out.

Throwing off her cloak and boots, she used the length of cord around her waist to tie up her skirts and with a grimace, she plunged into the waves. The freezing water snatched the breath from her lungs, stung her bare legs, weighed down her skirt. She fought the draw of the undertow, the slap of the surf, dragging herself toward the bow of the little boat. It slid toward her on a cresting wave; she grabbed at it and missed. She eyed the surf, judging her moment, and grabbed again. She caught the side of the boat, pulled herself up for a brief glance inside.

Nothing. No body.

She released a sigh of relief and worked her way up to the bow. Using the strength developed from long hours of physical labor at the convent, she dragged the vessel in to shore. The crunch of the wooden bottom on the sand was the sweetest sound she'd ever heard, and she groaned as she pulled it up on the beach, placing it well away from the greedy waves. Wiping her hands against her bodice, she turned—and a man loomed over her.

She screamed.

He jumped back. He wore coarse, damp, wrinkled clothes. He had big, broad shoulders. His pungent odor reminded her of rotten fish and seawater. A dark, scraggly beard rimmed his chin and a mustache overhung his upper lip. He'd tied a rag over his head and half his face.

He looked like a monster.

She screamed again.

"Don't do that!" He extended his rough, working-man's hands, palms up, and in a reproachful tone said, "You scared me."

"*I* scared *you?* You scared *me.*" She placed her hand over her racing heart. "Who are you?"

"I'm Arnou the fisherman." He spoke in English, but with an odd accent, an accent she couldn't quite place.

"What are you doing here?"

"I wanted that boat." He pointed and grinned like an idiot. "I've been watching it bob around the island. I thought it was a goner for certain. What you did was brave!"

In a flurry and a fury, she let down her skirts. "You mean you watched me?"

"Well...yes." He frowned as if puzzled. "What else should I do?"

"Help me?" Picking up her cloak, she flung it over her shoulders. Her teeth were chattering and the wind plastered her wet clothes to her frigid body.

"That water's cold. I didn't want to go in."

"But it was all right for me to do it?" Indignation rose inside her, but not even that could warm her.

"I didn't ask you to, but I'm grateful you did!"

Her indignation faded. The man was amiable, bumbling, and appreciative. He seemed like an affable little donkey except...well, he was big. Tall, muscular, with the hardness of body brought by years of too much labor and too little food.

Still he grinned, a big, stupid oaf who hadn't the sense God gave a pile of seaweed. "Guess I'd better pull the boat up on shore a little farther, eh?"

"I guess you should." She stomped her feet into her boots, groaning at the scrape of the sand against her skin and the cold ache that permeated her bones.

She didn't wait for him, but headed up the stairs cut into the rock. The wind pushed her up toward the lichen-covered walls of the convent and she hurried along with clumsy eagerness. She had to get inside—and fast. She'd started losing feeling in her fingers.

The strange man's odor caught up with her first, then she heard the stomp of his clogs. "So is this the famous Monnmouth Abbey that rescues sailors and sends them on their way?"

"Yes." How odd. He knew the name. Almost no one had heard of the abbey, and those who had, thought it was a sailors' myth.

"Do you live here?" The narrow stairway kept him behind her, but he was close, almost breathing down her neck.

"Yes." He would assume she was a nun. The men always did, and she let them believe the lie.

"With hair like that?" He chortled.

He set her teeth on edge. "What's wrong with my hair?"

"It's as orange as a carrot."

She swung around to face him.

He had that dim-witted grin on his face again.

"It is not!" She hadn't heard that stupid insult since the last time she'd met that superior beast Crown Prince Rainger de Leonides...and he was now dead.

"Has to be a carrot." The fisherman's brow wrinkled in earnest thought. "A beet is too red."

And not that she rejoiced in Rainger's death—if he hadn't been her fiancé, she could have ignored his smirk more effectively—but she hadn't missed being compared to a carrot.

She said a quick prayer for his soul and one for her own uncharitable thoughts. She turned away from Arnou, took two steps—and slipped backward on the slick rock. She flailed her arms. Tried desperately to gain her balance. Experienced the horrifying sensation of falling.

He caught her.

In fact, his hand must have hovered at the base of her spine, for in one smooth motion he grabbed her, set her on her feet, and helped her find her balance. Then, with a funny expression of mortification and distress, he wiped his hands on his shirt.

Two impressions struck her in swift succession—that he smelled much, much worse than she'd first realized, and that he was impossibly warm. "Who are you? What are you doing here?"

"I got caught in the storm." As if expecting a sudden gust, he looked up at the sky in alarm. "Aye, in the storm. It whistled and blew, and my boat sank."

"Your boat sank? What do you mean?" She pointed toward the skiff. "That's your vessel."

"No, it's not." He gave a decisive shake of his head. "Or it wasn't before now. Of course, if no one else claims it, it is mine."

"You said you wanted the boat, that you watched it bob around the island…." He *hadn't* said it was his skiff. She'd just assumed that it was. "Whose vessel is it?"

"Dunno. Someone who doesn't know how to secure his possessions, heh?" He chuckled.

Her gaze flicked to the boat, then to his face. "How did you get here?"

"I clung to the debris from my skiff and the wind blew me to your shore."

"Then where's the man who came with the boat?"

"I dunno. Maybe he fell out."

"You haven't seen any signs of another man?"

"No."

So a sailor *was* dead. She shivered and started toward the convent again. "How long have you been here?"

"A few hours."

"Why didn't you come right up to the convent?" The wooden gate rose before them.

"Because I wanted the boat." He was talking in circles.

She made an exasperated sound.

The fisherman lifted the great iron ring attached to the front of the gate and let it fall against the boards.

The sound echoed through the inner corridors.

Turning suddenly, she caught him staring at her through his one exposed eye, and for a single, frightening moment, nothing about him seemed foolish. Once again, he was a monster.

"Why do you wear that scarf over your face?" she asked sharply.

With an amiable grin, he tugged at his forelock. "I lost an eye. 'Tisn't a pretty sight, all red and scarred, so I keep it covered." He started to lift the rag. "Want to see?"

"No!"

From within the abbey, she heard a sound like the shuffle of dry leaves—she knew from experience a starched habit made just that noise. The door swung wide. An elderly nun stood back, her gaze lowered, her hands tucked into her sleeves.

"Sister Theresa, we have a traveler cast upon our shores." Sorcha stepped into the foyer. "Tell Mother Brigette he requests shelter until he can return to his own world."

At the sound of Sorcha's chattering teeth, dear Sister Theresa looked up. Her reserved demeanor fled and she crooned, "By our Lord, darlin', did ye fall in the drink? Hurry, we need to get ye warmed and bathed before ye catch yer death." She wrapped a dry blanket over Sorcha's shoulders and gave her a hug. "To the infirmary wi' ye!"

"Yes, Sister." Sorcha was in no condition to argue. Great shudders wracked her.

Now Sister Theresa looked at Arnou. She caught her breath at his stench. Pointing to an invisible spot on the floor, in a tone of pure steel-willed command, she said, "Ye! Traveler! Stand right there until someone comes to get ye. Don't move! Don't touch anything! And don't get anything dirty."

Arnou shuffled inside.

Sister Theresa joined Sorcha and helped her down the corridor. "Keep yer chin up, dear, we'll get ye there."

Sorcha nodded, knowing that in the infirmary heated bags of sand would warm her feet. Sister Rebecca, the infirmary director, would dose her with honey collected from the bees in Sorcha's own garden. Yet her footsteps dragged as she walked through the stripes of sunlight that shone through the high windows. She couldn't rid herself of the feeling she was abandoning Arnou.

"Miss!" he called in his rough voice.

She turned back to face him, ridiculously relieved at the chance to check on him once more. "Yes?"

He stood in the foyer where Sister Theresa had told him to stand, his neck craned, watching her with such desolation it seemed as if she walked away with his salvation in her hands. "I never asked your name."

"Sorcha." As she stared through the alternating light and shadow, something about him seemed familiar. The way he stood, his legs apart as if he laid claim to the very earth, his fist carelessly clenched at his hip. The way he held his head, his chin held at an arrogant tilt. And that eye…his unblinking, wide, and mesmerizing eye…it seemed as if in a long-ago dream Sorcha had seen his eyes, *both* his eyes, staring at her while the hand of Death reached out….

Sister Theresa squeezed Sorcha's arm.

Torn from her contemplation, Sorcha jumped.

"Dear," Sister Theresa said, "ye're going to catch yer death of cold if ye don't hie yerself to the infirmary."

When Sorcha again looked at Arnou, he grinned and bobbed his head. Again he was a simple, foolish fisherman.

Yet on her chest, the silver cross burned.

Chapter 2

The next morning, Sorcha stood with her hoe in her hand and watched Arnou as he hefted blocks onto the partly built low rock wall around the herb garden. His strength impressed her; it had taken three nuns and Sorcha, all their combined power, to budge a single stone. Yet he chipped and lifted and placed without ceasing, getting more work done since breakfast than Sorcha and the nuns had all summer.

He smelled much, much better—before Mother Brigette had allowed him to eat, she'd made him bathe. He also looked very silly—his clothes had been taken away to be cleaned and when they were boiled, they'd fallen to shreds. So Mother Brigette had given him a monk's humble brown robes. But they didn't fit his lanky frame, so his wrists stuck out of the sleeves and his calves stuck out beneath the hem. He wore the hood hanging down his back. The rag covered his eye and forehead and lent him the clownish air of a child playing blind man's bluff. His dark beard covered his cheeks and chin. Occasionally he looked up at the sun as if checking to see if it was still day.

Nevertheless, he toiled willingly, ate heartily, and grinned good-naturedly while waiting either for the owner to claim the boat or for Mother Brigette to grant it to him.

Sorcha wished Arnou would take the boat and row away. Yes, she needed the help in the garden, but somehow his presence contributed to her restlessness.

And why? He was just a fisherman. He knew nothing of Beaumontagne, of the palace with its long curved stairways and its marble columns, of the riding paths that wound through the mountains, of the primal woods and the thundering waterfalls. Beaumontagne...

Last night in her cell, she'd dreamed of home. She ran down endless palace corridors looking for her sisters, her father, her grandmother—and realized at last something hunted *her*. She had woken with her heart pounding and her senses humming. Sitting up, she'd stared at the high, small window in her door. She'd listened to the silence outside. She'd been convinced she had heard footsteps outside her cell. Slowly, timidly, she'd crept to the door.

The convent's buildings were arranged in an open square around the courtyard, with the chapel in the center of the complex and the meeting rooms and sleeping cells fanning out on the wings. Her cell was at the end of one wing, and when she peered out she saw the gardens wrapped in darkness, the starlit night, the setting moon. The wind moved the treetops, but on the ground, nothing stirred.

She heard no more footsteps, but she would have sworn—

"What do you think of him?" a composed, French-accented voice asked.

Startled, Sorcha turned to see Mother Brigette standing on the stone walk. Mother Brigette always moved with grace and deliberation, but Sorcha must have been deep in thought not to notice her approach. Removing her large straw hat, Sorcha turned it in her hands. "He's a good worker and we can always use help."

"Sister Theresa thinks he's touched." Seating herself beneath a twisted crab apple tree, Mother Brigette indicated the bench beside her. "Do you?"

"No, not at all." Touched? No! "He's just...easily distracted. And he talks too much. He's..." Sorcha sat, also, and searched for the right word to describe Arnou. "Annoying."

"I see." A brief smile lit the winter of Mother Brigette's face. "He says he's from Normandy, and although it's been years since I visited there, I believe that could be the peasant accent." She sounded like a French aristocrat, her face was richly lined with experience.

"So you...do you think he's who he says he is?" Sorcha had grown to respect Mother Brigette's opinion in all things.

"Why?" Her gray eyes scoured Sorcha. "Do you think he's lying?"

Sorcha shrugged uneasily. "If that boat isn't his, whose is it?"

"That's a question I would like answered." Mother Brigette was thin—all the nuns were thin, for this was a poor convent—and she sat with her spine straight, never allowing herself the comfort offered by the back of the bench. "I walked on the shore this morning. There were the fresh marks of a man's boots."

"Boots." Sorcha looked at Arnou's feet. They were clad in leather clogs and he'd come with nothing except the clothes on his back. "Two men on the island?"

"So it appears."

"But why? If there's another man stranded, why wouldn't he come to the convent?" But even before

Mother Brigette could speak, Sorcha's memory flew back to her dream, to the fear that something was chasing her.

"Perhaps because of you?" Mother Brigette suggested gently.

"Do you think I have to go back to…" Sorcha hesitated.

"To the throne of Beaumontagne?" In the face of Sorcha's astonishment, Mother Brigette smiled austerely. "Did you think I didn't know?"

"You've never before mentioned my title. I've always wondered if you knew. If Godfrey had even told you."

"He did not. He gave me money, a great deal of gold, and told me that you were given to fits of madness, and that I should keep you safe from yourself."

"What?" Sorcha half rose. "Godfrey said *what*? He said I was given to *madness*? Why would he say that?"

"That is a question worth pondering. At that time, I concluded he thought it would ensure I would watch over you closely."

"Did you?" Sorcha recalled the friendship that had developed between her and Mother Brigette during the first year. "You did!"

"I'm charged with the safety of each nun under my care, and I would never put them in danger from a madwoman."

"I thought you spent time with me because you…"
Liked me.

Mother Brigette laughed softly. "Within the month I knew you were quite sane, and I had the added benefit of enjoying your companionship. You're not an ordinary young woman. You're learned. More learned than I, and I had an exemplary education. Before the revolution, I spent time in the Paris salons with philosophers and scholars. That in itself alerted me to the possibilities of your station. Then I noted that you most assiduously read the newspapers which Mr. MacLaren brings, and you cut out and keep those articles relating to Beaumontagne. From that point, it was a short leap of logic to the realization that you were an exile and perhaps one of the Lost Princesses."

Sorcha mulled that over, then whispered, "I think it's time for me to go out into the world." She waited, wanting Mother Brigette to disagree.

Instead the nun smiled and nodded.

"Yet of course I can't go." Sorcha clasped her hands in a spasm of denial. "You need me. The convent needs me. I negotiate with Mr. MacLaren, trade our herbs for his supplies. I tend the garden. I help in the infirmary."

"You're very skilled, but we did all those things for ourselves before. We can do them again."

"But if I leave…" Sorcha had grown to love the nuns, and they to love her. Beaumontagne was far away in the Pyrenees Mountains. She'd never see them again.

Even without words, Mother Brigette understood. "We always knew we would lose you, and we're not of the world. We accept loss. We expect loss."

But what about her? What about Sorcha? "*I like it here.*"

"In your heart, do you believe this is the right place for you now?"

"Yes. Yes!"

"Sorcha, do you know what I am?" Mother Brigette asked. "Or rather, who I was?"

"No. I…" Sorcha hadn't ever thought about it. Mother Brigette had been the superior of this convent for all the time Sorcha had been here, and she couldn't imagine Mother Brigette doing, or rather being, anyone else.

"My name was Laurette Brigette Ann Genevre Cuvier, countess of Beaulieu in Provence in France. When I was thirty-two years old, I lived in a chateau in the summer, I visited Paris in the fall, I lived at court when I pleased, I was a friend of the queen, and I wore jewels in my hair, on my shoes, and on my fingers." Mother Brigette smiled as if the memory were pleasant, or perhaps as if Sorcha's blank astonishment amused her.

"Of course. You were an aristocrat." That explained so much about Mother Brigette—her education, her speech, her disciplined mind.

"I had a large family—a husband whom I didn't love, a father, mother, and sisters whom I adored, a young son, heir to a prosperous estate and the dearest boy in the world."

She didn't have them now, and Sorcha braced herself to hear a terrible tale.

"The revolution swept through France in a great wave. I saw my queen and friend Marie Antoinette guillotined, as well as my husband, my mother, my father, all of my sisters. In 1795 I was under house arrest with my son, my Tallas, when the chance came to escape. I was to take Tallas and go to the coast. I told no one but Fabienne, my trusted maid, asking that she help me pack. That night when we tried to leave Beaulieu, we were captured. For a few coins and her own redress, Fabienne had betrayed us to our deaths."

Sorcha made an incoherent sound of shock and horror.

In the same calm voice, Mother Brigette recited, "That winter I held my son in my arms as he expired in prison of a fever. I no longer cared if I lived or died. Nevertheless, I was rescued by an Englishman who put me on a ship to Edinburgh. The ship was blown off course and wrecked on the rocks of the Orkney Islands. There were other trials, but somehow always I was driven westward, toward Monmouth, and when I arrived on this island and looked at the convent, I knew I had been called to serve God. I didn't know why, yet I've done my duty. In every way I could, I did His work. I've helped rescue more than a dozen men and women and children from shipwreck. I've kept you safe. So perhaps that is God's plan."

"I am grateful." Sorcha's brief rebellion against her duty faltered under the weight of such a story. "So you think I should leave the convent."

"It's your duty, but more than that, you have a family you must find. Family is so precious, and you can't allow yourself to think they are stronger than you and braver than you. Perhaps even now they need you and your valor."

Sorcha imagined those words repeated in her grandmamma's voice, and she shriveled at the condemnation. "You're right. I should go forth and find Clarice and Amy. But I have no courage."

"Courage isn't a lack of fear, but rather taking the right action despite your fear."

Sorcha didn't for a minute believe that.

"And everyone is afraid of something."

"Not my grandmother," Sorcha said with stout certainty. "Not the dowager queen."

"The only person who fears nothing is one who has nothing to lose. Perhaps that does exemplify Queen Claudia, but I think as long as you're alive in this world and she doesn't know where, she has her fears, too." When Sorcha would have argued, Mother Brigette lifted a hand in admonishment. "You underestimate yourself. When you first arrived at the convent, you were young, you had lost everything dear to you, you cowered because you were still a child. Time has passed. You've matured, and now you hear duty calling. It's only natural to be afraid, but you know what you must do."

Mother Brigette might say she'd matured, but in the face of Mother Brigette's great and prolonged anguish, Sorcha felt inadequate. Once again, she wasn't good enough.

"Our guest is coming this way." Mother Brigette indicated Arnou shambling toward them.

He sidled to a place directly before them, then stood awkwardly. He pulled his forelock and bowed. He dragged his robes down as if trying to cover his muscular legs. Finally, with a triumphant grin, he knelt and looked up at them. "Greetings, Your Honors. Lovely day, isn't it?" He looked cheerful. He sounded chatty. "A wee bit nippy, of course, but that's to be expected so late in the year. We'll be having a storm again before the Sabbath comes."

"Why do you think that?" Mother Brigette asked.

"About the storm, you mean? Because I'm a fisherman. 'Tis my job." He bobbed up and down as if kneeling weren't humble enough.

In the sunlight, his bold features easily marked him as a lout: his nose was long and thin, his jaw was broad, his lips were well defined...and rather pleasantly pliable-looking. The rag that covered his eye and crossed his forehead was bunched and tattered, but long lashes flattered his remaining wide brown eye. If his robes fit him, if he grinned less, if he had an ounce of sense, he would be attractive...for a man who had proven himself to be a fool.

"I was wondering, Miss Sorcha, if you'd like me to dig out that old dead stump in the middle garden," he said. "When I'm done with the fence, I mean. It looks as if someone's already been scratching around it. I might as well do the job."

"It's not as effortless as you think, Arnou." Sorcha had wanted that stump gone for as long as she'd lived here, and she'd dug for hours while it clung stubbornly to the ground. She'd sometimes wondered if the spirit of the long-dead tree returned at night to send out new roots.

"I've looked it over. I can have it out this afternoon," he promised.

How easily he dismissed her toil! Irritated, Sorcha said coldly, "Indeed?"

"I'm a man who's used to keeping busy. Might as well pay for my provisions with a little bit of labor."

Before Sorcha could retort again, Mother Brigette intervened. "That would be lovely, Arnou. Thank you. Why don't you go to the kitchen and get your dinner now? Tell Sister Mary Simon I give my permission."

Arnou went into a veritable rapture of bowing and scraping, walking backward on his knees. Stumbling to his feet, he shambled away, making a beeline toward the kitchen.

Sorcha sighed in exasperation. "He hasn't another thought in his head but food. He's like a dog drawn to a meaty bone."

"He exasperates you," Mother Brigette observed. "Yet he seems to mean well."

"He babbles so much it's difficult to tell." And that babbling made Sorcha clench her teeth until her jaw hurt.

"I wish you had kept secret that you weren't a nun." Mother Brigette's voice held the sharp edge. "A habit provides you with protection you might not otherwise possess."

"I didn't tell him I wasn't. I just didn't tell him I was."

"How astute of him to discern the difference." Mother Brigette's gaze swept Sorcha's face and lingered on her hair. "With your coloring and your delicate features, you're distinctive. I fear for you when you leave."

"Perhaps the whole world has forgotten."

"You have the clippings to prove they have not. Besides"—Mother Brigette's face grew still—"enemies never forget." Standing, she fixed Sorcha with a stern look. "So prepare, Your Highness. When the time comes to leave, you'll probably be forced to leave as quickly as you can, and perhaps—"

A shout echoed through the hallowed silence of the cloister. Arnou came running back, his feet kicking up clumsily, his fingers pointed back toward the cloister, his one eye wide and terrified.

"Fire!" he hollered. "There's a fire in one of the cells! There's a fire!"

Sorcha came to her feet. Smoke billowed out of the cloister, out of the high, small window in the door of one of the cells. Out of…

"No," she said. Then, more loudly, "No!"

The smoke billowed out of *her* cell. It was *her* belongings that were ablaze.

Nuns poured from inside the convent, for fire was their greatest fear. If the thatch on their roof caught flame, it would leave them at the mercy of winter. Sister Mary Simon grabbed the filled bucket by the kitchen door. Sister Margaret ran to the well and started pumping water into the cistern. The metal clanged rhythmically. Arnou yelled and danced like a marionette on a string. Mother Brigette shouted directions and shoved Sorcha's shoulder hard enough to wake her from her petrified state.

Sorcha raced to grab another bucket. She filled it and ran to her cell, the water splashing on her hem and shoes.

A single glance proved her worst fears were fulfilled. The room had been ransacked, her bedclothes scattered, the mattress tossed aside, the small stand toppled. Her wooden chest had been opened and dumped. In one corner, red flames licked the meager pile of her belongings and up the gray stone walls.

Sister Mary Simon had already flung one bucket on the fire. Sorcha flung another. The flames hissed as the water subdued them. Sister Mary Assisi used an iron poker to drag the paper and cloth apart. Sister Theresa and Sister Katherine stomped on each piece until even the faintest glimmer of embers had faded.

As quickly as it had started, it was over. The fire was out. Sorcha and the nuns stood panting from fear as much as from exertion. The other nuns crowded the doorway, buckets of water in their hands. Smoke curled toward the wood beams and left a dark spot on the thatch.

As the immensity of her loss struck Sorcha, she trembled. Her clothes, yes, but more than that…. Dropping to her knees, she picked up a half-burned piece of paper.

It was not what she sought, but an article from the newspaper.

She picked another charred remain, and another, moving more and more quickly as frantically she searched for at least one of her most important possessions.

"What're ye looking fer?" Sister Theresa asked.

"For my letters from my sisters and my father." They were Sorcha's last connection to her family. "I want my letters. I've got nothing else."

But everything was gone.

As the realization struck her, she drew in a long, quavering breath. "Couldn't he have left me my letters?"

"Ye puir dear." Sister Theresa rubbed her shoulder.

"He who?" Sister Dierdre always kept an eye to her own well-being.

"It's only worldly possessions that you lost." Prune-faced Sister Margaret was easily the most sanctimonious of the nuns. "Ye should be more concerned about your salvation."

Sorcha lifted her hurt, incredulous gaze. "My father is dead. It was his last letter to me." The pain bit so deep, she couldn't even cry.

"He who?" Sister Dierdre repeated.

Sister Mary Simon shoved Sister Margaret aside. She stooped, picked something up, and gave a cry of delight. "Is this it?"

Sorcha snatched it from her. She unfolded the heavy sheet of paper. She read, *To Sorcha, the most crown princess of Beaumontagne and my darling daughter...* "Yes! This is it. Thank you, Sister. Thank you so much!" She pressed the scorched sheet to her heart and, as relief swept her, so did her tears. She closed her eyes and allowed herself to mourn for...

Amy's letter written in a childish scrawl and full of schoolgirl events and a young girl's confidences....

Clarice's letter in her own graceful penmanship, expressing worries about their futures, about their father's safety—expressing the thoughts Sorcha so often thought herself. And wishing the three could once more be together....

Sorcha would never see those letters again. She'd read them over and over so many times she had them memorized, but she wanted to hold the tenuous connection between her and Clarice and Amy.

The Lost Princesses.

That was what Mother Brigette had called them, and so they were—lost, and until Sorcha somehow reunited them, lost they would remain.

"Sorcha?" Mother Brigette called from outside. "Could you come here?"

Sorcha tucked her precious letter into her pocket and hurried out.

The air was clean out here, free from the noxious smell of scorched wool and burned dreams. The nuns looked alternately horrified and worried. Arnou stood on the outskirts, doing a jig to some inner rhythm.

Mother Brigette had her sleeve rolled up. Her hand was black with dirt. And she wore a pinched expression. "Follow me." She marched along the outer wall.

Sorcha marched behind her. The nuns followed, curious and murmuring. Arnou danced at the very end of the line.

He had not, Sorcha noted, helped put out the fire. He was as useless as he had been when she rescued the boat.

Mother Brigette stopped behind the crab apple. She pointed. "Look."

Someone had dug a small hole close to the wall. A man's boot marks marked the ground around it. Suspiciously Sorcha glanced at Arnou.

He stopped in his tracks. "What?" He pointed to himself. "I don't own boots!"

More important, the marks were undersized compared to his immense feet.

"Look in the hole," Mother Brigette said.

Sorcha knelt, pressed her fingers into the black powder piled in the bottom, and sniffed. The recognizable odor of sulfur, charcoal, and potassium nitrate filled her head.

"Gunpowder," she whispered.

The nuns had seen the boot marks, and they knew what she'd found, for she heard the murmur go through the small crowd. "Gunpowder." "Gunpowder?" "Dear holy Jesus, save us. Gunpowder."

"Wow. Really? Gunpowder?" Arnou said loudly.

Mother Brigette knelt beside Sorcha. In a low tone, she said, "Whoever set your cell on fire also intended to blow up the wall."

Sister Dierdre recoiled from Sorcha. Wide-eyed, she crossed herself.

"Who would do this?" Sister Theresa whispered. "There's only that young half-wit here, and he's been underfoot all day."

"Why would someone do this?" Sister Mary Simon was slightly deaf and considerably louder. "What does he want? We're a convent. We have no valuables to steal."

Of course not. Whoever had done this wasn't after valuables. He was after...Sorcha.

Mother Brigette was right. It was time to leave— before Sorcha brought disaster on the convent that had sheltered her for so long.

Chapter 3

Sunset found Sorcha inside the quiet glass greenhouse, kneeling, holding a trowel, her eyes fixed on the grooved brown stems and lacy green leaves of a valerian plant. Yet her hands, clad in rough garden gloves, were idle. She had come here to be alone, to think, to plan.

She had to leave Monnmouth as soon as possible, yet her mind was petrified with fear—fear of the stranger who stalked her.

Who was he? How had he found her? Had he left the island or was he lurking out there, waiting for darkness to fall so he could do harm to one of the nuns? Or to her?

Yet what was the alternative?

A long, treacherous road filled with danger.

She shivered as the sun slid behind the naked branches of the trees and cast long, fingerlike shadows groping through the glass.

To get back to Beaumontagne, she had to somehow cross the rugged Highlands of Scotland to Edinburgh, take passage on a ship to a port in France or Spain, then travel into the mighty peaks of the Pyrenees, and from there to her home. In the normal run of things she would be beset by discomfort, robbers, and the onset of winter. Now, with a possible assassin chasing her, the difficulties doubled and tripled until she couldn't imagine how she would take the first step.

She halfheartedly stirred the dirt around the valerian. She, who was so soft-hearted she could scarcely bear to pull a plant up by its roots, might have to use force against another human being.

She used to love twilight: the vivid blue sky turning to purple, the golden clouds, the anticipation of a quiet evening spent reading and in prayer. Now the skin between her shoulder blades prickled. She glanced nervously about her. And jumped.

A man stood behind her, his face pressed against one of the windowpanes. The glass distorted his nose. His breath painted the glass with frost, hiding his features, but his single brown eye was almost black.

She gasped. Her heart slammed against her chest.

Then he pulled back and waved frantically.

It was Arnou.

The dolt. He had startled her again. She glared at him. It almost seemed as if he were *trying* to spook her into leaving.

He gestured toward the door and, after a grudging hesitation, she nodded her permission.

Viciously she rammed the trowel into the ground and uprooted the valerian plant without a thought to its death.

Since the time she was a child, she had hated to be startled. Prince Rainger had known it, too, and taken pleasure in jumping out at her from behind closed doors or lurking beside the stairways and unexpectedly grabbing her skirt. The last time she'd seen him, he had drawled he was too old for such silliness; he had given her to understand he was too sophisticated to be bothered with her.

Too bad. There had been times when she had liked the rascally boy-prince. But she had despised the affected young man.

And she was sorry that Arnou and her return to Beaumontagne brought Rainger to mind, for Rainger's death at the hands of the revolutionaries reminded her of her own possible fate. Royalty was supposed to face adversity with equanimity; Sorcha's quaking dread proved her cowardice, and by the time Arnou had shambled around the greenhouse, opened the door, and made his way toward her, she had convinced herself she was unfit to rule.

"*Bonjour, mademoiselle*, it's warm in here." Arnou looked around at the glass and wood enclosure. "I like the smell. But it's damp."

He had a way of pointing out the obvious that was so annoying. "It *is* a greenhouse."

"Are you busy?" Arnou sidled closer.

"As you see, I am." She smiled tightly and flung the hapless greenery into a box. "I gather the valerian. Sister Rebecca dries the roots for a sleeping draught."

"Oh." He stared at the plant. "That little thing will do that?"

"In the right hands, it's very potent."

"Oh," he repeated. Lowering his voice, he said, "I have a question. Is it always so terrifying here?"

"Here?" She blinked at him in astonishment. "At the convent?"

"*Oui*. Because I don't like it when a man sets fires and digs a hole and puts gunpowder in the bottom and tries to light it." Arnou's one eye got big and round. "You're only an unworldly woman, but I can tell you a man who does things like that is the kind of man who could try to hurt somebody!"

"I suspected that," she said dryly.

"The thing is, I don't like staying here." He moved his shoulders uncomfortably. "It makes me wonder when a knife will slip into my back. So I was wondering—can I leave?"

He was such a coward! She despised cowards...as she despised herself. "You should ask Mother Brigette, not me."

"She's strict. She scares me."

"Would you like me to ask for you?" The darkness was falling fast, but being with Arnou made her feel brave by comparison.

"I was hoping you would offer. You talk to her so freely!"

"Actually, she's very kind," Sorcha assured him.

Arnou looked unconvinced. "How soon can I go?"

"Mother Brigette will raise the flag to signal Mr. MacLaren. You'll have to wait until he arrives tomorrow or the next day—"

"I can't wait that long. That man, the one who set your room on fire—he's going to do something else. Something worse. I'm scared. I don't want to be here." Arnou's voice trembled and he talked faster and faster. "I have my boat—"

"*Your* boat?" Her suspicion of Arnou leaped to life.

"Yes, the one you got for me." He knit his brows as if surprised she didn't comprehend.

She relaxed. How foolish, to be dubious of this simple soul!

"I can row to the mainland tomorrow morning. If I put my back into it, it'll only take an hour or two," he said. "Then I'll be away from here. I want to go back to Burgundy, where everyone knows everyone else and no one does crazy things like set fires and use gunpowder to kill people."

"To Burgundy..." *In France.* She needed to go to *France.* "It's a very long way."

"I'll get across Scotland and take a ship."

"You're going to get across Scotland?" She marveled at him—he spoke so casually, as if it were a ride in the woods. "How?"

"Walk. Catch a ride when I can. Farmers go to market and they don't care if I ride along."

She pressed him for information. "Aren't you afraid of robbers?"

"No one tries to rob me." He spread his broad hands wide. "I don't have anything."

Yes, and his clothes and demeanor made his poverty obvious. Sister Margaret had dug deep in the convent's stash of clothes and located a pair of brown breeches, patched at the knee, but she'd been unable to find any-thing that fit his big chest and shoulders. So she'd stitched together a tunic of sturdy wool cut from an old brown blanket. All the nuns took turns knitting a pair of black hose tall enough to fit his long shanks. Sister Margaret had insisted he tie a clean rag around his face. With his clogs to complete the outfit, he looked the pic-ture of a sturdy peasant.

Sturdy…. Arnou was big, strong, with long arms—the kind of man no fool would attack without a pistol or a gang, and even then he would make trouble. His size probably contributed to his safety more than his poverty.

"I don't want to go alone." He sighed and shuffled his feet. "I like to talk, and I hate it when there's no one to listen."

It was almost completely dark. She should go in. Yet she stood limply holding the trowel, wondering how and when the idea of traveling with Arnou had occurred to her.

"You could come with me." He spoke so softly, so hypnotically, he might have been a voice in her mind. "I would protect you."

"Why would I leave the convent?" How odd to think that Arnou, of all people, could guard her from harm. Yet right now, she almost believed it.

"Why would you want to stay? Someone's after you here." His deep velvet tone seduced her into a feeling of security. "It would be safer on the road. For you. For everyone. You should go."

Was he giving her advice? And in such a tone? Jerking her head up, she stared searchingly at him. She couldn't see the details of his face, but something about the way he stood…He seemed to have a natural arrogance, a balance and a build natural to a fencer or a lord. *Was he more than the humble fisherman he appeared?*

"This wool is itchy. I wish I had a different shirt." With a whimper, he stared down at his chest and scratched heartily. "Do you have clothes left after the fire? Because I need a cloak for travel and maybe I could have yours. I'm scared of this place. When will you talk to Mother Brigette for me?"

"I'll talk to her after matins." Sorcha stripped off her gloves and prepared to dash toward the dining hall.

"*Merci, Mademoiselle.*" He grinned engagingly.

She saw a flash of strong white teeth.

He walked to the door.

Almost without her volition, she called, "If I went with you, you'd have to swear with your hand on the Bible that you'd treat me honorably and do all in your power to protect me."

"I'll swear, of course." He sounded bewildered and hurt by her suspicions. "But I don't hurt girls and I would never let a companion come to harm."

"Good." Perhaps her courage would rise in his company. "In the morning, I'll let you know if I decide to join you."

With her hands folded on the desk before her, Mother Brigette listened quietly as Sorcha proposed her plan. When Sorcha was finished, Mother Brigette studied the princess who had been her charge for so many years. She had seen her grow from an adolescent who cowered at a kind reprimand to this beautiful young woman, untried by life. The years of simple living had given Sorcha a serenity that glowed like pure candle flame beneath her pale complexion. Her beautiful copper-colored hair hung in a thick braid down her back, and her blue eyes showed no awareness of self. Mother Brigette and the other nuns had raised Sorcha to be one of those rare and noble beings, an innocent who saw the best in everyone.

Perhaps, knowing what Mother Brigette knew of the world and of Sorcha's eventual fate, that had been a mistake. But Sorcha's grandmother had been her first teacher, and she had added the necessary reason and intelligence.

Unfortunately, the princess was completely untested and now…well, now she would have a trial by fire. Mother Brigette had no way of foretelling what would happen to her, but she could protect Sorcha on her first steps into the world.

"So you wish to cross the channel and travel to France with Arnou the fisherman," Mother Brigette said. "Whose idea was this?"

"It was mine." Sorcha sat in the hard chair, her feet firmly on the floor, her chin lifted as if proud to point out her own bravery.

"I see. How intelligent of you to take the initiative."

"Yes." Sorcha smiled, a shy, proud smile that Mother Brigette hated to subdue.

But she would. "You have to go, it's true. But while I admire your ingenuity, I have formulated a different plan."

Sorcha's pleasure faded.

Mother Brigette rose from her seat, came around to Sorcha, and stood over her. She needed to exert her authority in this, the most perilous moment of Sorcha's life. "Yesterday after you rescued the boat, God told me you must go at once." In fact, as soon as Mother Brigette had seen Arnou, seen the way he watched Sorcha, she had realized that the princess must leave as swiftly and as quietly as possible. "After the fire in your cell, I raised a special flag to signal Mr. MacLaren. He arrived this afternoon."

"This afternoon? I never saw him!"

"Years ago, not long after you first arrived on Monnmouth, I gave Mr. MacLaren special instructions. If I raised the scarlet flag, he was to come as quickly as possible and land surreptitiously on the far side of the island. He did so and has remained hidden since." Mother Brigette raised her voice. "Sister Margaret, would you come in here?"

Sister Margaret bustled in, a variety of freshly washed and ironed clothes draped across her arm. She and Mother Brigette exchanged a smile. "Here we are, Sorcha. We'll have you ready to go in no time." Pulling Sorcha to her feet, Sister Margaret pushed her behind the screen. "Strip down and I'll help you with your clothes."

"I can dress myself," Sorcha protested.

"You'll need help with this," Sister Margaret answered.

Indeed she would. "As soon as Sister Margaret has dressed you, Mr. MacLaren is going to row you across to the mainland," Mother Brigette said.

"In the dark? But it's dangerous."

"He is very skilled."

"I don't understand. This is happening so fast." Panic edged Sorcha's voice.

Mother Brigette and Sister Margaret exchanged measured glances. In a stern voice, Mother Brigette said, "It is happening at exactly the rate at which God wills it."

Sorcha didn't reply. Either she couldn't speak or she refused to agree.

Yes, the child had her moments of rebellion. Perhaps, in the trials that faced her, that was all to the good.

"It's necessary you leave at once. Whoever is following you must be thrown off the trail." Mother Brigette waited, but still Sorcha didn't agree. Even now, the princess didn't truly understand her peril. "Tomorrow morning before dawn you'll take the horse MacLaren gives you and ride with his escort as far as Hameldone, two days' hard ride. From there"—Mother Brigette could scarcely bear to say the words—"you'll make your own way to Edinburgh and a ship."

"Alone?" Sorcha's voice squeaked a little.

"Yes. Alone." If only Sorcha knew how much Mother Brigette feared for her! "I have no one to send with you. That's why desperate measures are necessary."

"What desperate measures?"

Sister Margaret stepped behind the screen, Sorcha's costume in hand.

Mother Brigette waited, half smiling.

"What's that?" Sorcha's horror was audible. "You want me to wear *that*?"

"Don't worry, it'll fit," Sister Margaret said serenely. "Put your arm in here."

"But I don't understand," Sorcha protested. "This is absurd. No one will believe this!"

"People believe what they see." Mother Brigette tucked her hands in her sleeves and listened to the rustles and whispered protests.

This was not the way she would have chosen to send Sorcha out into the world, but it was the only way. Mother Brigette's life had required that she make a study of men, asking questions, probing their minds and their hearts, listening to the tones of their voices, and weighing their truths.

Arnou was lying. She didn't know why, but he was not who he said he was—and that made him dangerous. Dangerous to Sorcha.

Unfortunately, Mother Brigette also judged Mr. MacLaren to be an inferior implement. He brought them supplies, but only because he made a good profit selling their herbs at market. He did as she commanded, but only out of superstitious fears involving papists and holy women and the evil eye. And she would not now use him if she had any other method to get Sorcha away from here. Away from the threat Arnou posed. Away from the threat posed by Sorcha's title and fortune.

When Mother Brigette judged Sorcha had gotten over her shock at her new wardrobe, she continued, "You'll have a small bag of coins on a belt tied around your waist. Never dip into this fund except in the direst of emergencies. I cannot emphasize that enough. You must have money to get home, and that will cover your passage." She subdued her fierceness and gently reminded Sorcha of her obligations to the nuns who had cared for her for so long. "I expect that when you've reached your destination, you'll wish to reimburse the convent."

"Well. Yes. Of course. But why can't Arnou travel with me? He wishes to leave the convent. He's strong. He'll frighten off attackers."

"He definitely would frighten off attackers, but Arnou is not bright. You realize that."

"I have enough intelligence for both of us." Sorcha sounded confident in that.

She was right. She had intelligence. But her argument proved how unworldly she was. "That you do. But he wouldn't understand the reason for your garments and I fear in his simplemindedness"—that simplemindedness she found so suspicious—"he would reveal the truth."

"*I* don't understand the reason for these garments!"

"Yes, you do." Mother Brigette grew anxious to see the results of Sister Margaret's handiwork. Would this camouflage be as successful as she hoped?

"All right." Sorcha sounded sulky. "Perhaps I do, but this is so...I look so..."

It was time to ignore the protests. "I'm also sending a saddlebag filled with medicinal herbs. You can sell the herbs as you need for food or use them in case of illness. You're leaving on the brink of winter, the worst time of the year for traveling, and while I hope that lessens the chance of robbery, I'm afraid you'll suffer days of misery and cold."

"Misery and cold I can endure, but this!" Sorcha's voice went from dismayed to huffy.

"'Twill be charming," Sister Margaret said.

Mother Brigette paced across the room, then stopped in her tracks. Pacing was a waste of time and energy. Yet she now wished she'd spent less time encouraging Sorcha's artlessness and more time warning her about the ways of the world. She had so much she wanted to say, but it was too late for regrets, so she chose her words carefully. "Travel in secret and in shadow."

"I understand." Sorcha sounded patient. "I remember Godfrey's warning about the assassins. I remember the fire in my cell."

"Be strong in your mind," Sister Margaret said.

"Keep your knife sharp and utilize all your skills. Fix your mind on the goal of returning to Beaumontagne and let nothing turn you aside," Mother Brigette added.

"I'm unproven, but not without resources." Sorcha seemed to understand their concerns and bent her talents to reassure them. "At the bedrock of my being I have my grandmother's teachings. In addition, I've lived the last years with the strongest, kindest, most assiduous women in the world."

Yet not the most wary. But Mother Brigette said nothing of that. "Most important, remember my tale of my maid Fabienne, and trust no man with your truths."

"But Mother Brigette, I must trust the man who has proved faithful and kind or I'll believe in no man and in nothing." Sorcha sounded incredulous and perturbed. "I can't be like that. That would be a sin in itself."

"Dying before you reach the end of your journey would be a sin," Mother Brigette said sternly. "Anything else is forgivable."

"She's ready." Sister Margaret stepped out, beaming. "I know I suffer from vanity, but I also know I've done a marvelous job."

"Come, Sorcha. Let me see you." Mother Brigette waited with hope and anticipation.

Sorcha stepped out from behind the screen, her cheeks rosy with mortification, her head bent, her fists clenched at her side.

Mother Brigette circled her, examining every detail.

Sister Margaret had wrapped Sorcha's waist in a length of cotton. She'd dressed Sorcha in a rough brown shirt, loose wool breeches held up with rope suspenders, a black cloak that hung to her knees, and three pairs of socks inside black boots. Her brown, wide-brimmed hat had wool earflaps and tied under her chin.

Mother Brigette smiled gently at Sister Margaret. "Thank you, Sister, you've done a marvelous job. Sorcha is, in every way, a convincing young man."

Chapter 4

'Tis the only horse ye can safely ride, Miss, er, Miss, er…" Flustered by her disguise, MacLaren gestured to the pony.

"I was trained to ride before I could walk." Incredulous, Sorcha circled the hairy little beast MacLaren had declared to be her mount on her flight from Monnmouth.

MacLaren's eyes shifted off to the side. "It's the only animal I can spare."

Sorcha looked across the back of the pony. The sun rose behind her, illuminating MacLaren's squat figure. He looked as if God had taken a man of normal height, lifted His mighty hammer, and with a single blow driven him down toward the earth, compressing him, widening him…driving the goodness out of him, and leaving only dull, damp clay.

Grandmamma would never allow herself to be placed on such a nasty little horse by such a nasty little man. He'd already loaded her saddlebags on the pony, but those could be moved. Straightening her shoulders, she asked coldly, "MacLaren, did Mother Brigette not tell you to mount me on a horse? A real horse?"

"I'm sending my best man to escort you to Hameldone. Ye should be grateful."

Grateful she was not. Last night Mother Brigette had feared too much of a fuss would alert the enemy about Sorcha's departure, so Sorcha had bidden a tearful farewell to Mother Brigette and Sister Margaret. The other nuns, the women with whom she'd spent so many years—they would wake soon and discover she was gone, and never would they see each other again. Sister Theresa, so small, so dear, so Scottish. Sister Mary Simon, Sister Mary Virtus, Sister Patricia—all gone from Sorcha's life forever.

And Sorcha had suffered too much loss; this new blow brought into sharp relief her grief for her father, her worry about her sisters…even her distress that her grandmother had had to bear the burden of rule by herself.

Grateful? To MacLaren? No, she was not grateful.

"Who is your best man?" she asked.

"Sandie the blacksmith." MacLaren gestured to the broad-shouldered, barrel-chested blond fellow who loaded his saddlebags for the long ride.

"A pleasure to meet you, Sandie." She smiled.

Sandie did not. A dour lot, these Scots. Or was it only the people forced by birth and circumstances to live close to stingy and cheerless MacLaren?

"Sandie's riding a pony, too." MacLaren spoke as if that would sugar the pill.

Unfortunately, instead it made her realize she'd allowed MacLaren to distract her. In her best authoritative tone, she said, "You have real horses in your stable. I saw them. I'll ride one."

"I have two horses, Miss, er, Miss, er..." He squirmed as if he couldn't bear to look at her. "One for me and one for me wifey. Which one would ye have me give ye?"

"Oh. Only two horses. I didn't realize. I can't take your wife's. Of course not. I suppose this pony will do me very well as long as—" As long as she didn't have to run away from a pursuing villain. "Well, the pony will do." Despite the fact the pony's belly hung loose and her ribs showed. "Thank you, MacLaren."

He nodded. "Aye."

"What's her name?" she asked.

"Whose name?"

"The pony's."

"She doesn't have a name!" He snorted and stumped his way down toward the harbor. "A name for a damned pony!"

Sorcha watched him go, then turned to face Sandie. "Well, I shall name her St. Donkey, for the animal that carried Mary to Bethlehem."

"Think well of yerself, don't ye?" Sandie asked sourly, and with a bump of his knees urged his pony up the road.

Hurriedly, she mounted and joined him. St. Donkey's gait jarred her teeth almost loose and Sorcha suspected the poor dear had a limp, but she was determined to make the best of this journey. It was, after all, a real adventure.

At the top of the hill, she turned in the saddle and looked across the rambunctious ocean to the rocky island where the convent buildings lifted their arms to God. As she watched, a mist enveloped it, and it disappeared into the swirling depths like a dream she could never revisit.

"C'mon, then," Sandie said roughly, "or I'll ne'er get back before the Sabbath."

Sorcha sniffed back her tears, pulled a white handkerchief from her sleeve, and blotted her cheeks, then rode toward Sandie.

He stared at her watery eyes.

"What?" she asked.

"Ye'll ne'er convince anyone o' yer disguise if ye keep on that way." Shaking his head, he urged the pony down the narrow path.

She looked down at herself. She was dressed just like a man. It was the perfect disguise. So what did he mean?

"What way?" she called, and hurried after Sandie. "Why can't I convince anyone of my disguise?"

He hunched his shoulders and kept riding. "Ye cry like a girl."

"Only once! And not for very long!"

He didn't answer.

"I won't do it again."

Still he didn't answer.

"I'll be as tough and coarse as any man!"

At last, one more gruff sentence issued from his mouth, impressing on her how unalterably easy it was to dupe her. "MacLaren's na got a wife."

You can go in now." Sister Theresa smiled at Arnou as she opened the door to Mother Brigette's dim office.

He stared at her as he walked through the door. Never in the two days he'd been here had she smiled at him, and he found her civility almost spooky.

No outside light pierced the cavern of the chamber, and he blinked as his eyes adjusted from bright sunshine. A single candle flickered on the desk where Mother Brigette sat, her pen scratching across a paper.

He was on a mission, but he didn't forget his disguise. So he shuffled forward to stand before her. He grinned. He pulled his forelock. He pretended to be a fool. "Mother Brigette, where is Miss Sorcha?"

Mother Brigette placed the quill in its stand, sanded the letter, and corked the ink. She looked up. "Why do you ask, Arnou?"

"I was supposed to row her to the mainland today and she's nowhere to be found." He bobbed his head, rearranged the rag over his eye, and did an absolutely smashing imitation of a fisherman who'd been smacked in the head by one too many cod.

"There's a good reason you can't find her." With elaborate care, Mother Brigette folded her hands on the desk before her and examined him with all the charity of a rat dog examining a rodent.

The first pinpricks of danger crawled down his spine. "Why is that?"

"She left last night."

Forgetting his disguise, he straightened. He bent a fierce glare on the commanding woman. "*What?*"

"She is beyond your reach." Mother Brigette returned his glare—and in her cool gray eyes, he saw fierce intelligence.

The pinpricks became jolts of alarm.

"You've lied to us, Arnou. You're not who you say you are."

Her glacial voice cooled his wrath, made his sense of self-preservation kick in.

He glanced around. A nun lurked in each corner.

But what threat were they?

Mother Brigette continued, "And I know a man can force his feet into small boots if the reward is great enough."

Damn! This woman with the perceptive gaze knew what he'd done.

He glanced up.

A fishing net hung from the ceiling. A rope dangled from it.

He looked back at Mother Brigette.

She held the end in her hand.

A trap.

"No!" he shouted.

"Yes." Her voice was flat. She pulled.

He tried to run, but it was too late. As if he were a tiger marked for death, the net enveloped him.

This had happened before.

But he wouldn't go back to prison. Not without a brawl.

Maddened by panic, by fury, by anguish, he fought, growing more and more tangled.

"Arnou, that's enough." Mother Brigette's voice slapped at him. "Calm down. We're not going to hurt you!"

Nothing she said could mitigate his terror. *He would not be snared again.*

A short, burly Scotsman stepped out from behind a screen. He flung a rope around Arnou's chest. The bastard gave a jerk, tightening it.

Between the net, the rope, and the panic, Arnou choked. He tried to claw himself free.

"MacLaren, don't kill him!" Mother Brigette warned.

"He's crazed," MacLaren rasped.

Arnou saw the gleam in MacLaren's eyes. MacLaren liked trapping a man. Liked choking him. Forgetting the net, Arnou lunged at him.

Because MacLaren was right. Arnou *was* crazed.

He wouldn't go back. He would not return to hell.

He tripped. He fell. He thrashed on the floor, intent on killing MacLaren.

He heard high, chirping cries of anguish.

But they didn't come from his mouth.

Four nuns rushed forward from every corner of the room.

The net tore at his face, snagging the rag over his eye, ripping it away.

He froze, aware of what had been revealed.

Sister Theresa gasped. "His eye. He has an eye!"

"A perfectly good one." Mother Brigette's wrath pierced his fear, bringing him a moment of lucidity. "I was right. He's lying."

The nuns threw wool blankets over him.

Darkness enveloped him. Smothered him. Panic returned with renewed strength. Again he fought his bonds.

The heat built up. The air slipped away. He couldn't breathe. And before he lost consciousness, Arnou grimly reminded himself—he'd lived in the dungeon in a cell the size of a coffin. For years, he'd survived without light, without warmth, without decent food. His spirit had taken blow after blow. Friends had died. He'd been beaten year after year with a whip, with a cane… finally, after an interminable time filled with blackness and depression, his spirit had broken, and nothing mattered anymore.

But somehow at that moment when all hope was gone, he'd discovered a tiny light within himself. Slowly, painfully, he'd come back from the brink.

He would come back again.

Because he was different now. Hardship had burned away his soft, privileged self, leaving nothing but steely resolve and a cool killing instinct.

He would have Sorcha. He would save his kingdom.

He was, after all, Prince Rainger.

Chapter 5

The Gala Palace in Beaumontagne
Three years earlier

With one skinny fist, Rainger punched a hole through the glass, then listened for a shout, which would betray that the guards had heard the crash.

Nothing. For now, his luck held.

Snaking his arm inside, he unlatched the window. The window swung open easily at his urging. He slithered into a dark, cavernous room and took a long breath of air rich with the scent of money. He was in the antechamber of the Gala Palace, where even in the depths of night the walls glinted dully with gold. No candles lit the darkness, but his eyes easily adjusted. He'd been staring into darkness for so long, he no longer recognized the light.

He had only a few minutes to find the fragile old queen and force her to do as he commanded. For if he was taken, he would be thrown into a prison cell—and he was far too familiar with prison to go quietly.

She lived in the west corner, where she received the afternoon sun. He remembered her needle dipping into her embroidery, over and over, dragging thread behind it while her cold, clear voice nagged on and on....

Stopping, he closed his eyes and swayed, lost in memories and sick with the need to avenge himself. And sick with hunger. God, it had been two days since he'd eaten, eight years since he'd eaten well.

Then his eyes snapped open, and swiftly he moved into the corridor. He moved without sound through the silence, halting to listen at every corner. The guards were outside on the castle walls. In the palace, nothing moved. Not even a mouse dared disturb Queen Claudia's rest.

The door of her chambers opened beneath his touch, and he knew at once he'd come to the right place. The scent of lavender was overwhelming. Dainty feminine furniture crowded every inch of the sitting room, and the single night candle that burned in the next room showed a rumpled, massive bed with a replica of the ornate crown carved on the headboard.

As he made his way toward the bedchamber, the scent of lavender grew stronger. He stepped across the threshold. The queen's bedchamber was huge and high, not the most comfortable room in the palace, but certainly the grandest, and that was what mattered to that damned old queen. He glided forward, toward the mound of blankets that covered her reclining figure.

He had dreamed of this moment. In the depths of his prison cell, where the light seldom shone, where the gray walls closed in and the ceiling was not quite tall enough for him to stand—he had dreamed of being here, staring at the old besom and knowing that at last he was going to get revenge.

For one moment, his eyes clouded and the blood thrummed in his veins. He took a long, slow breath. His head steadied.

And behind him, he heard the hammer of a pistol click into place.

Swinging around, he saw the white-haired lady sitting in a chair by the window, wrapped head to foot in a wool blanket, the barrel of her pistol protruding from its folds.

In her hoarse old voice, she commanded, "Put your hands up, or I'll shoot you where you stand."

Distantly he noted at least two bloodstains on her Aubusson carpet—he didn't make the mistake of disbelieving her. Lifting his hands, he watched as she reached for the bell cord, and said, "But Your Majesty, don't you recognize your only godson?"

She paused. She stared at him.

He knew what she saw. His gray rags hung on his bony form. His eyes burned with fervor. A beard covered his chin and a mouth that had forgotten how to smile. And he smelled. Smelled like a man who hadn't seen soap and water for years.

He was not at all the noble edifice her godson should be.

"What are you babbling about?" she asked.

He bowed, as best he could with his arms up. "Prince Rainger de Leonides, at your service."

"You insolent imbecile. My godson was shot dead by the revolutionaries eight years ago."

"The rumors of my demise are greatly exaggerated."

She gave a brief cackle and said, "Light the candles." The clawlike, bejeweled hand that held the pistol was so steady she might have been twenty, and not the eighty-two he knew her to be. "Move carefully. I would hate to get nervous and shoot my godson by mistake." Disdain dripped from her tone, but she didn't shout for the guards.

He did move carefully, taking a taper and lighting it in the fire, then igniting as many of the candelabras as he could see.

"Turn around," she said.

He faced her. She was old, so old, and so thin. Her once-handsome face had fallen into a mass of wrinkles. Her fingers were twisted with rheumatism. But he knew she wouldn't surrender. At the age of seventy-six, she had fought back the revolutionaries. She had reclaimed power, and now, six years later, she wouldn't surrender to anyone. Certainly not someone who had broken into her castle. Not someone she imagined to be an imposter.

She searched his features, seeking some confirmation that he told the truth.

Her face fell, and again she reached for the bell cord.

He tensed, and in a cold, dead voice said, "I'll attack if I have to."

"Very princely," she said with a sneer, but she drew her hand back. Sighing, she gestured to the window. "I saw you coming. I always see them coming, these noble young women tripping bravely across the courtyard with tales of being one of my long-lost granddaughters. You're the first man to think of this angle, of claiming to be Rainger. What made you think it would work?"

She sounded so weary he pitied her. He knew better; by sheer ruthlessness, Queen Claudia had survived the revolutions that wracked their two countries. But on his desperate journey through the countryside, he'd heard the gossip. Her son, the king, had died. The weight of ruling rested on her skinny shoulders. And no one talked about the girls. About the princesses. "Let me light you a cigarillo," he urged.

"How nice of you—and how convenient for you. You would have to come close to give it to me, and what would you do then? Snap my neck?"

He would have said her experiences had made her bitter and suspicious, but she'd always been that way. "I don't want to snap your neck, or at least not for the reasons you imagine. You're my only hope. I want my kingdom back. I want revenge on the rebels who killed my family and put me in prison for eight long years. And I can't do it without your help."

Her heavy gray eyebrows rose in regal astonishment. "Even if you were Rainger, what makes you think I would help you?"

Again, faintness came over him in a wave. Backing up to the table, he propped himself against it.

"One does not sit in the presence of a queen without invitation," she said.

"I'm leaning." He folded his arms. "I know you, Grandmamma. The first time I met you, you dragged me in from my perch atop the highest banner pole and whacked my legs with your cane. You said I was the only heir to Richarte, and I would take care or answer to you, for God had given me the kingdom next to yours and you wouldn't allow me to ruin God's plan with sheer male stupidity. Then you made me write out the whole Book of Kings from the Bible. I was six."

She looked thoughtful, although whether that meant she remembered or not, he couldn't begin to guess. Mildly, she asked, "Do you think I've changed?"

"Not particularly. You look as ancient as you did the first time I saw you."

She gave a dry cackle. "You always were a snot-nosed little brat." The pistol drooped, and she propped up her wrist with her other hand. "All right, here's what you'll do. You'll wash, shave, and dress, and if I think you pass muster—"

She wasn't going to have him killed.

"—then I'll allow you to perform a quest to prove yourself."

"A quest?" The room was spinning—or was it his head?

"*You do remember my granddaughters?*"

"*Very well.*" Three little princesses, one of them full of mischief, one forthright and determined...and one who was destined to be his queen. Sorcha.

Sorcha.

"*Ten years ago, as the troubles grew too great, I sent my granddaughters to England for safety from those bastards, those marauding rebels, those ungrateful peasants who imagined they could be royal by owning a crown.*" Little drops of spittle flew from her mouth as she spoke of the rebels, and her eyes glowed evilly.

"*They're gone? The girls are gone?*" He hadn't known that, for his country had been swept by rebellion at the same time, and he hadn't retained the throne. He hadn't gone into exile. He'd been condemned to a living death.

"*They're gone. England was safe, so I sent them to separate places around the country, to people I paid to care for them, but it was five years before I regained control and could send for them.*" Her lips curled in disgust. "*They've disappeared.*"

"*The people you paid—*"

"*Were not trustworthy. When the money stopped coming, they sent them away, put them adrift, let them go. One couple even died to avoid their responsibilities. I've lost my granddaughters. I haven't been able to find* them." Queen Claudia's voice dropped an octave. "That's where you take over."

He understood. He understood at once. "You want me to find them." He straightened his shoulders. "Very well, but first you must help me retrieve my kingdom."

Mouth puckered, she shook her head slowly. "I think not."

"But my people are suffering! A tyrant cruelly rides them for taxes—"

"Find my granddaughters, bring them home." She leaned forward, her eyes gleaming intently. "When you do, I give you permission to wed whichever one you want. Then, and only then, will you be able to use the powers of Beaumontagne to recover your kingdom. That is the deal I offer you, Prince Rainger."

The old lady was implacable—and she held the trump card.

He made his decision. "Done."

She leaned back. It was almost as if his ready agreement changed her mind about him.

He laughed. Dear God, he laughed with dark, harsh amusement. "Did you think I would rail against your decree? Throw a tantrum and pout? Do you know what I've done for the last eight years? I've lived in a dungeon, always dank and cold, usually dark, tapping messages to my friends in the next cell, digging a tunnel with my fingernails, existing on the edge of despair. Once a year, the tyrant whose traitorous ass sits on my throne came down to mock me and watch his men beat me." Lifting his shirt, he turned his back to her.

"Jesu. He did that to you?" As she viewed the mass of scabs and scars that crisscrossed his back, her voice shook with revulsion. "It's one thing to flog a man, but once only. More breaks his spirit, makes him an animal who knows nothing but loathing or—" Her breath caught.

He faced her. "Or madness." He allowed the raw hate to seep into his eyes...and perhaps she saw that edge of madness in him.

But whether he was mad or not—and he didn't know—she needed him. She had no one else.

He knew it.

She knew it.

"Yes, Grandmamma," he said, "I am Rainger, but not the Rainger you knew before."

"No. I see that now." Slowly, she put the pistol on the table.

"After the lessons in patience and control I've been forced to learn, do you imagine I see difficulty in bringing you your granddaughters? That is nothing compared to what I've already done. You have the troops. I'll do as you say—but after that, you will do as I demand. I'll find your granddaughters. I'll wed the one of my choice. And you'll give me the men and troops to win my kingdom back."

"Agreed." She beckoned him closer.

Cautiously he came forward, staggering a bit, and leaned over her.

Her claw settled on his arm, and she squeezed it hard enough to bruise. "But be aware—you're not the only one who's hunting my granddaughters."

Chapter 6

MacLaren was a worm—and not just any worm. He was a cheap, spiteful, malicious worm who enjoyed having a prisoner in his dungeon, keeping Rainger down in the dank cell, feeding him gruel and water, giving him nothing except a thin wool blanket to keep away the chill of night. Making someone miserable let MacLaren feel like a man of power.

What he didn't realize was that Rainger had been in this situation before. The walls oozed moisture when the tide came in—that was a new irritation, but other than that, Rainger recognized the bars, the sneers, the darkness.

The first day, he explored his cell beneath MacLaren's miserable castle. Rainger found no way out, but he knew how to bide his time. Hell, he'd bided his time for eight years in a deeper, darker dungeon than this one.

Only one inexorable torment visited him here.

His princess. Where was Sorcha? He could find her again—only one road wound away from MacLaren's castle. He knew from MacLaren's taunts that he'd rowed her to shore and sent her on her way. But could that wide-eyed innocent fool of a girl survive long enough for Rainger to rescue her?

She hadn't recognized him. The voyage to Edinburgh, the ride through Scotland, the sail across in the tiny vessel, had given him the grime and the aura of a workingman. His beard and the rag he'd tied around his face had covered his features. Most of all, he'd changed. The dungeon, the beatings, the loneliness, the despair, the desperation had changed him beyond all belief.

On the other hand, Sorcha hadn't changed at all. He hadn't expected her to look so very much like the princess he'd known—bright blue eyes, fair skin with a dash of golden freckles, copperred hair.

Beautiful. So beautiful. Like a dream he'd once had.

When he'd been a prince, honored, feted, respected, most of all, clean, he hadn't cared about the crown princess. He'd been in love with other girls, other women, older women who taught him the pleasures of the flesh…and eventually the meaning of treachery.

But when the first disbelief and anguish of prison had ceased and he found himself sleeping alone night after night, he'd begun to dream of Sorcha. Of his betrothed. For eight long years of imprisonment, for another three years of searching, he'd dreamed of her. And to so suddenly see her on the beach, to watch her tie up her skirts and plunge into the icy water after a boat with the possibility of saving a stranger's life—by all the saints, it was better than beef, better than soap, better than sex.

Well, not better than sex, but damned good.

Most important, she was single.

Her sisters hadn't been. Both of them had found men to love, Englishmen who wed and worshipped them. Clarice and Amy had taught him caution, and now as his crown princess moved farther and farther away from him, he weighed his options and made his plans.

He slept. He preserved his strength. And he waited. On the third day in MacLaren's prison cell, he lay on the cot, his eyes closed.

He heard the rattle of keys. Every sense went on alert. He caught the scent of strong whiskey—MacLaren—and the murmur of another voice—MacLaren's manservant.

Rainger could probably take both of them, but he remained somnolent. Now was not the time to make his move. Not while in MacLaren's crumbling castle with all of MacLaren's servants and kin roaming above.

MacLaren stuck a musket into Rainger's face and said, "Don't stir or I'll blow yer head off, and with pleasure." He wore a sturdy oak truncheon on a belt at his waist and a knife in a scabbard tied on his wrist. Apparently he wasn't going to be caught without a weapon should Rainger attack. "Brian, tie him up."

Rainger's gaze slid to Brian. His large ears, balding head, and sunburned skin glowed with the privilege he'd been granted. He wrapped rope around Rainger's wrists, his grin showing black gaps where his teeth had rotted away. While Rainger made the obligatory feeble struggles, Brian threw a blanket over his head.

Rainger went limp as they lifted him, pretending unconsciousness as they carried him from the cell.

"Quite the wee coward, isn't he?" MacLaren panted under the effort of hauling Rainger along.

Rainger's butt dragged in the dirt and hit each step as they carted him up the stairs. Despite the bruises, he knew that was a good thing; it meant they were short, both a good eight inches shorter than him, and when free of MacLaren's fortress, he would hold the advantage.

"I wouldn't be for letting ye oot at all," MacLaren informed Rainger's limp form. "But Mother Brigette said I should and the papist woman has a way o' knowing what I do. 'Tis almost spooky how she knows."

Rainger bitterly reflected that she'd known he lied, but not his motives. As far as he was concerned, she had damned poor intuition.

But at least she'd kept Sorcha hidden for him. At least there was that.

The first fresh air he'd breathed in three days seeped through the dusty wool cloth. The first sunshine came through, tinted with brown, but welcome. So welcome.

The two men draped him facedown over a horse.

No, a donkey.

No...well, Rainger didn't know what it was, but it was short and his toes dragged on the ground. In this godforsaken country, it might well be a barrow hog. As the creature trotted along the trail on a harness behind the other two men, the dust rose beneath its hooves, settling into the blanket and making Rainger sneeze. The two Scotsmen brayed with laughter, but Rainger didn't care. The sun warmed his blanket-clad ass. His legs were free...and the knots around his hands barely held him. He worked them, amused by Brian's incompetence, furious with every mile that carried him farther away from Sorcha.

The hour dragged on. The trail wound up into the hills. The men gave up laughing at Rainger and talked to each other. Rainger heard the discussion of crofters, of Englishmen, and the '46, of whether the rain would be enough for the crops. And when he finally slipped the ropes from his wrists, he had the satisfaction of knowing the men were paying him no heed. He pulled the blanket out from underneath him, freeing himself for action. He looked around. He was draped over a shaggy pony. The men rode a few feet ahead of him on horses. He'd have to move fast to knock Brian into the dirt, hoist himself into the saddle, and take MacLaren out.

Then MacLaren said, "This is far enough. Dump him here. Take his boots. See how long it'll take him to make his way back to Edinburgh barefoot and with his hands tied."

Bastard. Rainger held each end of the rope tightly in his fists. *I'm going to make you sorry.*

Brian chortled, pulling Rainger's creature to a halt. Rainger listened as the men dismounted. Brian walked toward him. Rainger tried to judge his location, and Brian made it easy—he patronizingly patted Rainger on the rear.

Like an avenging god, Rainger rose from the pony, threw off the blanket, whirled the horrified Brian in his tracks, and wrapped the taut rope around his stout neck.

Brian choked, grabbed at his throat, and futilely tugged.

MacLaren's face turned ruddy with horror and fury. He scrambled for his musket hung on the side of his saddle.

Rainger laughed. At this range, with the horses plunging and Rainger holding Brian in front of him, MacLaren had no chance of hitting his target without killing Brian, too. "Go ahead," Rainger taunted. "Shoot."

"Ye big bloody arrogant ass!" MacLaren kicked his feet free of the stirrups and threw himself out of the saddle. He pointed the musket at Rainger and stalked forward.

Rainger had to give it to MacLaren. He wasn't intimidated by Rainger's size or prowess—and he was none too bright, for he should be.

But Rainger had no time for a fight. He tightened his grip on the rope.

Brian kicked in abject silence, his shrieks silenced by the pressure on his windpipe—and went limp.

Rainger threw Brian at the approaching MacLaren.

The dead weight sent MacLaren staggering.

Rainger leaped and grabbed the muzzle. He twisted the musket free of MacLaren's grip, then smashed the stock into his chest.

MacLaren fell with a hard thud. Dust rose around him.

Rainger rammed his knee into his chest. He smashed his fist into his face.

MacLaren's head smacked the ground hard. His eyes rolled back, showing the whites.

Rainger laughed again, glad to finish this business. He unbuckled MacLaren's leather belt and truncheon. He ripped the knife and its scabbard off his wrist.

And fingers grabbed his hair and yanked him onto his back.

He didn't have to think. Instinct took possession of him. He waited until Brian leaned over him, then kicked straight up, catching Brian under the chin.

Brian's jaw broke. He screamed.

Rainger didn't waste any more time. Musket in hand, he mounted MacLaren's horse. He took the reins of Brian's horse. And with their saddlebags and their supplies, he rode hard back toward the road.

He had a princess to rescue.

Sorcha rode down the main street of Hameldone, turning her head from side to side, trying to take in all the sights. It had been so long since she'd seen two houses together she could scarcely contain her excitement. The narrow street, dirt road, and cramped, narrow shops gave the place an almost medieval feel, and as she neared the market, the noise of many voices raised to sell and buy sent a shiver of exhilaration down her spine.

Each sound struck her ear, transporting her back to Beaumontagne, to her capital city of Beauvallee. She could almost imagine that when she rode around that corner, she would see the colorful market with the royal palace perched high on the crag above the town, see Clarice and Amy with their arms full of flowers, smiling as they walked toward her—

Clutched by an unreasonable excitement, Sorcha urged the pony forward, around the corner—and almost ran into Sandie, seated on his pony, glowering and surly. "Keep up, young man."

After their first day, he'd never again referred to the fact he knew she was a woman. In fact, despite her cheerful attempts to start a conversation, he'd hardly spoken to her for the two and a half days it had taken the poor ponies to plod their way into Hameldone.

She, who had lived in a convent and dreamed of meeting people, of learning new ways and seeing new places, had spent the first leg of her journey in silence. If he'd been trying to make her glad about his impending departure, he had gone about it the right way.

Now he turned back in his saddle and urged his pony into the depths of the market.

Sorcha's nose twitched as she smelled fresh-baked bread and roasted venison. She would eat here before she took the road east toward Edinburgh. Eat, and buy some rosy apples and some potatoes and some dried beef—

"Are ye going t' ride that beastie up my back?" Sandie asked. "Because if ye are, we can part ways right now."

Startled at his harsh tone, she stared at her traveling companion. At the convent, she had imagined she would hate to part from whoever brought her so far. Actually, she'd be relieved to see his back. "We can part now." With tardy courtesy, she added, "If you're amenable."

He narrowed his eyes.

Belatedly, she realized he might not know the meaning of *amenable*. "I mean, if you don't mind, I'll go on without you."

"I know what ye mean." His gaze flicked over her mount. "Ye'll be taking the pony, then?"

"St. Donkey? Why, yes!" Sorcha could scarcely believe he asked. The poor dear still looked gaunt and at first she'd shown nothing more than a wary acceptance of Sorcha's petting. Now her eager affection made her follow on Sorcha's heels like a dog, and Sorcha wouldn't let her go to a cold fish like Sandie the blacksmith.

"'Tis an expensive gift from MacLaren," Sandie said.

Presumptuous man! "She was not a gift. Mother Brigette paid MacLaren good money for her!"

Sandie grunted and headed for a squat building with a horseshoe nailed on the door.

She followed. "Is that the stable where I should leave St. Donkey?"

"Aye."

"Can you tell me the best place to trade my herbs?"

"Mrs. MacDuncan's."

"And is that the best place to buy supplies for my journey?"

"Aye."

"Can you recommend an inn where I can spend the night? Because I'd like to have a good place to sleep with clean linens and a fine meal before I take to the road."

Sandie stopped. He slewed around in the saddle. He scowled. "If this is what ye mean by parting ways, ye'll be for following me all the way home."

She drew up. She watched him dismount and lead his pony into the stable. She waited until he came out and headed into the crowd. And she took St. Donkey inside, rubbed her down, put her in a stall and fed her, paid the hostler for the straw and the oats, and headed for Mrs. MacDuncan's to sell her herbs.

Sorcha didn't notice the broad-shouldered, well-dressed stranger standing in the shadows, watching her, or see Sandie take a small purse from him and, in an unusual burst of loquaciousness, gesture to her and then to the road out of town.

The road into the wilderness and toward Edinburgh.

Chapter 7

From the moment Rainger fought himself free, it had been a grueling day, but he was rested and the horses were good—MacLaren knew his horseflesh. The pony Rainger abandoned close to Castle MacLaren, figuring the beast would return to its stables if it had any sense. He led the second horse, riding the first one, then the other to keep them fresh. Now he kept an eye on the rocky path and urged them along as quickly as he dared.

But when the sun dipped toward the horizon he had to stop for the night or risk laming the horses on the rocky, pockmarked trail.

Four men sat outside a squat stone farmhouse smoking pipes and watching him; when he asked if he could get lodging, one pointed toward the door with the stem of his pipe and said, "As long as ye've got coin, Mrs. Gurdey will feed ye, and ye can sleep in the hut before the fire."

"I'll sleep in the stable with my horses." Rainger wasn't fool enough to leave the valuable horses alone in this poverty-stricken country.

"As ye like, young firebrand." The spokesman, an older man with as many crags in his face as the Pyrenees Mountains, puffed a smoke ring into the air and let the breeze carry it away. "Where are ye going?"

"To Hameldone." Rainger dismounted. "How much longer will it take me?"

"Riding those fine beasties, ye'll be there before the sun sets tomorrow night."

Two men nodded.

Another said, "Ach, Feandan, he's young and in a hurry. If he hastens, he'll be there by early afternoon—if he doesn't break his neck first."

Rainger smiled a chilling smile. "It's not my neck I'm likely to break."

At the implicit threat, all four men lifted their bushy eyebrows, but they appeared neither worried nor alarmed. Of course not—there were four of them and one of him. They could bring him down if they wished. It was Rainger's task to make them believe such action would cause them more harm than profit.

"All right, then," Feandan said. "Ye'd best tend yer horses. We'll tell Mrs. Gurdey to set another place fer supper."

Rainger turned away, then turned back. "Have any of you been to Hameldone?"

"We're coming back from market," Feandan said.

"Did you see a girl with hair the color of the sunrise?"

"In Hameldone or on the road?"

"Either. Have you seen her? She'd be traveling with a man."

The men exchanged glances. "Nay. Havena seen her."

But they should have—if she hadn't already been attacked.

"Mayhap Mrs. Gurdey will know." The elderly man jerked his head toward the dark, open doorway. "She's the only wayhouse between here and the market. She sees everyone pass."

Rainger took the horses to the stables, curried and groomed them, gave them oats, and returned to the little hut, his thoughts grim. Surely Godfrey wouldn't have traveled so far into the Scottish wilderness after his prey. Yet he'd traveled the road before when he had taken Sorcha to the convent....

The men had disappeared and a tall, stout woman stood in the doorway, her beefy fists resting on her hips. "Show me the color o' yer money. 'Tis na charity house I'm running here."

Rainger kept his gaze on her, not backing away from her hostility, and dug a coin from the pouch he'd taken from MacLaren's saddlebag.

She grunted at the sight, palmed the coin, and disappeared into the hut.

He stepped inside and blinked until his eyes adjusted to the dim light. Smoke swirled up from a small peat fire in the middle of the single primitive room. A pot bubbled on a hook over it. Sausages fried on a hot, flat rock.

The men were gathered around a long, rough table, slurping stew with wooden spoons, scoops of bread, or their fingers.

Rainger did not regret his decision to bed down in the stable.

He joined the men. His hostess slapped a bowl in front of him. Digging out MacLaren's spoon, Rainger joined in the slurping, too hungry to bother with manners that would be ill-appreciated here anyway. When Mrs. Gurdey placed a platter of sausages on the table, his knife held the others at bay while he stabbed the largest.

It was a crafty display of skill, for he trusted these men not at all and they needed to know he was not easy prey.

When he had satisfied his hunger, he sat back, fixed his most princely expression on his hostess, and asked, "Have you seen a young woman with hair the color of sunrise riding the road?"

She stared sullenly at him, a woman who obviously hadn't smiled since the day she first looked in the mirror. "No women ride this road. 'Twould be foolish."

"She was with a man named Sandie."

Mrs. Gurdey stared at him. "Sandie? Aye, Sandie's been here."

"But no woman?"

The female snorted. "Sandie hasna got a woman o' his own. He's a surly bastard, he is."

She returned to the fire to fling on another sausage, leaving Rainger to stare after her and wonder what Sandie's temperament must be to have this woman think he was surly.

Feandan wiped the gravy off his beard. "Did ye lose yer woman, lad?"

"Yes." Years ago. "Yes, I did."

"'Tis a shame when a filly goes astray." He cocked a knowing eye. "Still, there are always others."

"Not for me." Rainger had only the one princess left.

"Ah. 'Tis like that, is it? Well, then, I'm afraid I didna see yer woman, but perhaps she covered her hair."

"Perhaps." Rainger had been so frantic to find her, he hadn't thought that the nuns might have dressed her in a habit or disguised her as…as what?

From the woman by the fire came the answer. "Sandie had a lad traveling with him. Sandie was coming back, but the lad said he was going on t' Edinburgh."

Horror lifted Rainger to his feet. "Did the boy have hair the color of sunrise?"

"I don't know aboot that," she said, "but that lad had carrot hair fer sure. Do ye think that could be yer woman?"

Rainger died a thousand deaths at the thought of Sorcha dressed like a lad. Did Mother Brigette not realize a pretty boy was as likely to be raped as any girl?

But at least Sorcha was a woman who'd had little contact with men and would have the shy nature of a cloistered nun. She would keep to herself, barely speak to strangers, tremble at the idea of interaction with an unfamiliar man—and for her, all men were unfamiliar.

Slowly Rainger sank back onto the bench.

That was what he needed to remember. Sorcha might be untutored in the way of the world, she wasn't bold, and she was very, very wary.

Luckily for Rainger, he didn't know that at that moment, Sorcha stood in the common room of the Brown Cock Tavern, her arms draped around the shoulders of her new best friends, Mike and Haverford, singing the ditty called "Your Bubbies Look Like Melons, But They're Lemons In My Mouth"—and she was having a marvelous time.

The next morning, Sorcha shook hands with Mr. and Mrs. MacCutcheon. "Thank you so much for allowing me to stay in your marvelous accommodations. I can well see why your inn was recommended to me."

"Ach, 'twas a wonderful night we had wi' ye." Mr. MacCutcheon's round face beamed like the full moon. "The best I can remember." He nudged his wife. "Heh, Nellie?"

"I canna remember a better." Mrs. MacCutcheon, as tall and thin as her husband was short and round, wiped her hands on her apron, reached out, and gave Sorcha a jerky hug. In Sorcha's ear she whispered, "I'll remember what ye said about shrieking at the pig rather than MacCutcheon—they're enough alike I'll get me satisfaction and MacCutcheon will stop scowling."

Sorcha hugged her back. "He's a fine man, to have such a fine woman for his wife."

"I'll remind him of that, too." Mrs. MacCutcheon smiled at her spouse, who smiled back with the blissful expression of a man who, the night before, had been well loved.

Sorcha turned to Davis, the blacksmith. "Thank you for recommending this place. It was wonderful getting to know you. I hope someday we can meet again."

Davis rumbled, "Aye, little lad, if ye ever come through Hameldone again, ye must come find me and we'll lift another pint and we'll sing another song."

She punched his meaty shoulder, located at least a foot above her own, and turned to the spry old apothecary. "Mike." Opening her arms, she hugged him as hard as she could. "You dear man, I promise I'll write you when I get home and you must promise to write back and tell me if Miss Chiswick has favorably responded to your suit."

"I still say if she hasna forgiven me after forty years, she's na likely t'." He sniffed as if in disdain.

But Sorcha understood he was actually brokenhearted. "And I still say if you don't try, you'll die regretting it. Besides, I think all she's been waiting for is a simple 'I'm sorry,' and she'll fall into your arms."

"She's a bonny thing." Mike's smile stretched his wrinkled mouth. "She'd look beautiful in orange blossoms."

"That's the spirit." Sorcha turned to Haverford.

Lord Haverford, actually—tall, handsome, a man of wealth, and an Englishman in exile. A knowing smile played across his lips and his blue eyes looked into the depths of hers as if he were trying to tell her something.

He'd been doing that all last evening, too, but last night she'd been tipsy enough not to understand, and today, sober as she was, she still couldn't comprehend what it was he thought he knew. "Haverford, my friend." She extended her hand to him, for Haverford winced whenever she embraced him. "I'll miss you most of all."

Taking her hand between both of his, he cherished it. "I think you should wait to travel on until next week when I can escort you."

"There isn't time for that." Now that she'd left the convent and shed the company of Sandie, she felt the pressure to go forward, to get to Beaumontagne before something dreadful could happen. "I'm in a hurry."

"So you've said. But sometimes it's better to be safe than arrive on time."

All around her, the others nodded.

"'Tis a road fraught with danger that ye ride," Mike said. "And at the end o' it, ye have Edinburgh, the most sinful city in the world."

"I won't be in Edinburgh long," she said. "Just long enough to catch a ship to my destination."

Haverford groaned. "A ship? Like that?" He ran his gaze over her from head to toe. "I should keep you here by force."

"But you won't." She grinned at him. "That would make me unhappy."

Haverford sighed. "No. I won't."

It wasn't that she didn't take his concern seriously, but she easily read his character. Haverford was bone-lazy and without resolution of any kind, and although she had hopes for his future, at the moment she could command him with a crooked finger.

The serving maids waited outside to bid her good-bye, so Sorcha gave her new friends a last wave and escaped through the door to more affectionate farewells.

Then, with a spring in her step, she headed for the stable, where she settled her account. St. Donkey greeted her enthusiastically, shoving her head under Sorcha's arm in search of treats. Sandie's pony was nowhere in sight, and she asked the hostler, "Is Sandie already gone?"

"Yesterday," came the answer.

That surprised her. What had sent Sandie off in such a hurry? Was he so pleased to be rid of her he couldn't wait to leave her behind? It pained her to sit in judgment of her fellow man, but what an odd, nasty sort of person he was!

Yet she had an adventure lying before her, and she cheerfully saddled her pony and rode toward the outskirts of town.

As the last building disappeared on the horizon, she found Haverford mounted on a beautiful horse, his broad shoulders stiff, his posture erect.

Bringing St. Donkey to a halt, she grinned up at him. "Are you waiting for me?"

"I'll ride with you until midday." He lifted one hand. "Don't argue. A young woman of your quality shouldn't be riding about the wilds of Scotland on her own."

"You…you know?" She couldn't believe it. She'd been absolutely manly last night, eating with her fingers and a wooden spoon, singing tavern songs, drinking ale…although Haverford had taken that second pint away from her. "Ohh." No wonder he'd been gazing at her so meaningfully. "*That's* what you were trying to tell me."

"Among other things." He gestured to the road ahead. "Please, ride on."

She urged her pony forward. "What gave me away?"

"What didn't?" He rode behind her.

"Do you mean *everyone* knew?" But she'd been so proud of her disguise!

"No, but last night most of them couldn't recognize their hands in front of their faces." He sounded wry as he said, "You have a way of making a night in a pub into a party."

"It was my first time to spend an evening in an inn." She slewed around in her saddle. "Do you mean it's not normally so jolly?"

A spasm of something that might have been amusement passed over his face. "First, calling that place an inn is like calling a sow's ear a silk purse, and second— it's usually surly drunkards and belligerent blackguards crouched over the cups until they pass out or stagger home. I know. I'm one of the staggerers."

She chewed on her lower lip and worried about the elegant young lord stuck in this tiny burg. "This cannot be good for you. I still think you should apologize to your father and see if he'll relent."

"He relents about nothing, certainly not about a gambling debt so large it stripped him of an estate." Haverford's lips curled in scornful disparagement—of himself.

She hated to see him so disparaging of his weaknesses—and his talents. "Then, much as it saddens me,

I must urge you to move on. Find yourself a wife who loves you regardless of your wealth or lack of it. Or travel to India or the Americas and make a fortune of your own."

He pulled a handkerchief from his pocket and held it to his nose as if he couldn't bear the reek of her schemes.

Irked, she faced forward and urged St. Donkey onward. "Well, do *something*—paint a picture or write a book that will bring you fame and fortune."

The silence that followed her suggestion lasted for several miles and had her turning around in the saddle several times to examine his thoughtful expression.

At last he said, "I hadn't thought of that—the book-writing, I mean. At Oxford, I was considered a fair scribe with a quill. Perhaps I could write about my travels and sell that, then get enough money to travel some more and write yet again."

"That's the spirit!" She rejoiced to see him lifting himself from the despondency that had draped him like black crepe.

"You could come with me on my travels."

"You don't know how wonderful that sounds to me!" To travel where she wished, see strange lands, meet new people, be free of responsibility.... "But I have a destiny that must be followed or I fear the consequences will be dire."

"Damn it!" He cantered forward, close to her side. "Don't you understand? This isn't safe. There are wild animals and dangers you can't imagine."

"I can imagine dangers, believe me."

"But you don't see the obvious dangers. You think people are good. They aren't. They're all out for what they can get, justifying the most horrific deeds so they can sleep at night. Lying, gambling, cheating, stealing, fornicating—oh, I know I'm not supposed to say that to a lady, but you have to think that some man will try to...to hurt you."

"It doesn't do any good to distrust every man I meet," she said gently. "If I did, I wouldn't have you for a friend."

He groaned in frustration.

"But I'm not a complete fool. I do know what you mean." Recalling the fire at the convent, she glanced around. The road here was still rutted with many wheels, but the farther she went from Hameldone, the higher the mountains rose around her and the more isolated she became. "But dear friend, do you know the meaning of destiny? If I don't go and embrace it, it will come to find me."

"How do you know your destiny doesn't lie with me?"

"Oh, Haverford, I wish it did." She grinned at him, but his ardency made her uncomfortable and she pulled up. "It's midday and it's autumn. It'll be dark before you reach Hameldone if you don't turn back now."

"I have been dismissed."

"Yes. It's time for us to part."

"It sits ill with me to think of leaving you here." He waved a hand at the emptiness that surrounded them. "There's not one habitation, not one human soul anywhere in sight."

"Then, according to you, I have nothing to worry about." She smiled bracingly at him.

"Except wild animals and a possible accident." He looked searchingly at the rocks that broke the soft earth like fractured bones through flesh. "And the humans who hide themselves waiting for prey."

"Haverford, I have to ride by myself sometime." She reached up from her pony and patted his knee. "Don't worry."

"But—"

"Nothing will happen to me." She rode along, sending a backward wave at him, but when she glanced back he was still watching her. "Go on, now."

Still he remained in place until she rounded the corner and lost sight of him, and only then did it occur to her that she hadn't pressed him for details as to how he knew she was a woman—and that was information that might come in handy later.

It didn't take Rainger long to discover where Sorcha had spent the night. The whole town of Hameldone buzzed with last night's celebration at the Brown Cock Tavern, and when he asked why the evening had been so special, people were eager to inform him about the carrot-topped lad who'd infused the taproom with his enthusiasm and joy.

He rode at once to the inn itself. It was small, dark, and common, not at all the sort of place where a princess should reside for even one night, yet as he gave the horses a rest and swallowed a hasty dinner, he listened to the innkeeper and his wife chuckle at the young man's easy intoxication and his pure-voiced singing...of songs a sailor would blush to sing.

So much for hoping Sorcha would have the good sense to keep her head down and her wits about her. Apparently she was embracing her newfound freedom with open arms.

God help him.

He hit the road toward Edinburgh as soon as he could, hoping to hell she would manage to stay out of trouble long enough for him to catch up with her, because the idea of her on the road by herself…what had Mother Brigette been thinking? Sorcha was a babe in the woods.

He was an hour out of Hameldone, riding through an increasingly isolated landscape, when he heard a horse galloping toward him. He rounded the corner to see an elegant gentleman galloping along as if the devil himself were on his heels.

Without being told, Rainger knew it was Sorcha who had caused this flight. So he placed himself across the road and when the gentleman slowed, he shouted, "Have you seen a young lad riding a pony on the road ahead?"

The gentleman pulled the horse to such an abrupt halt the gelding almost sat on his haunches. "What do you want with her?"

Her. Damn her, had she trusted this slick, handsome fellow? "I'm her guardian," Rainger shouted, "and I demand to know—"

The gentleman rode right at Rainger and took a wild swing, catching Rainger's cheek with his fist before Rainger jerked backward. "What the hell are you doing, letting her go off on her own like this?" the fellow shouted. "Don't you know how dangerous it is, letting her traipse through the wilderness on her own?"

Temper ignited in Rainger and he swung back, smacking the man squarely in the chest. "What the hell are you doing, leaving her out there on her own? At least I'm going after her!"

"Go after her, then! Take care of her! Someone needs to. She won't let me close to her!"

"She's not yours to keep!"

"No, damn you, she's not. But you'd better be good to her, for God needs her in this world." The gentleman turned and rode toward Hameldone, fleeing like the coward that he was.

Rainger didn't waste time watching him go. Sorcha was safe, or had been when that cad left her alone. Now the bastard was right—it was up to Rainger to keep Sorcha safe. He rode like the wind up the road, concentrating on making good time without laming the horses in the muddy ruts. The wind picked up, whistling in his ears, and that masked the warning sounds ahead, but when he came over a ridge he saw the sight he feared most—he saw Sorcha fighting for her life.

Chapter 8

The black-clad horseman barreled down toward Sorcha. Screaming, she dug her heels into St. Donkey's sides. St. Donkey, bless her, did her best to flee, but even if she'd never suffered malnourishment and ill treatment, she had short legs, a droopy belly, and was ill equipped to escape the unwavering pursuit of a healthy young horse. Sorcha's wide-brimmed hat flapped in the wind. The attacker caught Sorcha before they'd galloped ten yards, lifting her out of the saddle and onto the horse before him.

Furious that Haverford's prediction had come true so soon, she screamed again, a scream laden with frustration and temper. Her cloak tangled around her waist. Flinging herself at the long-armed, ugly villain who gripped her, she had the satisfaction of seeing his expression change from a leer to astonishment. She smacked him under the chin with her head. She heard his teeth clink together.

He spit blood. His blue eyes turned redrimmed. His face contorted with rage and he made a fist.

The horse galloped. They were headed for a corner, a dropoff, a tumble of rocks.

For the first time she realized—he was going to knock her out. Kill her. This time she screamed in fear.

She twisted in a desperate bid to free herself—and beneath her, the horse balked and reared. She found herself airborne, her cloak wrapped over her head. She curled into a ball, braced for the agonizing impact of her bones on brutal rock. She landed, hard, on a patch of grass.

It took a minute to catch her breath. Another to realize she was alive and well. Another long, torturous minute she spent fighting with her cloak, trying to escape the dark folds so she could see which way to run. She jumped when something snuffled at her.

St. Donkey.

"I'm hurrying!" she yelled at the beast. Throwing aside her cloak, she came to her feet.

In the distance, she heard the thunder of galloping hooves, felt the pounding beneath the ground. Her eyes were blurred with tears of pain and shock, but she looked for a safe place. She glimpsed two strange rider-less horses running loose.

She stopped. She tried to understand what had happened.

In the distance, on the rocks, the limp form of her attacker lay smashed.

Was he dead?

His head was cocked at an odd angle.

He *was* dead.

A man stood over the top of him. It looked like Arnou. Arnou...it couldn't be. Impossible. She'd left him behind at the convent. Besides, this Arnou was different. He looked tall, strong, stern, cruel. A wise woman would be as frightened of this man as Sorcha was of her assailant.

"Arnou." Her faint voice couldn't reach across the distance. That irritated her. If this was Arnou, she had nothing to fear of him. She hollered, "Arnou!"

He turned to face her, then turned away. In that quick glimpse she recognized the dark hair, the chis-eled features of the man she'd met at Monnmouth. But he didn't wear the rag that covered half his face. From her vantage point, it appeared he had both eyes.

She blinked.

Lifting his arms, he tied the rag around his face, and when he faced her again, his menacing demeanor dis-appeared as if it had never existed at all.

"What happened?" she shouted. She found herself running toward him. "Did you kill him?"

St. Donkey trotted after her, then stopped to graze.

"What?" Astonishment etched Arnou's face. "I didn't kill anybody. I came riding over the hill and saw you struggling with him. You shoved him and jumped free of the horse. He swayed back and forth, couldn't get control, and his horse bucked him off."

She stopped running. "Are you saying *I* killed him?"

"No, miss. I'm saying you saved yourself, because it sure looked as if he was going to kill you." He bobbled his head as if he were amazed and in awe.

"I think he was." As the realization sank in, her knees wobbled.

"But you saved yourself," Arnou repeated.

"That's right."

"You're a really good adventurer."

"I never knew I could do anything like this."

"You're a heroine."

"Yes, I think I am." His words battered at the wall of her fear, and replaced it with a guilty sort of pride. "We should find him a priest."

"It's too late for a priest. Besides, he's not a good man." Arnou put a gentle hand on her arm and turned her away from the sight of the broken body.

"Do you suppose he was the one who set the fire at the convent?" Her head buzzed with the possibilities—or possibly because of the fall.

"I suppose he is. Him or the guy who hired him." He gave her a little shove. "Go on. I want to see if the blackguard has anything in his pockets that would tell us about him or why he was after you. Why don't you go and catch the horses—there are three, his one and my two—and I'll let you know what I discover."

"All right." She could do that. She'd be *glad* to do that. Capturing the horses would keep her busy and her mind away from the awful results of her flight.

As she wandered away, Arnou called, "You took care of yourself."

Sorcha nodded.

"Mother Brigette would be proud of you."

Mother Brigette *would* be proud of her. She was proud of herself. She'd met her first challenge—and that challenge had been an attempt on her life—and she'd triumphed.

And now she had a job to do.

Sorcha caught the first horse easily. An unsaddled mare, it stood patiently waiting at the top of the hill and when she took its reins, it followed her like a lamb.

Catching the other horses wasn't quite so effortless. One of them, a fine gelding, was saddled and nervous, prancing in an excess of nerves. It took Sorcha several tries before she managed to catch the reins, and a long, soft-voiced discussion of the gelding's beauty and good nature before the horse allowed her to take it to grass and tether it there.

The last horse, her attacker's, was raw and wild, a horse broken too soon, still rebelling against the restraints. She caught him at once, but he reared and fought, and it took all her skill and concentration to bring him down and gentle him. When at last she'd coaxed him into a tether, she found Arnou standing, hands on hips, watching her. "You didn't help me," she said.

"You didn't need it." That foolish grin he wore so convincingly spread across his face. "You're as good with horses as you are with boats."

Like a splash of icy water from the Irish Sea, she remembered that he had let her dive into the ocean to bring in the boat he wanted, and the familiar sense of exasperation settled in. This was Arnou. He was satisfied to let someone else, particularly Sorcha, perform the labor to make his life better.

She pressed her aching palms together. "How did you find me?"

"I didn't do it on purpose. I wanted to go home, that's all."

"How did you get two horses?" Horses worth a lot of money.

"I traded the boat for them."

Hm. She wouldn't have thought that boat would be the worth of two horses. "That must have been a fine boat."

"It was!" he said enthusiastically.

She studied him. He was dirty again, but he didn't smell. Instead, he was splashed with mud from the road. A sturdy truncheon, about a foot long, hung from his leather belt and he looked capable of using it. In fact, out here Arnou seemed large and reliable. She'd thought about traveling with him for safety; now it appeared she could. "How did you recognize me?"

A frown knit his brow. "Why wouldn't I recognize you? You look like yourself."

Logical answers that made her want to shriek imprecations at him. "Have you noticed how I'm dressed?"

"Like a boy, but you still look like yourself. I suppose you're dressed that way for travel, heh?"

"That's right, and you mustn't tell anyone that I'm a girl."

"All right." Going to the still-fractious horse that the attacker had ridden, he laid gentle hands on him. The young horse jerked and shied, but Arnou petted him, spoke to him, until he calmed.

Sorcha wouldn't have thought that a sailor would have so much experience with horses.

"You have an awfully high voice for a lad," Arnou said.

"Oh." Arnou had a good point. Perhaps her speech was the reason Haverford had penetrated her disguise so quickly. "I can make it deeper."

"That would be a good idea."

"Did you…did you find anything on that man that explains why he attacked me?"

"He had money." Arnou lifted a laden purse off his belt. "Lots of money."

Shocked by Arnou's callus action, she asked, "You took his money?"

"He's not going to use it where he's going." Arnou sounded logical and looked indignant.

"No." Abruptly she turned away. "So he was paid."

"I suppose, but I don't know why anyone would try to kill you. You're so pretty and nice!"

Should she tell Arnou the truth?

No. This most recent threat proved the truth of Grandmamma's ironclad adage—royalty trusts no one.

"If we hurry, we should be able to find shelter before nightfall." He walked around her pony, then around the stranger's young horse. He looked them over with an assessing eye. "And if we sell these two beasties, we'll have enough money to finance our journey."

"Sell St. Donkey? I can't do that!" Did Arnou mean he would travel with her? Her heart lifted at the thought of having him at her side. This hearty man would discourage attacks from robbers and assassins, and the road wouldn't be nearly so lonely.

But…oh, dear. Her conscience wouldn't allow her to let him ride into danger with no warning. Even Mother Brigette would agree, she *had* to tell him the truth. "I'm a princess," she blurted.

Grinning, he nodded.

"Someone wants to kill me."

He nodded again, his face falling.

"They're hunting me right now."

Once more he nodded, his lower lip sticking out.

"That man"—she gestured toward the broken body—"was undoubtedly the vanguard of something much worse, and if you go with me, you'll be in danger." She waited for him to say something, to somehow indicate his horror at her situation, and his.

Instead he said, "I *knew* you weren't a nun."

"Is that all you have to say?" He hadn't understood a word she said!

"What else?" He scratched his ear.

"Doesn't the peril on the road worry you?"

"As long as the men who chase you carry these kinds of purses"—he lifted the laden pouch—"I'm well paid for traveling with you. And as long as you knock them out like you did today, I'm safe enough."

She didn't know what impressed her more—his foolishness or his greed.

Going to the gelding, he removed the saddle, then placed it on the mare and cinched it tight. "Tomorrow we'll be in Glenmoore, a fair-sized market town. I can trade the horses—"

"*You* can trade them? Are you better at trading than you are at fighting?"

He hesitated, then shrugged sheepishly. "I'm pretty good at all kinds of things."

"That what I thought." If she had to sell St. Donkey, she intended to make sure Donkey's new owner would love her properly. "I'll do the trading."

"You'll do the trading," he repeated. "I'll just trail along."

Chapter 9

Glenmoore was a den of thieves.

The streets were narrow. The houses small, dark, and mean. Every citizen prided himself on his ability to pick a pocket or cut a purse.

As Rainger and Sorcha rode into town, Rainger kept a sharp eye out. With no more than eight hundred people living here and the promise of winter discourging the travelers, he suspected they made their livings stealing from each other. If he weren't on his guard, he and Sorcha would be fresh victims on which the bloodsuckers could feed.

And clad in her silly boyish disguise, Sorcha was determined to set off alone and sell the assassin's horse and her own pony.

She didn't know it, but he wasn't going to let her leave his sight.

When they reached the town square, she instructed, "You stay here. I'll find a buyer for St. Donkey and Wulfgar."

She'd already named the assassin's horse. The horse trader would know at once she was soft. Once she forgot to keep her voice at a low pitch, he'd know she was a woman. The sale was doomed, and Rainger wanted to smack his head against the nearest wall.

"You guard Conquest"—she petted the gelding she'd claimed as her own—"and Alanjay."

She'd named their horses, too. Of course. But at least he didn't have to call either of them *St. Donkey*. A man had to draw the line somewhere.

Warily, she glanced around the street. "I suspect this town has more than its share of villains."

At least she had the good sense to recognize that!

"I'll be back as soon as I can. Don't wander off!"

"Aye, Sorcha." He found it wasn't difficult to fake compliance when he had no intention of obeying.

"Don't talk to strangers!"

"Aye, Sorcha."

"And whatever you do, don't let the horses out of your sight!"

"Good luck, Sorcha!" he called, and waited only until she turned the corner before eyeing the available scum and making his choice.

A pickpocket worked the meager crowd: a youth not yet twenty, burly, selecting his victims with an eye to the best profits for the least trouble.

That was Rainger's man.

Rainger made a great show of counting his coins, then carelessly stuffed the pouch on his belt. He could only hope that in this crowd his man would be the first to the bait.

When he felt the weight of the pouch vanish, he whipped around and nabbed his pickpocket by the ear.

The youth struggled and howled.

"Shut up." Rainger tightened his grip, rescued his pouch, and led the wincing lad around the corner to a quiet street. "What's your name?"

"Farrell."

"Farrell, you're a lucky young man." Rainger grinned at him. He didn't grin as he grinned at Sorcha, broadly and stupidly. For Farrell, he used a toothy grin that showed his sharp white teeth and predatory nature. "I've chosen you to be the guard for my horses."

"Why would I do that?" Farrell's eyes shifted back and forth as he sought an escape.

"Perhaps because I caught you cutting my purse and I'd be glad to give you up to the constable. I'm sure the constable would be pleased to get his hands on a man of your reputation and skills. He might like to make an example of you—I hear hanging is painful and lasts a long, long time." Rainger let Farrell mull that over. "But you should guard my horses because I recognize a youth with talent and want to pay you five shillings for the privilege of caring for these fine beasts."

The youth stopped fighting and eyed Rainger suspiciously. "Let me see."

Rainger pulled the coins from his pouch. "Five shillings." He tossed them in the air, let the sun glint on the edges, and caught them with one hand. "Two right now, three when I come back and you, and my horses, are still here."

"That sounds easy!" Farrell's eyes gleamed with avarice and an ill-hidden laughter.

"And if you and my horses have disappeared"— Rainger used Farrell's ear to bring them face to face— "I'll hunt you down and shake my shillings and whatever you were paid for my horses right out of your arse."

Rainger knew very well the effect of his icy stare on a younger man, and he wasn't disappointed now. Farrell blenched. He tried to duck away, but couldn't tear himself free. "Dunna fancy the job," he muttered. "I could get hurt."

"That's too bad, because as far as I'm concerned, the job is yours—whether you want it or not."

Impatient with Rainger's lack of understanding, Farrell snarled, "No, ye dolt, ye dunna understand. The others'll steal the horses from me and there's na a thing I can do aboot it, or not much."

Rainger showed Farrell the two shillings, then shoved them in the youth's pocket. "What do you think would be our horses' best protection? Running with them from one place to another or putting them in a stable and guarding them there?"

"Stable," Farrell squeaked. "Na, wait. Keeping a move on. Then everyone will think I'm taking them t' sell."

"Good idea." Rainger shoved the reins into Farrell's hand. "Start moving and I'll find you when my business is done. And remember what I told you. If my horses are gone, I'll hunt you down. Do you believe me, Farrell?"

"Aye! I believe!" Farrell started toward the square. "I believe," he called back again.

Satisfied he'd frightened Farrell enough to keep him honest for at least as long as the bargaining required, Rainger walked after Sorcha. Two women gossiped by the well; he stopped, bowed, and asked, "Have either of you two women seen a young man, about so tall"—he indicated Sorcha's height—"with blue eyes and—"

"Ach, ye mean the beardless youth with the horse-flesh t' trade." The woman who spoke should recognize a beard; she sported a heavy mustache as well as wild, iron-gray eyebrows and a scarf tied over her dirty hair. "He asked for the most honest buyer in Glenmoore. We sent her t' MacMurtrae's Stable."

"He's na honest, but he'll na kill the young man for the gold in his teeth, either. Besides, he's the only buyer in Glenmoore." The younger woman had no mustache, but Rainger had no doubt it would sprout soon. "He's a nice lad and doesn't deserve that fate."

"Follow this street almost t' the end and take a left," the older woman instructed. "You'll recognize the stables when ye get there."

"Thank you, ladies." Rainger tipped his hat and stalked grimly toward MacMurtrae's. After not even an hour in town, Sorcha had made herself known to half the citizenry. How did she do it?

He knew he'd found his target when the houses thinned, the street grew ever more muddy, and he rounded the corner to find himself staring at the back end of St. Donkey and Wulfgar. Lurching to a stop, he backed into the shadows and surveyed the scene.

Sorcha stood with her back to him, the reins in her hands, arguing vehemently with a squint-eyed, ill-dressed, middle-aged horse dealer.

MacMurtrae, Rainger assumed.

MacMurtrae wasn't arguing back. He just stood with his thumbs tucked into the lapels of his plaid jacket, shaking his head with a smug expression on his face.

If Rainger had interpreted the scene correctly, that expression meant MacMurtrae knew he was dealing with a woman—in Sorcha's indignation, she had forgotten to lower her voice. And as all men knew, women were always easy to gull.

But last night Sorcha had prepared for this trade, asking Rainger what he thought the horses were worth and adding her opinion based on the discussion she'd had in Hameldone with the stable owner. To Rainger's surprise, she shrewdly discussed the process of selling the beasts, and it was only MacMurtrae and his monopoly that held her back now.

"That's outrageous!" Sorcha's light, cultured, very feminine voice carried clearly to Rainger. "These horses are worth twenty times what you're offering."

"They're worthless beasts, old and bandy-legged."

"They are not!"

"Yet there's na one else t' sell them t'." MacMurtrae sighed in fake sadness. "So I guess ye'll take what I'm offering."

"I'll ride them all the way to Edinburgh before I sell them to you!" She meant it, too.

Rainger would have to step in.

"What will ye feed them, young man?" MacMurtrae asked. "Between here and the capital there's little but rain, mud, and soggy grass. No shelter, barely a path through the dales and o'er the passes. Ye'll have trouble riding those other two animals ye brought int' town, so ye might as well offer *them* t' me, too."

She laughed, and the carefree sound startled Rainger—and MacMurtrae, for he jumped and nervously fingered his stained cravat. "We'll eat the horses first."

"Don't say that, lad! Ye don't eat fine beasts like these!" Realizing what he'd admitted, MacMurtrae swore long and colorfully.

With a smile, Rainger backed up again.

Sorcha *was* good at barter, but she couldn't win in this town with this buyer. Not without some help, and Rainger was the man to give it.

"I'll give ye twenty-five guineas for the two o' them," MacMurtrae declared.

"I want twenty guineas for the pony and two hundred guineas for the horse."

"Twenty pounds...and two hundred...." MacMurtrae sputtered at her cheek. Trying to regain control of the situation, he said firmly, "Twenty-five guineas and na a tuppence more."

Stepping out of the shadows, Rainger stared long and hard at MacMurtrae.

MacMurtrae's eyes narrowed, and he laid his hand on the pistol at his side.

Sorcha swiveled to see why MacMurtrae glared over her shoulder.

Rainger slipped back around the corner.

He heard her say with authority, "Two hundred and twenty guineas for the two of them, and not a tuppence less."

Rainger moved back into view. With the tip of his knife, he indicated the price should rise.

The horse trader glared, his male pride offended.

Rainger grinned at him, that toothy grin he had perfected which didn't indicate happiness but rather a willingness—no, a desire—to beat MacMurtrae into calf's-foot jelly.

Amazing, how an unspoken threat could make a bully like MacMurtrae straighten up and take notice. The color drained from his face and as quickly as he could he said, "As a favor t' ye, I could give ye an extra twenty guineas..."—at a gesture from Rainger, he changed it—"twenty-five guineas. But no more!" He pointed his finger at Sorcha and tried to ignore Rainger, but when Rainger's grin changed to a snarl, MacMurtrae jumped like a hunted rabbit.

Sorcha recognized that she'd suddenly developed the upper hand. In a persuasive tone, she said, "The pony's well broken in, the perfect mount for a child or as a beast of burden. The horse is young with good lines, with years of service ahead of him, and MacMurtrae— you should see him run. He's like harnessing the wind!"

By the time the negotiations were finished, Sorcha had over two hundred guineas for both beasts and Mac-Murtrae was sweating like the horse when it had run flat out for a mile.

When the final terms had been agreed upon, Sorcha petted St. Donkey. "MacMurtrae, this sweet girl has to go to a good home, and Wulfgar needs a good master, one who'll understand his wild spirit."

"Would ye like t' interview the buyers?" MacMurtrae asked sarcastically.

Rainger sighed at MacMurtrae's folly.

"Can I?" Sorcha's eager question echoed up the walls.

"Nay." MacMurtrae took the reins from her.

"But you'll make sure St. Donkey has a good life, won't you?" Sorcha gave the pony a last long, loving pet. "She was named after the donkey that carried Mary to Bethlehem."

Rainger thought it was probably the first time since MacMurtrae was out of diapers that his expression softened. But it did and he, too, petted the pony. Then his face regained its usual surly scowl. "Do ye want me t' interview the children she'll carry t' make sure they're kind?"

"That would be lovely." Sorcha beamed at him. "I knew that gruff exterior hid a kind heart."

"Buried deep," MacMurtrae growled. "Verra deep."

"It was a pleasure to deal with you, sir." Taking his hand, she pumped it enthusiastically.

When she released him and walked away, MacMurtrae wiped his palm on his pants.

Rainger relaxed and prepared to return to his horses.

Then Sorcha turned back to MacMurtrae. "You've been so fair, given me such an enjoyable barter, and I know I can trust you—so can you tell me, please, where can I get a meal? Someplace I can eat and pick up food for someone else?"

Rainger saw it happen before his very eyes.

An evil scheme took root and blossomed in Mac-Murtrae's head. With a cheerful gloat in Rainger's direction, he dipped his head and whispered in Sorcha's ear.

"Thank you!" She started toward the edge of town.

"Hell!" Rainger followed.

MacMurtrae collared him as he walked past. "Ye got what ye wanted, man—a blasted guid price for the horses and yer woman's pleased wi' herself."

In return, Rainger collared MacMurtrae. "She's a lad. Remember that. She's a lad."

"If she is," MacMurtrae reported, "she's a damned silly lad."

Rainger shoved past MacMurtrae.

But by the time he turned the corner behind Sorcha, she had disappeared.

Chapter 10

With her wonderful, hard-won two hundred pounds jingling in her pocket, Sorcha almost danced down the street and toward the inn recommended by Mr. MacMurtrae.

Arnou would be so pleased with her success! And surprised, too, for although he'd tried to hide his doubts, he clearly had misgivings that she could get the amount they'd decided would be appropriate. Plus she had the added satisfaction of knowing MacMurtrae would place the horses in good homes. Beneath that gruff, tough exterior, MacMurtrae was obviously a good man.

Sorcha knocked on the narrow door in the wall to which he had directed her, and when the serving girl opened it, Sorcha smiled. Careful to keep her voice at a masculine pitch, she said, "I've come to eat."

The girl looked Sorcha over, then said, "All right. I'm Eveleen. This way." Eveleen led her into a small, dim foyer decorated with two marble statues—nymphs holding water vases on their shoulders. An odd choice for an inn, but the whole place looked odd. Or rather— too nice to be a common inn.

As Sorcha followed Eveleen down a long corridor, she noted that this place was larger than it appeared. A series of closed doors lined one side of the hallway. A shut set of double doors were right in the middle of the wall on the other side. The walls were plastered, white-washed, and decorated with framed paintings of lovely women in various stages of undress. Sorcha lingered by one, a well-rendered scene of a female bathing in a moonlit waterfall wearing nothing more than a startled expression. On the cliff above her, a man and his horse stood in shadow, looking down at the girl. His air of brooding intent made Sorcha's heart beat faster. The woman had no chance; he would capture her and have his way with her.

"Come on." Eveleen grabbed Sorcha's arm and tugged. "Ye can admire the art on the way oot. There's better stuff ahead."

"Really?" Sorcha stumbled after her. "Because I know something about art, and that painting is amazing. It tells a story. Is it supposed to be Zeus and one of his paramours?"

"I dunna know." Eveleen was clearly a workingwoman who wasted no time. "Ye'll have t' ask Madam."

"Madam? Does she run this inn?"

"Wi' an iron fist in a velvet glove."

They passed an open door—a bedroom! how odd to find one on the ground floor—and the light from the open window shone on Eveleen. She was very pretty, even exotic-looking. Her clear skin was a lovely tan, her eyes were large, brown, and lined with dark lashes, and her shoulder-length hair was a magnificent mahogany color and caught at the nape of her neck with a bow. But her costume…it was very odd for a serving girl. Daring, even. Her dress was cut like a nightgown, with a low neckline, a marvelous amount of lace, and was created of a material that looked almost transparent. Perhaps the outfit might tease forth coins from stingy men's purses.

No—Sorcha had learned a lot since she'd left the convent. Without a doubt that outfit would tease coins from *any* man's purse.

"What's your specialty?" Sorcha hoped this place used herbs to cook. So far on this journey Scotland's cookery hadn't impressed her.

"My specialty?" The girl glanced at her. "Blowing the hornpipe."

"What's that? Some sort of sausage dish?"

The girl laughed. "Ye could say that." Then she stopped so quickly Sorcha, walking and gawking at yet another painting, almost ran her over. "Have ye done this before?"

"Eaten?" Surprise sent Sorcha's tone into a more feminine register. Lowering it again, she asked, "What do you mean? Of course I've eaten."

"Hmmm." The girl ran her gaze over Sorcha. In a voice laden with suspicion, she asked, "Who sent ye?"

"MacMurtrae the horse trader."

"Are ye sure it wasn't the constable?"

"No." *The constable?* Why would Eveleen think it had been the constable? "It was MacMurtrae. I just sold him two horses. Well, a horse and a pony." Sorcha couldn't resist bragging, "I got more than he wanted to give."

Picking up Sorcha's hand, Eveleen examined it. A sudden, gamine grin blossomed on her lovely face, and she folded the fingers into Sorcha's palm. "This is too guid. Madam will never forgive me if I dunna include her in the jest."

This place just got odder and odder. "What jest?"

Walking back to the big double doors, Eveleen knocked.

A low, cultured contralto voice called, "Come in."

Opening the doors with a flourish, Eveleen gestured Sorcha inside.

The small parlor was decorated in aqua and furnished with tastefully feminine furniture. Potted flowers grew and bloomed in massive porcelain vases. Heavy drapes covered the windows, and candles lit the room. Their dancing flames illuminated the face of the extraordinary woman—an immense woman in height and breadth, dressed in a loose flowing robe and an all-encompassing, paint-splotched apron that emphasized her tremendous proportions. Her chins stairstepped from her chest to her face with nary a glimpse of her neck. Her jaw was square, her mouth a tiny red rosebud. Her nose was an indeterminate blob, but her eyes…her wise brown eyes reminded Sorcha of Mother Brigette.

The lady stood before an easel, holding a small brush laden with scarlet paint, and the acrid odor of mineral spirits mixed with the scent of flowers.

Posed against a background created by blue velvet stood a young woman of perhaps twenty-five, clad in nothing more than a flower over one ear and a sheet tied at one hip. She stood in silhouette, her blond hair rippling down her back, her arms outstretched to capture some unseen treasure.

Sorcha's jaw dropped. She knew her grandmother would tell her that princesses were never nonplussed, but color climbed in her cheeks and she couldn't tear her gaze away from the extraordinary scene.

Tear her gaze away? She couldn't even blink.

"This is Madam Pinchon." Eveleen shut the door behind her and leaned against it. "Madam, this youth"—she winked at Madam Pinchon—"came t' the back door asking for something t' eat."

"Did he indeed?" Madam was the owner of the contralto voice—and, from the work on the canvas, also the artist of the paintings in the corridor. The canvas showed a pale nymph, surrounded the blue shadows of trees, reaching for a silver moon.

Enthusiasm swept away Sorcha's awkwardness. "You're a marvelous talent. But you don't need me to tell you that."

"Nevertheless, I appreciate the compliment." Madam extended a hand.

Sorcha took it and noted the short fingers, the broad palm, and spatulate fingernails with pigment under the cuticles. "Salt of the earth," she whispered under her breath.

Madam laughed, a full, hearty laugh. "Exactly."

"Madam has the sharpest ears in Scotland, so be careful what ye say," Eveleen advised.

The girl with the upraised arms spoke. "She knows more than any of us care t' have revealed. But she is most discreet about disclosing it."

"You, on the other hand, are not at all discreet about my secrets," scolded Madam. "I prefer my victims unaware."

"Victim?" Sorcha tried to take a step back, but Madam still held her hand.

"It's simply an expression." Madam released her. "I would never hurt you."

Sorcha believed her. With her voice, her size, her presence, it was impossible not to. But she also realized—this was not an inn.

She just couldn't put her finger on what it was.

The posing girl shifted uncomfortably. "Please, Madam, can I put my arms doon now?"

"We're done for today." Madam cleaned the brush with mineral spirits. When the girl started to walk across the room, seemingly unconscious of her nudity, Madam said, "Helen, clothe yourself. There's no need to discomfit our young client."

Helen stopped and blinked at Madam. "Ye think I'm going t' discomfit this youth? Because all the fellows I know would gladly pay t' see me—" Helen focused on Sorcha. Her green eyes grew wide and astonished, and she said, "Oh!"

"Yes." Madam washed her hands in the basin beside her brushes. "Oh."

Sorcha looked down at herself. Had she forgotten to button something? Then she caught Helen exchanging a smile with Eveleen. They seemed to speak without words, and in a way, this place reminded Sorcha of the convent.

Yet it wasn't a convent.

"Young man, sit." Madam lowered herself into a large armchair and waved Sorcha to the one opposite. When Sorcha had obeyed, she asked, "Do you believe in the art of palmistry—that is, of reading your fortune in your hand?"

"It's nonsense," Sorcha said firmly. Then she wavered. "But I have an immense curiosity about my future."

"Then you're in luck." Madam lifted one plump finger. "I'm a gypsy. What I see is not nonsense, and if you cross my palm with silver I can read your fortune. Have you any silver?"

"Yes, I have a lot of silver." Sorcha couldn't resist. She had to brag again. "I made a wonderful sale of two horses—not horses, really, but a pony and a horse—"

Madam waved her to a stop. "First—tell no one, no one at all, when you possess a wealth of silver. You never know who can hear you, and you put your life at stake. And second—all it takes for me to read your palm is one small coin. Do you have a small coin?"

Abashed, Sorcha sorted through the heavy pouch at her belt, brought out the smallest coin she could find, and handed it to Madam. "You remind me of Mother Brigette."

"Mother Brigette?" Madam placed the coin on the polished table beside her. "The mother superior of the convent at Monnmouth?"

Eveleen gave a snort, then covered her mouth with her hand.

Helen giggled and carried a candelabra over to place on the table beside them.

Madame's small eyes were alive with clever amusement.

Their glee hurt Sorcha's feelings and put her on edge. "Do you know Mother Brigette?"

"Yes." Madam's laughter died. "A woman of kindness and charity. She suffered much tragedy in the loss of her family."

Sorcha's wariness faded. Mother Brigette had made it clear few people knew of her misfortune. That Madam did meant somehow, sometime their paths had crossed. For Mother Brigette to confide in Madam meant Mother Brigette had respect for the huge lady, and that knowledge made Sorcha comfortable enough to place her hand in the cup of Madam's.

Madam turned it over, looked at the fingernails, then outlined the shape of Sorcha's palm. "Danger hems you all around."

Sorcha blinked in astonishment. "Yes!"

"But you miraculously survive. That's because— look at the stubbornness in this hand!"

Madam wasn't right about that. "I'm not stubborn. I'm most amenable."

"That's what you *think* you are, not *what* you are. The last years have changed you and fired the metal in your soul." Madam smiled as if well pleased. "You refuse to submit to death no matter how closely it presses you." Then she started. She turned Sorcha's hand toward the light of the candles. She paled.

"What is it, Madam?" Helen leaned close. "What do you see?"

Sorcha looked from one woman to the other in alarm.

"Your fingertips...they show the signs...you have touched death!" Madam stared at her. "When? When were you ill? When were you hurt? Your palm shows no sign of that!"

"I'm never ill and I've never been hurt. Not seriously." Ridiculous that Madam should believe such a thing. Yet...

She was buried alive.

And she didn't care. Somewhere close, water seeped into a pool, and the slow drip which had once driven her mad now contributed to her indifference. Her world was sorrow and loneliness. She was dying, and she welcomed the end of desolation, of grief, of anguish.

Her fingertips touched the skeletal hand of Death...

That dream. The dream that had brought her out of a sound sleep and haunted her ever since.

"Then you went with another to the threshold of heaven—or hell."

Madam's eyes stared hypnotically into Sorcha's, trying to force her to acknowledge something Sorcha didn't want to talk about. Didn't want to remember. "No. I didn't."

"Did you bring him back?" Madam whispered.

"I don't know what you're talking about, and you don't, either!" Sorcha closed her hand into a fist.

Eveleen and Helen gasped and looked warily at Madam.

So people didn't usually speak so bluntly to Madam. But Madam shouldn't be insisting when Sorcha wanted her to *stop*.

Madam straightened. "What temper!"

Sorcha took a calming breath. "I'm sorry, I shouldn't have snapped at you."

"No, I meant here." As if nothing awkward had happened, Madam opened Sorcha's hand and pointed to the pad under her little finger. "You have a terrible temper."

"I don't have a temper." *Madam must be reading the wrong hand.* "I am most affable. Everyone says so."

Madam traced a line that bit deep across Sorcha's thumb. "You are too quick to judge."

"That's not true, either. I think things through."

"You've never been tested," Madam answered firmly. Fixing Sorcha with a stern gaze, she said, "Remember, it is you who, at the crossroads, chooses your path. You cannot see clearly if the red mist is before your eyes. Wait until it dissipates, then make your decision and speak your mind."

"I'm almost too meek. Everyone says so." Sorcha added the ultimate argument. "*Grandmamma* says so!"

Madam paid no heed to her contention. "You have a great work ahead of you in your land, but first you must struggle through the challenges."

That was true, anyway.

"Put your faith in God, and your hand in the grasp of the one who loves you. You already know the one."

"You mean a man? You see a man?" Sorcha searched her own palm, trying to spy this man of whom Madam spoke. All she saw were calluses from the hoe and shovel, and lines crisscrossing the pale, dry skin. There was no man. The only man she knew was Arnou and he didn't love her. At least…he'd never indicated that he loved her.

"Take that hand. Then you will have great happiness. Great happiness!" Madam squeezed Sorcha's hand.

And Sorcha couldn't take Arnou's hand, not in the way Madam meant. He was a fisherman from Normandy. She was a princess.

"You'll want to hurt him, but don't. Teach him. He's been hurt enough." As Madam moved Sorcha's fingers and watched the changes in her palm, she shook her head as if she pitied this mythical man.

Oh, why was Sorcha even contemplating this? Obviously, palm-reading was absurdity at its finest. Again she pulled away.

Madam let her go. What Sorcha had assumed was a parlor game was now a celestial outline, and no matter how absurd Sorcha thought it was, Madam's small, dark eyes were completely earnest.

The other women must have seen the doubt in Sorcha's face, for Eveleen advised, "Ye should listen t' Madam. It's scary the way she's right."

"It's true," Helen added.

"But she can't be right this time," Sorcha said. "What she said just isn't true."

Madam smiled as if she weren't at all offended. "In the end, we'll see who is right."

"Besides," Helen said with sly amusement, "I'll wager she knows something about ye that ye never imagined."

"No one here's going t' take that wager." Eveleen smiled.

Madam chuckled, a warm, deep laugh that made her whole body jiggle.

Sorcha looked from one to the other. "You're laughing at me again and I don't know why."

"If I tell you your deepest secret, will you believe what I read in your hand?" Madam asked.

Madam knew her deepest secret? Sorcha pulled the collar of her cloak closer around her throat, lowered her voice, and said, "Sure."

Leaning forward, Madame touched Sorcha's cheek. "The clothes are a poor disguise for your beauty, Your Highness."

"How did you…?" Sorcha jumped. She stared at her palm. She saw no crown, no throne, no marking that signified her gender or her royalty. She thrust her hand at Madam. "Did you see that *here*?"

"We know a lot aboot the difference between men and women," Helen said. "Eveleen guessed ye were a lass. So did I."

Sorcha wore a boy's clothes. She had deepened her voice. Apparently that wasn't enough. "All right, you saw through my disguise. But why would you call me *Your Highness?*"

Eveleen sat in a chair.

Helen perched on the arm.

"Less than a fortnight ago, a man came to us. He had money. He had a good horse that ran like the wind. He was ugly as the devil, and he wore black. All black."

Sorcha took a startled breath. "The man who…"

"Tried to kill you?" Madam finished for her.

"How did you know?" Now Sorcha believed in Madam's prognostications. How could she not? Madam *was* telling her her deepest secrets.

"He drank deep," Helen said, "and he confided in me that he was an assassin sent to murder the princess of Beaumontagne. I urged him to tell me more." Helen's eyelids drooped in sultry invitation. "He said he was one of many men who were offered a reward to kill this princess who lived in a convent. He said a prince had been sent to bring you home, and that all he had to do was follow him, slaughter you, take your necklace as proof of his deed. He said he was the only one who'd taken to the road, that the rest of the shiftless assassins were waiting on the way to Edinburgh or in the city itself. He said he'd catch you for sure and he'd have twice as much money as before."

"The assassin found me." Sorcha wet her lips. "The prince did not."

"But you survived the assassin," Eveleen said.

"Yes."

"Good for you," Helen said. "He was a braggart and lousy in—"

Madam cleared her throat.

Helen snapped her mouth closed.

"We all have secrets here." Madam leaned back and folded her arms across her ample belly. "So, Your Highness, it is your turn. I'll give you a clue—this isn't a convent. Guess our deepest secret."

Sorcha heard the babble of women's voice as they passed outside the doors. The aqua in this room was flattering to Helen, to Eveleen, even to Madam, and probably to herself. The gold candelabra showcased the candles, and the soft brilliance they cast highlighted each seat so deliberately she detected a master hand at work. A love seat, the couch, and the chair were upholstered in dainty needlework, and the wood trim was a light oak, airy and open. The room was a gem in itself, and filled with lovely women, it would be a showcase.

Realization dawned. "You're...ladies of the night. And this...this is a house of ill repute!"

"The best house in Glenmoore," Eveleen said.

"The only house in Glenmoore," Helen added.

Sorcha couldn't believe her good luck. No woman she'd ever met had had the fortune of meeting a prostitute. She'd wager not even Grandmamma had visited a bawdyhouse and here Sorcha was, in the middle of the parlor with Glenmoore's finest! "I asked that horse trader out there where I could *eat*."

Eveleen and Helen collapsed in an entwined heap of merriment.

"That MacMurtrae." Madam smiled. "He's a sly one."

"Aye, ye can eat here," Eveleen said, "but ye can't *eat* here, if ye know what I mean."

Wide-eyed, Sorcha shook her head.

"Aye." Helen pushed at Eveleen's shoulder. "She's got *virgin* written all over her."

"That she does," Madam said.

Sorcha wanted to ask questions, to unearth all the mysteries about men and women, to be the smartest, most savvy princess in all of Europe. One question covered it all, and it burbled from her lips. "What do you *do* with men?"

Madam laughed out loud, something Sorcha thought happened but rarely. "The answer could take mere minutes or long days." To her girls, she said, "Take her down to the kitchen and feed her. She's hungry."

Someone knocked loudly and insistently at the outer door.

Madam used her hands to heft herself to her feet. "*I'll* go see who seeks to disturb our peace."

The girls took Sorcha's arms and led her toward the door. "We'll get ye a meal, and ye can tell us what ye do know about men."

"Thank heavens! I'm starving." But Sorcha had to tell Madam one thing. One very important piece of information. Turning back, she said, "My name is Sorcha."

Madam's eyelids drooped over her wise old eyes. She murmured, "Sorcha."

Sorcha knew her name was carved in the stone of Madam's mind, and if something happened to her in this bleak land, if one of the assassins succeeded, Madam Pinchon would know who to tell, and what to put on her lonely tomb.

Chapter 11

Rainger pounded on the small, inconspicuous door with the knuckles he'd used to knock the information and the smug laughter right out of MacMurtrae.

The horse trader had sent Sorcha to a whorehouse. A whorehouse! She'd been in there for a half hour while he'd been searching for her, and she hadn't come out—he'd knocked that information out of MacMurtrae, too. Dear God, what was she doing in there? What were they doing to her? He had visions of Sorcha *saying* things that would make the prostitutes laugh at her. *Seeing* things that would shock and dismay her. *Doing* things out of ignorance, things that would confuse her and destroy her innocence. If someone didn't open this door soon, he was going to kick it down.

The door opened beneath his fist, and he almost fell into the dim foyer.

He regained his balance and, for the first time in his life, he stared *up* at a woman. She was *tall*. She also outweighed him by five stones. She probably served as the guard for the whorehouse, and that meant she was physically powerful.

"Yes?" Her deep voice demanded respect and an explanation.

Rainger tried a lie first. "My…brother came in here not long ago. It's a mistake, he shouldn't be here…."

"Your…brother?" The huge woman imitated his tone. Before he could duck, she grabbed him by the collar and yanked him inside.

That settled the issue of her strength.

She slammed the door behind him. "Tell me about your brother."

"He's about so tall"—Rainger showed her with his hand—"with red hair and a black cape."

"I may have met him." The woman looked down her nose at Rainger. "What can you tell me that would convince me to let you see him?"

"He just sold two horses and he's proud of himself."

"If that's the best you can do, I'm throwing you out the door." The woman flicked her sausagelike fingers.

Damn. What did she know? Rainger improvised, "He's never been to a place of this nature and he's ill prepared for the rigors required."

She inclined her head. "What else?"

"He's traveling to Edinburgh with me. He probably mentioned me. I'm Arnou the fisherman."

"He said not a word about you." Opening the door, she grabbed the scruff of his neck and prepared to throw him out.

He probably could've hurt her, but he didn't fight women, especially not women who appeared to be protecting Sorcha. Hastily he said, "He's not what he appears."

The woman tightened her grip.

"He's a she!" Rainger blurted.

The woman shut the door...with him still on the inside. She let him go. "Now, why did you tell me *that*?"

He straightened his clothing. "Because I figured you already knew or you wouldn't be harassing me."

"I know a lot of things about that lass, and I know nothing about you, so you'd better start confiding your secrets or I promise you, you'll never see her again."

Possessive fury ripped through him. He stepped up to the woman. He fixed his gaze on hers. "Do not tell me I'll never see Sorcha again. She's *mine*."

For one scorching moment, the woman held his gaze. Then she blinked. "Come with me." Turning her back on him, she walked down the corridor, leaving him standing alone, fists clenched at his side.

What game was she playing?

Did she not fear that he would attack from the back?

Was she so sure of herself? Of him?

As he debated, she walked out of sight in the dim corridor. "Come!" she called.

He did. She led him to a well-appointed parlor of aqua and gold—but it was empty. The room smelled of paint and mineral spirits...and perfume. Sorcha wasn't here, and he stood in the doorway as the huge woman seated herself on a delicate chair that looked as if it would break under her weight. "Where is she?" he asked.

"She's here. She's safe. I intend that she will remain that way." The woman pointed to a chair opposite hers. "Sit and talk to me. Convince me I should allow you to see her."

Instead he stood. "If you'll just ask her, she'll tell you that I'm her traveling companion and your suspicions will be lulled."

"You're wrong. That girl is an innocent. She has no idea who her enemies are, and I do not intend to deliver her to you without assurances." Her voice flicked at him like a whip. "Sit down."

He sat.

"Give me your hand."

This woman made him wonder if he'd fallen into delirium. He gave her his hand.

She examined the shape, looked at his nails, turned the palm upward, and stared at it, apparently arrested by...the fact it was clean? The depths of the lines? The slash across the fingers of his right hand...the slash Count duBelle had made with his cane?

He waited for her to comment on it, but when her heavy lids lifted, she stared into his eyes and said, "Your fingers have touched death."

He stared back. His brain absorbed the impossible information: this woman knew what had happened. How was that possible?

It wasn't possible. Only one man living knew what had happened that night, and he was far away, and he never spoke of it. Not even to Rainger.

But this woman didn't wait for an answer. "You are Sorcha's prince."

Did this woman have sources he didn't imagine? Was *she* an assassin?

"No. I only suspected. I didn't know until this moment." She watched him as if she knew his very thoughts. "I am Madam Pinchon. I'm the owner of this establishment and have been for more than five years. Yes, I will kill you—but only if you have ill intentions toward that girl. Does that calm your suspicions?" When he didn't answer, she smiled. "No. Of course not. Your suspicions are well founded and part of your being. But I warn you, Prince, you're making a mistake not trusting that girl."

"I trust her."

"Enough to tell her who you are?"

"I have my reasons for not revealing myself to her." And he carried weapons on him right now. If this woman, this Madam Pinchon, tried to kill him, he would respond with all his strength. If she'd hurt Sorcha, she'd live only long enough to suffer.

She drummed her fingers on the arm of the chair and pondered him as if he were a puzzle. "So you're her prince, but you've never met."

"We grew up together." An exaggeration, for he'd lived in the palace in Richarte and Sorcha had lived in Beaumontagne, but at least once a year their parents had traveled to see each other. Rainger couldn't remember a time when he didn't know Sorcha.

"But she's traveling with you. Why doesn't she remember you?"

"I've changed." An understatement.

Madam scrutinized his face, half covered by a rag. "There's nothing wrong with your eye."

"No." Let her know he was a powerful, healthy man capable of defending himself and Sorcha.

"Just as she is disguising herself, you're disguising yourself. But why? Why don't you tell her who you are?"

"I have no assurance she'll meekly go with me to be wed, and I can't lose her now. Too much depends on our union."

"What masculine madness leads you to believe she'll wed a man who lied to her?"

"When we return to Beaumontagne, she'll have no choice."

"You're a fool. Too much royal crossbreeding, I suppose." Standing, she started for the door. "Come with me. Sorcha's downstairs in the kitchen, eating with the girls."

He followed on her heels, his mind whirling. He should be more alarmed about the possibility of walking into a trap, but—"*Eating?* With the *girls?*"

"Perhaps I should say—eating a meal with the girls." She burst into laughter and, setting her feet carefully on each tread, led him down the narrow stairway.

This easily could be a trap with Sorcha as bait, so he loosened the knife strapped over his ribs and sturdy truncheon hanging off his belt. The kitchen door was ahead. From inside, he heard the sound of light feminine laughter and, above that, Sorcha's voice telling a story.

Her glee stopped him in his tracks. She sounded young, carefree, and memory tossed him back to a day in the gardens of Beaumontagne....

He wandered the palace disconsolately. He was lonely. The adults were busy talking about the recent troubles in the kingdom and though he was sixteen, they'd told him he wasn't old enough to give his opinion. He was too old now to play with the princesses. They romped like puppies when they should show some decorum and when he told them so, they shredded him and his dignity.

Yet the sound of Sorcha's voice brought him to a halt, then had him sidling forward, keeping to the shrubbery.

When he got in position he saw that she stood on top of a wall, declaiming the part of Beatrice in Much Ado About Nothing *and doing so with such vigor, he cringed when she said, "I had rather hear my dog bark at a crow than a man swear he loves me."*

Her broad delivery and sweeping gestures made her sisters collapse with laughter, and he watched undetected, separated by two years and an inflated sense of superiority.

But that hadn't stopped him from noticing that his fiancée, though she was acting like a hoyden, had blossomed into a pretty girl. She had a shape, the kind of shape that made his body stir. His father said that a well-built barn made Rainger's body stir—which was true, but it was also true Sorcha had developed rounded breasts and a waist that Rainger could span with his hands. Her hair was still carroty, but her dark lashes and brows were like black velvet settings for her sapphire-blue eyes, and her smile warmed him.

Unfortunately, it warmed everybody. She was the perfect princess, and he got sick of his godmother and his friends and two courts, his own and Beaumontagne's, saying he wasn't good enough for her. Everyone always punched his shoulder to show they were joking—but they weren't.

She always did her schoolwork, behaved well at ambassador visits, and charmed his father.

He suffered from pimples, adolescent surliness, and inopportune cockstands that occurred during court presentations.

Only Countess duBelle really understood him. Her smiles, her stroking of his arm, her surreptitious touches on his knee had gone far to build his opinion of himself—and those inopportune cockstands.

Yet today, seeing the princesses being carefree and affectionate, he wished he could join them and that their lives could be like they had been when they were young.

Returning to the present, he grimly reflected that their lives would never be like that again.

Madam Pinchon indicated a carved wooden screen against the stairway. "Stay behind that. Listen. Do not speak. Do not reveal yourself."

"But why?"

"Because in this place and at this time, Your Highness, I am in command." She glanced at the truncheon hanging from his belt. "With that by your hand, you're safe enough."

"I do know how to use it," he assured her.

"I'm sure you do." She disappeared into the kitchen to a chorus of greetings and the clinking of silverware. "Dear Sorcha, are you satisfied with your meal?"

"It was very good," Sorcha said, "although not as good as Eveleen's explanation of blowing the hornpipe."

Rainger jerked his head back so quickly he thumped his head against the wall. Fortunately, with all the laughter no one heard him.

What had these women told Sorcha?

He heard a chair scrape across the floor. "They've explained men to you?" Madam asked.

"All about them." Sorcha sounded incredibly cheerful for a cloistered virgin who had just been told the facts of life. "I expect I'll now be able to manage whatever husband I have to marry quite well."

Rainger peered through a hole carved in the screen, but the angle was wrong to view the kitchen.

"Remember, managing a man is all about understanding his thoughts before he does—which shouldn't be difficult, because men have so few of them." The relish in Madam's voice told Rainger quite clearly how much she enjoyed tweaking his nose out of joint.

He moved from side to side, wanting to see Sorcha. He'd be able to judge her condition by her expression. And he needed to survey the situation, to judge the danger.

"So ye're bound t' be wed, are ye?" one of the ladies asked Sorcha.

"Eventually. I'll have to be. I have to give Beaumontagne an heir." Sorcha sighed with pathetic wistfulness.

Moving with the stealth he'd learned in the last few years, Rainger slid out from behind the screen and glanced in the kitchen. He saw tall windows at the tops of the walls, and a long table cluttered with dishes. Madam Pinchon had positioned herself in an immense chair at one end. Half a dozen scantily clad ladies were seated on benches. Sorcha sat in between a blonde and an auburn-haired beauty, and she looked perfectly at home. More than that, she looked happy and so feminine he wondered how she ever fooled anyone at all.

"Perhaps yer husband will be a prince." The lovely auburn-haired woman spoke.

"Yes, Eveleen, he'll be a prince." Sorcha grasped the female's arm and in a tone of mock dismay said, "But I've met my share of princes."

Madam shot him a meaningful warning glance.

He backed behind the screen again. The kitchen held nowhere an assassin could hide. He would keep his guard up, but for the moment he believed they were safe.

Sorcha continued, "Princes have warts and bad teeth and they're old and they smell…. The best prince I ever met was my fiancé, Rainger, and he was no prize—God rest his soul."

What had been wrong with him? All right, he'd been selfish, vain, and given to airs, but compared to the other princes, he'd been quite a catch. Pressing his ear against the screen, he silently urged her to expound more.

"What was wrong with this Rainger?" Madam asked.

"One shouldn't speak ill of the dead," Sorcha said primly.

"When you get right down to it, you shouldn't speak ill of the living, either." Madam spoke forcefully enough for him to hear. "If this Rainger was a waste of good teeth, then he was and it's too late for him to change."

"He did have good teeth. He was a very handsome boy." Sorcha sounded wistful.

"Good looks go a long way toward soothing my distaste," a pert voice said.

"So tell us what was wrong with him," Madam commanded.

Yes, tell us what was wrong with him.

"When we were children, he was all right. A tease, but not bad at heart. But he didn't have my grandmother to teach him humility, and as he grew, he believed the things his courtiers told him. He thought he was wonderful. He was *not*."

A little less eagerness to speak ill of the dead wouldn't be amiss.

"He believed he was better than me because he was a boy, because he was older, and because we were betrothed almost as soon as we were born."

"He didn't have to do anything t' win ye." Eveleen spoke again.

"Exactly. He was stuck with me—that's what he said, stuck with me—and he valued me not at all. Not as much as his horse or his dog."

But I value you now. You are my key to the kingdom. I'll make sure you know it, too.

"And I assure you, I'll be a good ruler. He wouldn't have been. He didn't understand tact or how to manage people."

But I've learned. I'm managing you right now.

"He believed his way was the only way and everything he did was right." Sorcha laughed, but her amusement held a bitter edge.

Sorcha's scorn flicked at Rainger's pride. Yes, he'd wanted her to explain what she disliked, but not so vehemently.

She finished with, "I would have done all the work and he'd have gotten all the credit."

A scathing review of his character, the kind that left him breathless and aggrieved.

"But all princes are much the same." Sorcha made a noise that sounded like a shudder.

"She's got a worse time of it than we do." The blond woman spoke.

"Poor princess." Madam sounded sympathetic. "We should give Sorcha a gift."

"Advice on how t' geld a man?" The pert cheerfulness in the lady's voice made Rainger flinch.

"No, Helen," Madam said patiently. "I was thinking a nightgown guaranteed to make the wedding night ordeal go quickly."

"But you've been so kind to me already."

Sorcha means it, the little fool.

"You're the most entertainment we've had in weeks. Come on, stand up, let's look you over." At Madam's command, chairs scraped again. After a moment, she said, "She's about your size, Helen. Give her that new lace nightgown."

Rainger eyed the screen, then the door. If he moved the screen a little bit, he could look inside the kitchen.

"Ah, not that one!" Helen's voice expressed disappointment.

"I'll buy you a new one." Madam's tone made it clear she'd brook no argument.

But if he moved the screen, he ran the chance of being spotted.

"All right!" Without sparing a glance toward the screen, Helen flounced out of the kitchen and up the stairs.

"I've met two men on this journey who've known I'm a woman," Sorcha said. "The nuns dressed me, but they must have made a few mistakes. You know the female form better than anyone."

"And the male form." Eveleen laughed.

"And the male form," Sorcha conceded. "Can you help me look less female?"

Rainger's princess was nothing if not practical.

"We certainly can," Eveleen said. "There're men who request that, ye know."

Rainger knew what Sorcha was going to say before she said it.

"Why?"

"Sometimes men like t' play games," one of the ladies told her.

"That's something to remember," Sorcha answered.

More of her note-taking on how to handle a man, no doubt.

In a brisk, no-nonsense tone, Madam said, "Let's see your hair. Hm, yes. The color of your hair's unfortunate, but it's thick. Let me loosen your braid."

Rainger hadn't thought he would see Sorcha with her hair unbound until their wedding night. Now, when he had the chance, he was eighteen frustrated inches away from the spectacle.

He heard a shuffling, a murmuring. Then the prostitutes gasped.

"It looks like a silk of indescribable value," Eveleen said.

Madam Pinchon cleared her throat. "The color's not so unfortunate after all. And it has a nice wave."

Picking up the screen, Rainger shuffled around until he had the kitchen, and Sorcha, in his sight. He shoved the rag off his face and pressed his face to the carved hole.

Sorcha faced him, an angled shaft of sunlight illuminating her features, and the shock of recognition purified him.

Madam had spread the strands across her shoulders. It was as beautiful as Eveleen said. The colors glinted in the candlelight. Gold blended into bronze and bronze blended into copper, and he wanted to bury his fingers in the molten metals of her hair until he burned himself to cinders.

His heart halted its beat. His breath locked in his throat. He clutched the edges of the screen so hard the wood dug into his flesh.

And something lightly touched him on the shoulder.

He jumped. With his fists up, he whirled.

Helen stood holding the folded lace nightgown in her arms. As intimate as a touch, her gaze ran up and down his body—and stopped at the straining buttons on his trousers. She smirked. "Excuse me." She slipped by him and into the kitchen as if a man standing behind screens and watching the ladies was nothing new to her.

And perhaps it wasn't.

She stopped at the sight of Sorcha's unbound tresses. "Ye could work here and make a fortune!"

Rainger wanted to strangle her.

Sorcha fingered the ends and grimaced. "But what has this to do with dressing like a boy?"

"The braid's the main problem—difficult t' disguise and no man wears a braid. But there're things we can do—smudge yer face, for one thing." Eveleen ran her fingers across the soot-covered fire poker and wiped Sorcha's nose and cheek. "No woman leaves a smudge on her face."

"And no man cares whether he's got one," one of the other ladies said.

Helen wrapped the nightgown in brown paper and tied it with string. "We can put her in a lot of old shirts and cut off the length so it looks as if she's got bulk in the shoulders and arms. She'll be warm, too."

Rainger should have thought of that.

The ladies rose and, like vibrant butterflies, surrounded Sorcha, tweaking her clothes and all talking at once. Then they broke, fluttering in different directions.

He stood behind the screen, not hidden, but the prostitutes ignored him. They came and went, chattering about Sorcha, her royalty, her prince, and her misfortunes. From their conversation he gathered that these ladies in a bawdyhouse in a crime-ridden town four days' hard ride from Edinburgh felt sorry for his princess. A sad turn of events, and one that someday he would be able to rectify.

Inside the kitchen, clothing flew.

Sorcha clucked out a constant stream of protests.

Madam rumbled with laughter.

And when the ladies separated to allow him a view of Sorcha, he blinked in surprise.

They'd performed a miracle. Her shoulders were bulky, her face dirty. Her hat covered her ears and was tied under her chin. She looked like a lad who'd been on the road, like a lad who'd weathered a rough life.

"No one will recognize you now." Madam handed her a mirror. "Not even the nuns."

Sorcha gazed at herself and laughed out loud. "That's perfect! You've done a wonderful job of making me a boy. I'll be safe like this."

It was true. Sorcha and he could pass through Glenmoore and along the dangerous road to Edinburgh with no fears that assassins would target her there.

"We've got one other thing to keep you safe." Madam gestured him in.

He acknowledged her right to test him. Madam wanted to be absolutely certain that Sorcha rode freely with him.

He adjusted the rag to cover his eye. Stepping around the screen, he called, "Sorcha."

Startled, the crown princess of Beaumontagne looked around and saw him. He stood in the doorway of the kitchen, hardened and changed from the vain boy she'd described.

Yet her eyes widened, then narrowed. For one moment he thought she recognized him. Knew he was Rainger.

He waited, wondered, *wanted*...

Then she passed her hand before her eyes. She looked again, and shook her head.

The moment passed.

He was still a stranger to Sorcha.

Chapter 12

Wind and rain.

Sorcha could scarcely remember a moment when she had not been wet and cold through to the bone—and now, on the third day out of Glenmoore, she was hungry. Today their provisions had run dry and the barren wilderness of the Scottish Highlands yielded no game, no shelter, no village, no light...only wind and rain. Wind and rain.

She stayed cheerful, and heaven knows Arnou never faltered in his belief they'd successfully make their way to Edinburgh. But what comfort was Arnou's assurance when over and over again he'd proved himself to be a fool?

That evening, for the first time, they didn't even find a shack or a barn to keep them off the ground. As they

huddled together beneath the bare overhang of a rock—
the shelter could scarcely be called a cave—she tried to
think of conversation. Anything that distracted them
from their misery, from the fire that barely smoldered
and the cold ground and the damp blankets.

Weighing the heavy braid in her hand, she frowned at
its color. "At the next village, I'm going to cut my hair."

Arnou whipped around and glared. "*What* did you
say?"

"I'm going to cut my hair. It's a bother, traveling
with it, and Eveleen said that the braid was the thing
that gave me away as a woman."

"No man has recognized you since they dressed
you." With the dark stubble of three days' worth of
beard on his chin and a gaunt cast to his face, he looked
as desperate and as dangerous as any assassin. His dark
eyes were harsh, and he clipped his words as if his lips
were stiff. He must really be cold.

"That's true," she conceded. "But it would certainly
help my disguise if I—"

"I forbid it."

Arnou's flat, imperious tone sounded not at all like
the fisherman she knew. "What do you mean, you forbid it?" She was laughing as she asked, but as he fixed
his eye on her, her laughter faded. He looked almost…
intimidating.

Then the image faded. He dropped his gaze, tugged his forelock, and sighed heavily. "I just meant…your hair's so pretty, like the sunrise that lifts night's shadow."

"How poetic." She didn't know what to say—or what to think. In the space of a minute, she'd seen two different faces to Arnou, and she recognized neither one. "But I thought you said my hair looked like carrots."

He grinned. "Carrots are good for you, so my mother always told me. Don't cut your hair. Trust me, I'll take care of you. I'll give my life before I'd allow anyone to hurt you."

"I know." Uncertainly, she dropped her braid. The cold pinched at her earlobes, and she shivered. "It just would be easier."

"I've got to check on the horses." He started out from beneath the rock, then he came back. He tucked her hair beneath her collar, straightened her coat, and pulled her hat over her ears. "Give a man something to dream about, Sorcha."

That night, as she lay wrapped in all the blankets they'd brought, with Arnou's arms wrapped around her for heat, his odd behavior came back to haunt her. She didn't understand what he meant—*give a man something to dream about.*

Did he dream about her?

She'd never inspired dreams in a man before. No one had ever valued her for her appearance, and most certainly not for her carroty red hair. Rainger had made that clear.

Yet Arnou seemed taken with her looks and her hair, so taken he had vowed to die for her—and that sent a secret thrill through her.

Not that Arnou was in any way appropriate. But when he was washed and didn't smell of fish and filth, and when he didn't slump and grin like an idiot, and when she could forget his poor scar and vacant eye socket, why, then she thought he was rather attractive…in a rough sort of way.

And he liked her hair enough to get sort of arrogant about it. She certainly liked that.

She liked him.

More important, she trusted him.

Arnou was honest and true, without pretense or deception, and she knew from Grandmamma's lessons how rare it was to find a man with those virtues.

But Arnou was a simple man. Sorcha had found a rare gem—a cavalier dedicated to her service. He would never betray her.

Plus, when she thought of him, of his strong, rough hands, his broad shoulders, his long legs, inside she felt sort of warm and gooshy.

She didn't know what that meant, but her reaction made her feel alive.

With a smile, she drifted off to sleep.

The next day Sorcha woke to find Arnou already awake, speaking softly to the horses. She peeked out from beneath the blankets and saw a skiff of snow in the cracks of the rocks.

Winter.

She groaned. Winter had caught up with them.

Arnou came and peered under the stony overhang.

"Do I have to get up?" she joked.

"No." He offered his hand and, fatally cheerful, said, "You can stay here and starve."

"If those are my choices..." Taking his hand, she marveled at its warmth. How could he be warm when every part of her was chilled?

In stages she rose to her feet.

As she stretched out the kinks, he supported her and said, "But be merry! The clouds are gone and the sky clear-washed. Look, the sun is rising!"

Sorcha did look. "A miracle." The kind of miracle only wet and weary travelers could truly appreciate. The sky clothed itself in gold, then blushed with pleasure to see the sun after so many days. The purple mountains turned ruby and orange in anticipation of warmth, and Sorcha found herself observing each ripple of color and wondering which one Arnou thought matched her hair.

But when she turned to him, he wasn't watching the sunrise, he was watching *her*. And he said, "All the colors."

Just as if he knew what she was thinking!

"You've got pretty eyes, too," he said.

That swell of unwilling pleasure he'd caused her only yesterday lifted her again. Flustered, she tried to pretend she was used to such compliments. "Courtiers…I mean, some people told me I have my grandmother's eyes."

"Do you?" His one eye was dark and, in this light, looked interested and intelligent.

"No." She gathered the damp blankets from their shelter and folded them. "Grandmamma's eyes are so cold they pierce one like a chill wind."

He laughed. "She sounds like a scary one, your Grandmamma."

"Puppies and young children flee from her." Sorcha was only half joking.

"Do you have family other than her?" Arnou had taken the horses from their shelter, wiped them down, and tethered them in the green grass.

"I have two sisters, Clarice and Amy. I'm on my way to see them now."

"Are you?"

She took a long breath. "I hope so. Amy was only twelve last time I saw her. Clarice was beautiful and she'll be more beautiful now, I know it. And I miss them...." Sorcha realized she must be weakened by hunger, for an unexpected surge of loneliness brought tears to her eyes. When she had control, she said, "I, um, had letters from them, the best company I could ever have. That fire...that fire at the convent burned the letters, and I feel like I was burned, too."

His gaze dropped. He adjusted the rag over his eye.

She sniffled. "I feel like there's a small, hot coal where my beating heart used to be, and until I see my sisters, until I know they're well, I won't be truly alive again. Silly, aren't I?"

"Not at all. Your affection is inspiring and not necessarily common." His words were kind and surprisingly sensible. "Sisters don't always love each other so well."

"We can't fight when we're apart." She wiped her eyes.

As if the subject made him uncomfortable, he changed the subject—but what did she expect from Arnou? Tact?

"After you went to sleep last night, I explored ahead. There's a village not far up the road. We'll circle around it, then I'll go back and buy supplies."

At the idea, her empty stomach rumbled. "Food?" she asked eagerly.

"Most certainly food." He smiled at her, a warm smile quite unlike his usual foolish grin. "You're a trooper, Sorcha. You don't complain no matter how hungry or wet or cold you are."

"What good would complaining do?" she asked, surprised. "You're as hungry and cold and wet, and there's nothing to be done about that, either."

Still he smiled at her as if she'd said something remarkable, until that warm, gooshy feeling spread through her insides again and she found herself glancing down in a sudden excess of modesty.

He said nothing more, and when she peeked at him, an uncertain frown knit his brow. The old Arnou was back—yet not the old Arnou. This Arnou seemed less of a fool and more of a…a what? A genuinely confused man.

"Come on, let's make the most of this weather." He helped her into the saddle.

They rode, leaving the path to take the long way around the village. When they were clear, he stopped. "I'll go in and barter for food. Over this rise, there's a long valley that parallels the road. Ride there, you can't get lost, and I'll catch up with you within two hours." His voice became stern. "Keep a lookout. If you see anyone—a farmer, a farmer's wife, a dog—*don't* stop to chat with them. If you see a man on horseback, *don't* assume he's your friend. He could very well be another assassin."

"All right," she said, offended. "You don't have to be nasty about it."

"Nasty?" He reared back as if she'd insulted him. "Woman, you ate a meal at a house of ill repute and by the time you were done, you knew all the prostitutes' names."

"Of course I did. Why wouldn't I?"

He seemed to be trying to answer that, but she noted with satisfaction he could come up with nothing, because nothing he could say would make sense. Finally, he pointed a finger at her. "You will please remain hidden and silent."

"I know there are men after me, and I'll be prudent," she assured him.

"Your idea of prudence and mine do not mesh." As he rode away, she thought she heard him add, "Thank God."

But that didn't make any sense at all, so she rode over the rise, fighting the ever-present wind, and dropped down into the long valley. Here, autumn's sun warmed her back, the wind whistled overhead, and the pleasure of the day brought a smile to her face. Around her, the land fought off winter's early effects, holding wisps of green grass in hallows protected by tall, gray, craggy stones. No scent drifted on the breeze; the air was so fresh it cleansed her lungs. She wandered along, taking her time, cherishing these hours for their peace. Small birds settled on the warm rocks, preening and chirping, so sweet and comical she laughed out loud.

Before she expected it and not far ahead of her, Arnou rode out from behind a boulder. "What's so funny?"

She jumped at his sudden appearance. "You scared me!"

"The road was smooth and fast."

She looked at his bulging saddlebag. "Did you get us something to eat?"

"We have a veritable feast." He searched her face. "Now—why were you laughing?"

"After so many awful days in a row, doesn't this make you want to dance and sing?" She threw out her arms to embrace the whole world.

He stared at her with that confused frown again. Then, as if he couldn't help it, he smiled. "It makes me want to eat." He pointed to a small rise surrounded by a ring of rough stones. "We'll sit there. We can see any-one who rides along the valley long before they get here, and—"

"Yes! That looks lovely." Sliding out of the saddle, she took her horse's reins and bounded toward the stone circle.

The boulders were huge, at least twice her height, and most of them still stood upright, reaching toward heaven like silent witnesses to the ages. She stared up as she passed between two of them, calculating how many men it had taken to stand them upright—when Conquest balked. Setting his hooves, he refused to enter the circle, and his abrupt refusal almost jerked Sorcha off her feet. "What is it, boy?" She backtracked, petting his nose, speaking softly to him, but although he accepted her comfort, still he refused to step between the stones. Brow puckered, she looked at Arnou.

"We'll have to tether the horses outside the circle," he said.

"But why?"

"I've seen stones like these before." He scrutinized them: tall, gray, covered with orange lichens and green moss. "The locals always tell me the fairies built the circle, or the goblins, or the priests of the old religion. I suppose the horses sense there's magic here."

She glanced around in astonishment. "The only magic comes from the beautiful day."

He studied at her, posed above him on the hill. "Tell the horses."

Did Arnou *believe* in fairies? Such faith from her fisherman-protector seemed absurd in the extreme, yet he set about tethering the horses in the good grass beyond the circle with cheerful acceptance. How odd.

Once again, but with more caution, she stepped into the circle.

She sensed nothing. No otherworldly wonder struck her, and that was good. When Arnou joined her, bag in hand, she said, "Grandmamma told me time and again no evidence of magic exists."

"Your grandmother doesn't know everything." Arnou's mouth puckered as if he tasted a particularly tart lemon.

"Do you really believe the fairies made this place?" Silly Arnou!

"The tales say that time stops in the land of the fairies. That they control the weather. That it's always spring there." He waved a hand at the nests of yellow flowers bobbing in the shadows of the stones. "For myself—I feel we're safe here. Don't you?"

Unreasonably, she did. "Of course, but because we've been cautious and this place is a lookout."

"Of course." He sounded amused and indulgent.

For the first time in days, she felt warm enough to strip off her cloak and her hat and peel off her top three shirts. Maybe, she thought in amusement, the fairies really did create this lovely weather.

Climbing to the highest point within the circle, she looked out to the countryside. To her surprise, the mount was higher than it looked. From here she could see the Highlands that stretched for miles in every direction. The sun stretched shadows across the land. Purple mountains and blue rivers dwindled into the pale horizon. She almost felt that if she concentrated, she could look toward the southeast and view Beaumontagne. The breeze whispered softly in her ears, urging her to try, and she strained, lifting her arms as if she could fly, wanting so badly to see Grandmamma, to hear Grandmamma's voice, to know the truth about her father, her sisters, the men who chased her....

Arnou's hearty tone broke her concentration. "Here's our dinner. I've spread it out on the blanket and you can have what you like. How about a beef pie? Or a haunch of roasted coney? I've got fresh bread and cheese..." His voice trailed off. "That's a funny look on your face, and you're standing on your toes."

Abashed, she returned to earth with a thump. Nonchalantly she strolled toward him. "I thought I heard something."

"Really?" He scanned the vista worriedly. "I didn't. Was it a fairy?"

"A fairy. Don't be ridiculous, Arnou." The scent of the meat pie struck her nose with sweet violence. She dropped to her knees on the blanket and considered the feast before her. "My heavens. You got so much. We'll never be able to eat all this."

"You'd be surprised." He tore a leg off the coney and handed it to her. "Besides, we don't know what's on the road ahead. I'll pack the leftovers and we'll have them until they're gone. By then we'll be in Edinburgh. For now—eat up, Sorcha."

She sank her teeth into the sweet meat, and her eyes closed as the rich flavor filled her mouth. Without taking a breath, she ate until she held only a bone, and opened her eyes only when she heard his soft chuckle. "What?"

"A man would pay good money to see that look of ecstasy on his woman's face."

"All you have to do is feed me," she said cheerfully, and extended her hand for more food.

He still smiled as if he knew something she didn't. He cut the round end of the bread, dug out the soft insides, and filled the makeshift bowl with a scoop of meat pie. Then he handed it across and as she ate with hearty enjoyment, he slowly did the same for himself. She thought it odd that he seemed to enjoy watching her more than filling his stomach, but she was hungry enough not to care. "Whoever made this was the real beautiful fairy," she said.

"Your beautiful fairy was the baker's wife, and she's ugly, talented, and amenable to a flirtation." Arnou mischievously wiggled his eyebrows. "I secured the baker's dinner for us."

That made Sorcha stop eating. "You flirted with the baker's wife?"

"I made the sacrifice for your appetite," he assured her.

A smile played at the corners of his lips and it struck her that here, in the sunshine with no threat for miles, he looked almost young. Beneath the black stubble of his beard, the deep lines that usually bracketed his mouth relaxed. His eye drooped with sleepy amusement. In the safety of the stone circle, he looked like a totally different person, not at all the buffoonish Arnou but rather a man who could romance dinner from any woman at any time.

"How old are you?" That sounded abrupt, and she stammered, "I...I mean, I thought you were younger than me."

"Why did you think that?"

She remembered his bumbling at the convent, his astonishment at her defense of herself during the attack, the way he'd looked plastered against the wall at the house of ill repute, surrounded by amused prostitutes. "You just don't seem to have too many…skills."

"I'm a man of hidden talents." He tore off a chunk of crust, thrust it in his mouth, chewed, and swallowed.

"So how old are you?"

He turned his dark gaze on her. "Twenty-seven."

Older than her. She would never have suspected. "Do you have any family?"

"Dead."

She regretted asking; his single, abrupt word disturbed the peace of this place. Yet she found herself driven to know more about this companion who had made himself her champion. "I'm sorry. Do you have anyone at all you care for?"

"I have a whole country of people I care for." He finished his pie, ate the bread, and dug around in the saddlebag, until he pulled out a squat brown bottle. He removed the cork with his teeth. "I also have whisky. Would you like some?" He offered it, his silly grin in place.

"Yes. Thank you." She didn't have a cup, but obviously he thought nothing of that. So she tilted the bottle up and drank. The whisky stung her throat, cleared her sinuses, made her eyes water and her head spin.

When she lowered the bottle, she discovered he watched her with his mouth half open.

"What's wrong?" she asked.

"Aren't you going to cough?"

"After so many days of dirty water and grainy wine, the liquor tastes clean." She drank again, then handed him the bottle.

Cautiously he sniffed the contents, then drank and wheezed.

She laughed, and, overcome with the joy of the meal and the company and this special place, and courted by the breeze, she stood, extended her arms, and twirled in an exuberant circle. She heard him call her name, but that sense of being lifted filled her again. She rose onto her toes and swayed in time to the music of the wind. And the wind responded, catching her in its arms and dancing with her. It sent her running through the springlike sunshine like an exuberant child, taught her to dip and sway, all for the pure pleasure of movement. The yellow flowers, the green grass, the ancient gray stones whirled across her vision, and all the while she was aware of the rough brown blanket and Arnou watching her as if he couldn't take his gaze away.

She didn't stop until the wind died, a slow dwindling that left her standing by the blanket, panting, exhilarated, and uplifted.

"Sorcha." Arnou's deep voice called her name with vibrant authority. When she opened her eyes—when had she closed them?—she saw him extending a rosy-skinned, perfect apple.

"Ohh." She sank to her knees beside him. Accepting the apple, she breathed in the scent of summer's heat and autumn's harvest. She sank her teeth into the ripe fruit. The taste slid across her tongue, the perfect blend of tart and sweet, and she'd never sampled anything as glorious as that single bite of apple—until Arnou removed the ripe globe from her fingers, leaned close, and put his mouth on hers.

Chapter 13

In the heat of the noontime hour, in the silence of the stone ring, Arnou's kiss seemed as natural as Sorcha's dance with the frisking breeze. She held herself still, absorbing the sensation of his lips on hers, wondering in an abstracted way what caused the humble, bumbling Arnou to take such an action. Then the warmth of the moment dissolved thought. Her lips opened under the delicate pressure of his and the flavor of him was like honey on her tongue.

He must have thought the same about her, for he murmured, "Sweet," and the movement of his lips plucked at nerves she hadn't known existed.

He smelled like this valley: fresh, wild, unfettered. Even with her eyes closed, she would always recognize his odor...and her eyes were closed now.

When had that happened? It seemed so natural to share this moment with him, to be intimate as she had never been intimate with any man.

His hand cradled her chin, and the calluses on his palm and his fingers paid tribute to the work he'd done as a sailor. As a man.

His lips left hers and coasted up to press on her cheeks, her eyelids...then down to caress the tender spot at the base of her ear.

As his breath caressed her neck, she shivered with delight. She knew that men kissed women; after being sent into exile in England, she'd lived with a kind couple who expressed their affections with an occasional peck on the mouth.

But this was different. Arnou's kisses were rich, laden with the cream of experience and the honey of desire. She wanted to revel in each moment that he pressed his lips to her skin. When he kissed her throat, she heard herself give a faint moan, as if her body couldn't resist giving the most primitive kind of applause for his skill.

And when she moaned, he lifted his head and stared down at her face.

She felt the heat of his gaze, but the warmth of his passion had permeated her bones and she could scarcely lift her lids. When she did, she saw that his pupil was dilated so large the deep brown of his iris was almost invisible. She fancied she could see right into the depths of his soul, and she smiled, a slow, languid curve of the lips, wanting him to know how very much his worship had meant to her.

"You silly girl." His voice rasped as if his throat were swollen. "Do you think that this is safe?"

"Safe? Of course. I trust you." The chill of doubt touched her. "Shouldn't I?"

"Not at all." Moving to his side of the blanket, he lay down, closed his eye, and was absolutely still and so rigid he seemed to be fighting against some great pain.

She didn't know what that pain could be, but it left her the only one on alert.

She glanced around her. The air was so clear, this place was so high, she could see for miles in every direction. Nothing moved on the road, nothing moved in the valley, nothing moved on the hills. Even the horses, grazing not far away, looked thin and small. It was almost as if the fairies really had created this place and wove spells to protect it. If someone out there hunted her, he was nowhere in sight.

With a sigh of relief, she cleaned up the dinner, wrapping the remains of their meal in brown paper. If they were careful, they had enough provisions for the next two days. The rain had slowed their journey into

Edinburgh, but if it stayed as dry as it was today, that would be enough. She brushed the crumbs off the middle of the blanket, placed the saddlebag beside them, and at last gave in to her most pressing need...and stared at Arnou.

Tension no longer gripped him. He had slipped into sleep, making up for the wakeful night spent scouting their next move. The rag over his eye cut her view of his face, but relaxed in slumber and untouched by foolishness, he had the appearance of youth, of nobility.

And Mother Brigette would point out that that was a lesson for Sorcha. She had listened to his inanities, been annoyed by his constant broad grin, and been unable to see the virtue of his features.

For some reason, she wanted to gaze at him, to linger over his face, his form...touch him, kiss him as he'd kissed her.

As she subsided beside him on the blanket, she wondered—why had he kissed her? It had seemed the act of a man driven by impulse. Knowing Arnou, that was what it was.

But why? Did he find her attractive? Did a man find her, with her carrot hair and pale, freckled skin...desirable? She could scarcely imagine such a thing.

Of course, it was just Arnou, and if Rainger were alive and here, he would point out that Arnou was an idiot.

Very well. It was true. But Arnou was a kind idiot. A brave idiot. He might cringe away from actual fighting, but even knowing full well someone stalked her, he still traveled with her.

And lately he hadn't seemed so ridiculous. He'd shown moments of intelligence, of shrewdness.

She flattered herself that the hours with her had improved his mind and his manner, and perhaps in the future he would be able to improve himself and his situation....

But none of that answered the question of why he'd kissed her—and when he would kiss her again.

Taking her hat, she placed it over her face, easing the sunshine that was bright even over her closed eyelids...and as she reminisced about that kiss, she slid into slumber.

Rainger knew where he was—asleep on a blanket in the middle of a stone circle in the middle of the Scottish Highlands.

He knew his mission—to retrieve Princess Sorcha, return her to Beaumontagne, marry her, and use her army to rescue Richarte.

He knew the danger—robbers, starvation, winter, assassins. Sorcha might rebel and decline, as her sisters had, to follow her destiny.

But he could meet every challenge.

Only his own weakness brought on the nightmare.

Only his own weakness….

"Rainger, you can't go see the countess." Marlon was the only one who dared speak as they all wished. "It's too dangerous."

"I have to." Seventeen-year-old Rainger stared down his nose at the small coterie of his friends: Cezar, Hector, Emilio, Hardouin, and Marlon. Men who had been raised with him and trained to serve and guard him at all costs. "I love her. She sent me a note. She's worried about me. I must have one more night in fair Julienne's arms." He was very aware of how romantic he looked: hanging from the trellis below Julienne's balcony, sword at his side, shoulders squared, dark eyes flashing with passion. He imagined himself to be the epitome of the quixotic cavalier, and his chest swelled with pride.

He was the crown prince of Richarte, marching off to war to save his country from the evil usurper, but first he would have one last night of bliss. His danger was great, yes, but her peril was even greater, for the evil usurper was her own husband, Count duBelle.

"Stand guard," he told his friends, and continued his climb up Count duBelle's trellis into Count duBelle's bedchamber, where he would pork Count duBelle's

wife. He grasped the heavy branches of the vine and lighter wood of the trellis with his gloved hands, boosting himself higher up the wall and closer to his love.

Cezar, Hector, Emilio, Hardouin, and Marlon. Three were older. Two were his age. All were dashing cavaliers of the realm.

None approved of this adventure.

"Where is she? If she wrote you a note, why isn't she hanging over the balcony waiting for you? I tell you, I don't like this." Cezar's dark hair and eyes most closely matched Rainger's; he was his third cousin, two years older, and the handsomest of the group.

But Rainger had been the man Julienne had chosen. "You're jealous," he said.

"For God's sake, Rainger, this isn't a game. They're hunting us." Cezar's voice lashed at Rainger like a whip.

For a moment, cold reason plucked at Rainger's mind. Since the death of his father the king, the insurgents had grown strong. They said he was young, spoiled, and unfit for rule. The royal Richarte army waited on the precipice of battle for him, their young prince, to lead them and prove his worthiness.

Instead he was hanging on a trellis following the demands of his cock rather than the thoughts of his brain. Staring down at his friends, he wondered if Cezar was right, if he should run while he could and take his pleasure later.

Then the branch he clung to broke. He lost his toe-hold, hung by the other arm, flailed about for a hand-hold...felt foolish.

Typically, his friends would be pointing at him, braying with laughter like the jackasses they were.

Instead they were deathly silent, as if they were too somber, too important, too weighed down with serious matters to behave normally.

And that infuriated him.

Did they really think they were so much smarter, so much more mature? Did they really think he was cosseted and indulged? He'd show them.

Gaining his balance, he continued his climb, more carefully now, with less concern for the way he appeared and more concern for reaching his destination.

He was grateful Julienne hadn't seen him make a fool of himself. But Cezar was right. Where was she? Why wasn't she waiting on the balcony?

He inched and scrabbled his way up and over the marble balusters. Lightly he landed on the balcony. He eyed the open door and the closed drapes. Warning jangled along his nerves.

Where was Julienne?

He glanced down at his friends below. They stood together in a little group, muttering disgustedly.

Rainger couldn't climb down. He couldn't admit he might be wrong.

He loosened his sword in its scabbard and crept forward. He parted the drapes.

And there she was, posed against the headboard, exquisitely nude and bathed in the glow of a single bedside candle—Julienne, Countess duBelle, his first and best lover.

"Darling." In that single word, her warm, rich voice promised every sort of pleasure. She held out her arms. "Come to me."

Prudence, deliberation, logic flew from his brain. He entered the room in a rush, intent on one thing—sinking into her body, riding her hard, then doing it again.

He put all his ardent admiration and desire into his embrace.

She chuckled and wiggled away. "Darling, so many medals and buttons. Quickly. Quickly! Disrobe for me. Show me your marvelous young body and your massive manhood."

For a single second, discretion returned. She had never wanted him to be quick before. If anything, she had complained about the speed at which his needs drove him.

Then she smiled…and leisurely licked her full, ruby-colored lips.

He didn't need a second urging. He ripped off his clothes, flinging garments willy-nilly across the room. His coat, his belt…his sword, his pistol…his boots, his breeches. In record time, he stood naked before her, strong, young, virile, flaunting an erection she claimed surpassed any she could imagine, and certainly Count duBelle's.

"Very good, darling. Now wait just a minute…." She stretched her arms above her head, lifting the heavy globes of her breasts in a glorious display.

Lust surged through him. He trembled, he needed, he could barely see, scarcely hear—

Until from behind him, he heard the snick of many blades being drawn.

Whirling, he faced seven swords pointed at him. Seven cavaliers dressed in Count duBelle's livery held those swords.

They looked him over, and they were grinning.

One thought flashed through Rainger's mind: He had to protect Julienne. "Get behind me, darling!" he shouted.

She slid off the bed behind him.

He placed himself between her and the sharp points.

She moved to one side, then to the other.

He moved with her, keeping his gaze on the swords. His own sword...he'd carelessly tossed it toward the windows. His pistol...he'd placed it on the bedstand, but every time he moved that way, the cavaliers drove him away.

They were laughing, the bastards. Laughing out loud. They were amused by the prince they'd trapped, naked and without resources.

But he wasn't without resources. "To me!" he shouted toward the windows. "To Rainger!"

It was the call of a desperate man.

Rainger's men would be here soon, climbing the trellis, evening the odds—

Just as that defiance crossed his mind, he heard the scream from below.

A death scream. He froze in horror.

Who? Who had died? His cousin Cezar? Hector, so happy, so generous? Emilio, Rainger's age and his best friend? Hardouin, sensitive and poetic? Or Marlon, intense, practical, and hard-headed?

Swords clashed. Men shouted. The ambush that had waited for Rainger included his men.

"Welcome, young prince."

At the sound of that urbane voice, Rainger's head jerked around. From behind the drapes, Count duBelle strolled forth. Women called the usurper handsome: blond hair, blue eyes, athletic body he kept well trained, and a sense of fashion that displayed all of his perfections. At the age of thirty-three, he was a man in the height of his power. Now he stood, slapping his palm with his leather whip, gloating over his new acquisition.

"I do believe we've snared the most important pawn in our game of chess." Count duBelle was smiling. He was smiling as if he'd won the war.

But he didn't know the facts. Rainger wouldn't allow him to take Julienne, to run her through with the rapier he held in his hand.

Oh, God. Oh, God. His foolishness had killed a friend. Maybe...all of his friends.

He faced death, and he wasn't romantic. He wasn't righteous. He wasn't heroic. His heart raced and his hands trembled.

Yet he could be gallant. He could protect Julienne.

He reached back for her, needing the reassurance of her flesh against his palm.

But while he had listened to the fight below, she had slipped past.

"Julienne!" he shouted.

With a teasing glance over her shoulder, she sashayed toward Count duBelle.

Count duBelle caught her around the waist and pulled her toward him. Together they faced Rainger.

They were smiling. Both of them were smiling.

Rainger struggled to comprehend this horror.

"My darling, you weren't lying," Count duBelle marveled. "You hold him by the ballocks."

Rainger's bile rose.

"Isn't he sweet?" Countess duBelle placed her hand on her cocked hip. "Even now he can't take his eyes off me, and he's erect and ready."

She had betrayed him. Julienne had betrayed him. And his men. Below the window, the sounds of the fight had faded. Not, he knew, because his men had won the day. Because they had been vanquished.

A trap. His men had tried to tell him, but he'd been too stubborn and too lustful to admit they were right.

She had trapped him. And he'd let her.

Count duBelle's gaze slithered down Rainger's body to his genitals, and his smile tilted down on one side. "Young Rainger proves the royal family didn't win their position by their impressive size."

"Darling, I told you that." Countess duBelle caressed her husband's arm. "He's nothing but a straw boy compared to you."

She had said those exact words to Rainger about Count duBelle.

She was naked in front of Count duBelle's men, and they acted as if the sight were a common one. Count duBelle stroked her flank, then slipped his hand behind her, manipulating her until she squirmed. For more than two years, she'd enticed Rainger, first subtly, then openly. She'd seduced him, taught him how to make love to a woman, flattered him, entrapped him.

She had meant nothing she said to him. She'd given her body carelessly because she valued her body not at all.

"You're nothing but a whore," Rainger realized.

She laughed, a frivolous ringing sound. "Everyone knows that except you, my darling. Everyone except you."

Count duBelle's men advanced, their swords out, flashing amused smiles.

If Rainger had any honor, he would impale himself on the points.

But he didn't have the courage. Even if his men were dead. Even if he'd ruined the nobility of his house, of his father, of his name—he was only seventeen years old. He was young. His whole life stretched before him.

Surely something would happen to save the day. Surely somehow he would rise to achieve his revenge and win back his honor.

Count duBelle must have seen Rainger's brief surge of hope, for he strolled out onto the balcony. "Ahhh. Two of your men appear to be dead. One is bleeding. Well, no. Let me take that back. They're all bleeding, but that one's wound seems to be rather messy."

Rainger started toward the window.

The sword points stopped him.

"Don't hurt yourself, darling." Julienne stepped in front of him and sank her claws into his chest. She left five small red crescents. Taking the blood on her fingertip, she licked it in a lavish display. "That's our task."

Catching her arm, Count duBelle jerked her to the side. To his guards he said, "Take His Highness Prince Rainger to the dungeon. Chain him to the wall. I'll be down...soon."

The men grabbed Rainger by his arms.

With Rainger in Count duBelle's hands, Richarte's army of noble soldiers would be forced to acquiesce to his demands.

Rainger—and Richarte—faced defeat. And it was all Rainger's fault.

Slapping his whip in his palm, Count duBelle smiled thinly. "When I'm done with you, you'll lick my boots and beg for your life."

Rainger struggled against the guards. "I will never beg you for anything."

But he'd been wrong.

Chapter 14

When Sorcha woke, it seemed hours had passed. She sat up in alarm, unease prickling along the nerves under her skin.

Were they safe? Had the assassins found them?

But when she glanced at the sun, it was still high in the sky. Apparently, she'd slept only a few moments.

Yet Arnou was gone.

She spotted him standing at the crest of the hill, the place where she had stood to look across the countryside and where she had imagined she could see all the way to Beaumontagne.

Like her, he'd discarded his outer garments. He stood in his thin wool shirt, absorbing the sunlight, his head tilted up, his arms outstretched.

He didn't notice her, but she took the moment to study him: his broad shoulders, his narrow hips, his long legs. He was obviously a fisherman, his strength inherited from years of lifting nets and fighting storms. He was strong, brave, and gallant. Perhaps not clever, but the royal princes she'd met were not necessarily brave and almost never valiant. She was lucky to have Arnou.

Making her way to his side, she slipped her hand in his. "It's beautiful, isn't it?"

"It's more than beautiful. It's crucial." Arnou's fingers felt cold and still. His voice was harsh with agony. "A man must lift his eyes to the horizon or the whole world shrinks to the size of a coffin and life becomes nothing more than a living death. A man can pound his fists on the unforgiving walls until his hands bleed and cry for help, until he has no voice, but without the wind and the sunshine, the grass and the birds, he'll never break free."

She didn't understand his words. Didn't understand his mood. "It sounds as if you were in a prison."

Gradually, he turned to look at her. His single eye seemed not a window to his soul, but a shutter to hide his pain. Then, as he stared at her, he came to life. His voice grew rich and benign like the Arnou she knew.

"There are prisons of rock and prisons of the soul. A man can chip rock away, but only a miracle opens the prison of the soul." His fingers hovered the barest space below her chin. His thumb stroked her cheekbone, a slow, steady motion that soothed and aroused her.

"What kind of miracle?"

To answer, he kissed her. Again.

He spoke to her with his lips, but without words. He spoke to her of all the marvelous wonders Madam's ladies had promised, and he used his tongue to express nuances they had not mentioned.

His tongue…he pressed it between her lips, opening her to his breath and his taste. He taught her things with his tongue. He drew her out, showing her how to duel and how to soothe. She would start to feel comfortable, think she understood what to do. Then he'd angle his head differently, use his teeth, change the pressure…and she followed as if he were her professor and she his student.

After long moments of suspense and exhilaration, he drew away, apparently satisfied with such an imperfect contact. He smiled as if he'd conquered some special madness. He pinched her cheek as if she were his favorite cocker spaniel.

Didn't he know? She couldn't stop now. His kiss was temptation itself, drawing her into him. She pressed her body against his, seeking the warmth he promised.

His arm hovered above her, then reluctantly slid around her waist. "I shouldn't…" he muttered.

"Only for a moment," she coaxed. "Just show me again."

He lifted her up on her toes, up against him, her chest against his chest, her hips against his. Layers of clothing separated them—his clothing, her clothing, but that didn't seem to matter. After so many years of the cool, cloistered isolation of the convent, touching another human being, really *touching* him, was part delight, part torture. Her hands rested on his forearms.

She stood on her toes to return his kiss, and at first that was enough. Gradually, she moved her hand up his biceps, exploring his strength. It wasn't an actual thought process, more of an instinct that made her want to hold him in her arms as he held her.

Sinking her fingers into his shoulders, she kneaded them like a cat and moaned into the sweet cavern of his mouth.

Something broke in him, some restraint he'd put on himself, for he yanked her more tightly against him. He deepened the kiss and moved her hips against his, a slow grinding motion that seemed animalistic—and embarrassingly arousing. She broke the kiss. She whispered, "Arnou, I don't think we should do this."

"I don't think you should think." He kissed her again, his tongue creating a steady rhythm into the depths of her mouth and somehow, that rhythm echoed in her belly.

She wrapped her leg around him, trying to get close enough to alleviate the itch between her legs.

With a gasp, he lifted his head.

He stared down at her. The skin of his face was taut across his cheekbones. His chin thrust forward determinedly. And his eye was dark and focused—on her. Ruthless—about her. Determined—*to kill her.*

She caught her breath in an onrush of fear.

No, not to kill her. To take her.

Yet her body seemed unable to make the distinction. Violence shimmered in the air around him, and she was afraid. Her blood darted about frantically, seeking oxygen from nonfunctioning lungs.

He wanted, *meant* to take her. To put her under him, to thrust inside her and possess her.

The ladies had told her about that. They'd described sex and all the trimmings in great detail. But she hadn't understood until now. Intimate? Yes. Beyond any imagining. She backed away from him, pressed her knees tightly together, trying to keep him out…trying to relieve the anticipation that built regardless of the fear.

It didn't work. Rather, this Arnou dominated her, taking her on a journey whether she wished to go or not. He stared as if he wanted to devour her.

Her anticipation built. And she was still afraid, but for once in her life, she faced her fear and the challenge life presented her.

Was she willing to follow Arnou's lead? Was she willing to take this man into her body and find pleasure, give pleasure in equal measure?

She had to marry a prince, yes. She had to have children for her country. She had to sacrifice the rest of her life to duty. But she was trained to be a princess, to recognize opportunity and use it to her advantage.

This was a moment of opportunity. The sun shone. The breeze blew. She was alone in the middle of the wilderness with a good man, an honest man, a man she liked and who, it seemed, worshipped her.

Opportunity. She would seize it.

Or rather—he seized her. He pushed her over onto the grass. There was no finesse about his gesture; he moved efficiently and without any worry for her delicate sensibilities. When she was stretched out, he knelt beside her and took away her clothes. The two shirts, the breeches, the hose, the shoes. She was naked in the sunshine, not knowing where to look, how to act, where to put her hands.

Yet at the sight of her reclining before him, his wild, fierce expression faded. Touching the silver cross that hung from the chain around her neck, he said, "Pretty."

She touched it, fingering it uncertainly. "My sisters wear one, too."

"A timely reminder." Sitting back on his heels, he looked at her body. *Stared* as if she had lived in his dreams and now lived in his reality.

She thought she saw the glint of tears in his eye. Lifting herself onto her elbows, she scrutinized him. Yes, those were tears. In a voice soft with concern, she asked, "What's wrong? Are you weeping?"

"Have you ever cried for pure pleasure?" His voice rasped as it dragged across a powerful emotion. "I have never seen anything as beautiful as you are today."

Flattering? Exhilarating? Yes, and yes. He was so kind, so gentle. The lump of her fear melted.

He gave her what she wanted before she realized that she wanted it.

She wanted this place and this time, hidden from real life and guarded by standing stones. She wanted to be nude, bathing in sunshine, reveling in the wonder of her warm skin on the cool grass. She wanted to display herself for Arnou and see this rough-edged, straight-forward man wipe the tears from his face.

He was handsome. And tortured. And desperate... for her.

Reaching out, he used one finger to leisurely circle her breast.

That single contact raised all the tiny hairs on her body. Her nipple contracted. Her eyes half closed and she was aware of every smell, every sound, of the heat of the sun above and the cool of the ground below. This man sharpened her perceptions, and through his touch she could feel the earth rotating, the seasons changing, the stones around them aging in a process so slow no one could know it.

But she did.

Because of him.

From beneath her, the scent of crushed grass rose around them. She let the weight of her braid tilt her head back, lifting her face to the sun.

She heard him take a deep breath.

She lifted one knee, knowing full well she lured him in a manner he couldn't resist.

He chuckled, a sound of pained amusement. At once, as if he feared her thoughts, he said, "I'm not laughing at you. I'm laughing at myself. I'm laughing at this day. My God, how did we get here? To this moment?"

"We rode here." Digging her toes into the grass, she waited and watched him.

His breeches bulged in a marvelously demanding way—the sign, Eveleen had told her, that meant arousal. Yet he seemed frozen in place, staring, clenching his fists....

Arnou was trying to gain control! This sweet, simple man didn't believe he had the right to touch her.

Placing her palm in the middle of his chest, Sorcha asked, "Would you like me to blow the hornpipe?"

"Blow the...you want to...Dear God." His heartbeat accelerated beneath her palm. "Yes."

Sliding her hand down, she pressed it against that bulge. Through the layers of clothing, she explored the length of him from the tip to the base. There was more than she could have imagined, and the thing moved beneath her touch, growing longer.

Arnou groaned and thrust into her palm. A sweet madness seemed to possess him. He rose onto his knees, caught her around her shoulders. He tipped her backward so she was off-balance. He cupped his hand against her throat.

He stopped. He wrapped his fingers around her chain. He looked at the cross in his palm—and a pang crossed his face. *"No!"* He rubbed his eye as if trying to block the sight of her. "Stop. Don't offer something you know nothing about."

"But I do know about it. Madam's ladies told me, and if it would relieve your discomfort—"

Lowering his hand, he fixed her with a gaze so wickedly intent she caught her breath. "Did the ladies also tell you that a man can blow a woman's hornpipe?"

Just when she thought Arnou seemed smarter than he appeared, he said something as ridiculous as that. In a patient tone, she said, "Now, now. You shouldn't discuss matters you don't understand. Women don't have a hornpipe."

"You'd be surprised." Placing his finger on her breastbone, he gently slid the tip down, down into the small nest of red curly hair between her legs and into the naked flesh hidden within.

Holding her gaze, he lightly touched the nub there. "There's a bit of a hornpipe here and when a man plays this instrument, his woman sings."

"I don't think that you ought to touch me like that." She wet her suddenly dry lips.

"Watch me." He wasn't challenging her. He was commanding her.

What had started out as a simple impulse had grown into an event far beyond her puny experience. Her insides rioted with a frantic tempo. It was amazing to discover, after all those sterile years, that her body was susceptible to the physical. That her body, in fact, had a vitality of its own, disengaged from her brain and defiant of reason. Caught by disbelief, she watched as, with great deliberation, he placed his hands on her knees. As his rough palms glided along the inside of her thighs, he flushed as if heat had flashed through him.

She understood that, because his touch sent a surge of warmth through her veins. Her skin grew sensitive to each brush of the breeze. Her nipples tightened to the point of pain. And her...her hornpipe ached with anticipation. "Arnou, don't." Her voice was so faint the wind blew it away.

"An almost silent protest." He slid between her legs and in the sunshine, he could see her private parts. "When you were alone, did you ever...?"

"Yes," she said hastily. Of course she had. She thought, sometimes, that that was the only thing that kept her sane in the isolation of the convent. But she didn't want to *talk* about it.

Unfortunately, he did. He caressed her thighs, breathed on the tight curls, touched her so delicately she almost couldn't feel him...and had never felt anything so acutely. "So at the convent, you touched yourself. Like this?" He slid both his thumbs along the crease of her womanhood.

She jumped. "Really, Arnou, I don't think you should...or I should..."

As she stammered out her protest, he watched his own thumbs moving, swirling, probing. "Should what?"

"Should, um, do things out here that I..." She caught her breath as he slid inside her a bare inch.

"That you what?"

"What? Oh. That I did in the deepest, darkest..." He made her feel so weak, so liquid with desire, she couldn't get enough air.

"Deepest, darkest...?"

With great effort, she finished, "Deepest, darkest moments of the night." Then she concentrated on breathing. Breathe in, breathe out. Breathe in. Breathe out.

Dipping his head, he used his tongue to caress her.

She whimpered. Nothing she'd ever done for herself equaled a single touch of his mouth. His heat, the dampness, his tongue, so rough and practiced....

His lips moved against her as he said, "Tell me what you did at the convent."

She could no longer hold herself up on her elbows. She slid flat onto the grass. "I...ah...I touched myself where you have your tongue."

"Did you press?" He demonstrated. "Or pluck?" He wrapped his lips around her and used a gentle suction.

Instantly, blood thundered in her ears. Desire clouded her vision. She arched up, supporting herself on her shoulders and her bottom.

He eased the ache with a gentle lapping motion. "Tell me," he murmured, his warm, deep voice inviting confidences she'd never told another soul. "Tell me."

"I was alone. The nuns...they prayed and served God, but I...I wasn't one of them. I wasn't even their religion. But I wasn't...in the world, either." She could scarcely articulate the words, but she needed to explain herself to him. Arnou would understand. "During the winter it was dark so much. No one spoke and I...oh, I would imagine a man...."

"A prince?"

"No." She half laughed, focused on the escalating sensation between her legs and barely aware of what she was revealing. "Just a man...who touched me and told me I was beautiful...."

"You are beautiful." His voice was enticement itself.

"And who lived with me my whole life and talked to me, and who did things to me...oh, Arnou, please!" Her fingers curled into the grass. The tiny stalks broke under her tension. "Please, Arnou. You have to...just a little more and I can..."

"In the deepest, darkest moment of night, did you make yourself shudder and come?"

"Yes!"

"Like this?" With his lips and his tongue, he suckled on her. He seemed to know how much pressure to use, what pace to maintain, how to spin bliss from chastity.

Great tremors swept her. She cried aloud, spasming, the whole of her being concentrated on that center he had found so easily and ravished so skillfully. He nourished her climax, teasing her along until she thought she would die of joy.

Finally he let her subside.

She lay gasping on the ground, and all the stress of long lonely years evaporated in the heat of the fairy ring.

But he didn't take his fingers away. Instead one circled the entrance to her body, over and over again, and little by little she found the demands within her building again.

His voice sounded as smooth and intoxicating as whiskey itself. "Did you put your finger inside?"

He was going to…going to…and she couldn't bear it. It was too much: the sapphire sky, the jade grass, the frisking breeze, the forceful man…her startling nudity, her shocking admissions, her insatiable lustiness. "Arnou, please, don't—"

He didn't listen. She knew he wouldn't.

His finger pierced her body.

She was damp, swollen, and ready, and as her passage closed around him, sensation, only just subsided, roared to life again. He set a rhythm her body somehow recognized—the rhythm of the ocean waves, the changing seasons, the passing stars. At his direction, her body surged and moved, rising and falling as his finger slid in and out. She shuddered in a completion that built and built...and paused...she hovered between disappointment and pleased exhaustion....

His finger remained inside, caressing her, but her perception of fullness increased. Increased to the point of discomfort. Even to...pain.

She squirmed, trying to find her way back to delight.

"Two fingers, that's all. Sweetheart, let me..."

"No!" She tried to scoot away.

He held her in place with one arm around her hips—and once again, he put his mouth between her legs.

At that moment she realized—everything he'd done before had been nothing but an hors d'oeuvre. He thrust his fingers in and out, in and out, and at the same time he sucked on her, creating heat and desperation. He was hurting her, yet at the same time, he fed her pleasure with his lips and tongue. She struggled against him, strove with him, wanting to be free, wanting to submit. Passion—inappropriate, marvelous passion—had vanquished the self-contained princess and Sorcha both fought the change and reveled in it.

Best of all, Arnou offered her no choice. He controlled the moment and she had to surrender.

When she did, the anguish and the glory exceeded everything that had gone before. She came in a magnificent rush, whimpering and moaning, coiling and fighting, spasming again and again until exhaustion brought her to quiescence.

When she reclined panting on the ground, unable to move, covered with perspiration and so exhausted she could no longer think, Arnou rose up and covered her with his body.

He weighed her down. The fastenings on his clothing dug into her skin. He held her in his arms and kissed her forehead, her eyelids, her cheeks, and her lips. "Shhh. Sweetheart, you're splendid. You're beautiful. All I want is you."

She appreciated his praise, yet all she wanted was him, and she had not had him. She wasn't so far gone that she didn't realize *that*.

She wrapped her legs around his hips and pushed herself up to him.

He answered, but the pressure of his clothed loins only drove her a little wilder. And it seemed he moved reluctantly.

Teetering on the edge of humiliation, she whispered, "Don't you want me?"

The arm under her head trembled. Against her chest, his chest heaved. "Not want you?" That marvelously attractive voice rasped with need. "I'm dying for you."

"Then take off your clothes and—"

"No." Lifting his head, he gazed down at her. "No!"

"But I want—"

"One of us has to show some responsibility, and apparently that person has to be me." He laughed harshly. "I should be stricken by a bolt of lightning for calling what I just did responsible, but we've got to stop, Sorcha. We've got to."

"I felt that bolt of lightning." She undulated her body against his.

"Dear girl, you were barely close enough to be singed."

"Then show me."

He stared at her as if stricken by a revelation, and not a pleasant one.

She didn't like being viewed as if she were the first ant at the picnic. "You're worried that I'm a princess and you're a common man, but there are precedents. Catherine of Russia took lovers—"

He placed his hand over her mouth, and if anything, his gaze grew more horrified. "We aren't going to make it all the way without…"

What was the man talking about? "Without…?"

His lips moved silently, as if he couldn't quite say what he meant. Then he heaved a huge sigh. Wetting his lips, he said, "We're going to have to make a little detour. You need to spend a night in an inn."

"A detour?" She lay naked in the grass with a man on top of her. The echoes of passion had barely subsided. And he was talking about their *route*. Urgently she tried to bring the conversation back to the *now*. "There was an English queen of French origins, Isabelle by name, and she took lovers, too."

"A detour will take precious time, which we don't have, but I can't fight this."

If he'd reacted with anger or interest or with any great emotion, she'd have continued to argue. But he sounded absentminded.

Mortifying.

She shoved at him, rolling him off her. With the painful care of a woman who'd recently suffered—and enjoyed—an initiation of madness, she donned the first of her shirts. "What about the man who attacked me?

You've been worried he had compatriots, and I'm sure he does. If we take a detour, we give the assassins more time to catch us."

"We also throw them off the track." Arnou handed her shirts to her as if he wanted her to get dressed, yet watched with such brooding attention she knew he hated every moment. "I know just the inn. It's run by a fellow I think you'll like."

"I'm sure I will."

"Who don't you like?" He shook his head as if exasperated by the fact she enjoyed meeting people after so many years hidden in the convent. "You have to stop trusting everyone."

"Madam said that, too. But it's so uncomfortable to look at everyone as a possible enemy." And Sorcha knew what it was to be uncomfortable. The touch of her tight breeches against her swollen tissues made her break into an unappealing sweat. Frustration made her malicious, and she said, "Besides, if I have to distrust everyone, shouldn't I distrust you, too?"

He stood, leaned down, and brushed off his knees.

Feeling vaguely ashamed of herself and sure she'd hurt his feelings, she whispered, "Arnou?"

He straightened. "Of course you should trust me. Don't you trust me?"

Relief rushed through her. He wasn't angry about her misgivings. "You know I do. I trust you more than anyone I've ever met!" Standing, she gestured widely, flinging her arms out to embrace the world. "You may be a simple sailor, but you're my noble cavalier."

As if he couldn't resist, he pulled her toward him.

She melted into his arms.

Then he thrust her away as if he didn't dare hold her. "Very well. You trust me. I say we go to this inn. So we'll go."

She surrendered. "All right, Arnou. We'll go."

Chapter 15

"**I**s your *cock* unusually large?" Sorcha asked in a chipper voice.

"What?" With every step his horse took, Rainger suffered a jolt that went right through his aching balls. They were blue. And swollen. And painful.

Worse, beside him rode Princess Cheerful Cherry, carrying on a jolly commentary and asking questions about his less-than-stellar behavior back at the stone circle.

What in hell had happened back there in the stone ring? He'd planned a kiss. A simple kiss. The kind of innocent lip-play that would soften Sorcha toward the foolish Arnou. He had thought that if she responded, he would move toward more intimacy...tomorrow.

Instead he'd kissed and tasted her like a starving man. He'd barely been able to pull back.

Now, obviously, his greatest fear had come true and he'd lost his mind, because…"What did you say?" he asked.

"Is your *cock* unusually large?" Sorcha seemed to take joy in emphasizing the word. "That's what Eveleen called it. A *cock*."

He cursed that horse trader MacMurtrae for sending Sorcha to a bawdyhouse. He cursed Sorcha's charm, her open-mindedness, her inquisitiveness, and most of all his own body, which demanded release and demanded it now. "That's not what princesses call it."

"There's always a separate rule for princesses," she said sarcastically. "I am sick of having to endure separate princess rules. When I am queen, I shall make a law that says: *Princesses may call a cock a cock and no one shall stop them.*"

"Fine. Then you can call it a—" He stopped barely in time. "You can call it anything you want. Until then, let us not discuss my—" He stopped himself again.

"*Hornpipe* seems unnecessarily colloquial." Sorcha's lips were puffy from the pressure of his. Her eyelids had a sexy, drooping slant.

Her boyish costume made no difference to his libido. To him, she looked like a well-loved woman, and he wanted to love her some more. "Princesses don't call it that, either," he said.

222 • CHRISTINA DODD

"What do they call *it*?" She sounded exasperated.

Staring doggedly at the road, he said, "Princesses don't talk about it at all."

"That's silly. How will I ask you questions?"

"You don't."

"But I have to ask *you*. Once I get to Beaumontagne, no one will ever tell me anything. As princess, I'm supposed to be pure and ignorant and sacrosanct." In a disgusted tone, she said, "When I get married, my husband will probably make love to me through a hole in the sheet."

"No, he won't."

"You can't promise that."

Actually, he could.

He risked a glance at her.

"So come on, Arnou." She was smiling at him, dimpling, coaxing. "I won't call it a *cock* if you don't want me to. But you have to tell me what I want to know. Is your *thing* unusually large?"

"My thing..." If he had a wall, he would pound his head against it. He'd be just as likely to win. "Please, Your Highness, call it a cock."

"All right." She seemed not at all surprised. "So is it? Because as we were leaving, Eveleen took me aside and whispered she thought you were particularly well endowed, and when I asked what that meant, she said—"

"Yes. It's huge." He would say anything to halt this discussion before he found himself compelled to show her his size. And shape. And the correct use for his... cock. "If all the men in Europe put their cocks on a table, mine would be the biggest."

"Really?"

Dear heavens. She believed him. "No."

"Maybe not, but I'd sure like to see the cast of performers."

Stunned by her comment, he stopped his horse.

She stopped her horse.

He stared at her, straight and strong and sober.

She stared at him and she saw...heaven only knows what she saw.

See the cast of performers. She wanted to see every man in Europe slap his dick on a table so she could see the cast of performers.

He had the strangest feeling in his gut. It seemed vaguely familiar, a feeling he'd experienced a long time ago. He didn't recognize it, but he couldn't contain it, either. A noise rose from his belly like an artesian fountain, a noise that was stunted, broken, uncertain. But as he continued, the sound grew in volume.

It was laughter. Whole-hearted, full-bodied laughter that shook the saddle and made his horse prance sideways in alarm. Laughter! He hadn't laughed like that since…he didn't remember when he had laughed like that.

She giggled, a festive sound that brought birds winging overhead and made rabbits poke their heads out of their holes in the ground.

He stopped, met her amused gaze, and whooped with merriment again. Only by an effort of will did he manage to stammer out, "If I ever get…all the men in Europe…together, I'll let you…buy the table."

"I'll hold you to that promise."

When he'd calmed enough to wipe the tears off his cheek, he said, "I haven't laughed like that for years."

"It's a surprise to me to discover you have a sense of humor."

It was a surprise to him, too. It was a bigger surprise to know she'd deliberately set out to make him laugh. She wasn't the same Sorcha he'd known as a boy. So who was she?

"Look at this road, Arnou! It's wide enough to ride two abreast." She gestured around them. "Look at the terrain! The mountains are falling behind and we're coming back to civilization. Once we reach Edinburgh, we'll not have another chance to be together."

Oh, no. Not again. Please God, she wasn't trying to seduce him again.

But she was.

His briefly revived humor failed him. "Once you get an idea in your head, you won't let it go." He urged his horse forward once more.

She rode with him, astride in the saddle as if she'd been born to it, the horse moving between her thighs as smoothly as Rainger would if he...Damn. If he couldn't stop his thoughts, he was going to explode. He had to stop thinking about having her in bed and undressing her. About her figure, so much more curvaceous than her boyish clothing had suggested, about her pale breasts with the freckles that reached almost to the pale peach nipples, about the flared hips and the fiery brush that begged a man to touch it and be burned to a cinder.

If the pain he suffered now was any indication, he *had* been burned. He'd touched her and the two of them had gone up in flames. Certainly her bewildered, amazed, passion-pouty expression had driven him on to greater heights of ardency—and folly.

Only that silver cross she wore around her neck had stopped him. It had seared his palm, and when he stared at it, he remembered seeing its glow in the darkest moment of his life.

"Grandmamma always told me I had to seize my opportunities." Sorcha made a fist as if she were seizing...something.

Seizing it lustily enough that he winced. "I very much doubt your grandmother was talking about *me*."

"No, she was talking about *me*, and I know we're facing a lost opportunity. If you had let me blow your hornpipe—"

"Would you stop jabbering about that?" he snapped.

Sorcha jerked back. First her lower lip stuck out. Then her eyes filled with tears.

And because she made him feel like a cad, he found himself explaining something he never wanted to tell any woman as long as he lived. "What I mean is—when you talk about that, my personal parts grow rigid—"

Craning her head, she looked at the bulge in his lap. "More rigid?"

"Yes. More rigid." He could scarcely stand to look at Sorcha for fear he'd launch himself out of the saddle and into her body.

She, of course, sounded thoughtful and curious.

"Frustration puts me in pain," he said.

She sniffed. "You don't have to be in pain. If I had—"

He lifted his hand in a stop gesture.

"But if I *had*," she insisted, "you'd be riding comfortably now."

"No, because I'm not going to stop wanting you because you satisfy me once."

"Really?" She sounded charmed by the concept. "You'll want me more than once?"

Because confessing would cause no harm and please her, he said, "Morning, noon, and night, my dear. Morning, noon, and night."

"Then I'm glad we're going to an inn. We'll spend the night together."

With minor modifications, that was Rainger's plan. But he ground his teeth at her perky suggestion.

"We should take the opportunity to enjoy each other." Sorcha seemed unconcerned with propriety. She seemed willing to give herself to a man she called honorable and kind. Apparently she had suffered no grief at Rainger's death.

And why not? True, before he hadn't cared what she thought of him. Now her indifference irritated him. "But what about your prince?" At her startled glance, he realized he had almost bitten off her head. Being the foolish Arnou was taking more and more effort, but he managed to sound sheepish. "I mean…you must care about your prince."

"What prince? The one I have to marry?" She shrugged with weary lack of interest. "I don't even know who that is, and I don't care. There's a good chance he'll make me miserable one way or the other."

"I meant the prince to whom you were betrothed." *What about Rainger? Tell me how you felt about Rainger.*

"Oh. Him. I never cherished girlish dreams about Rainger."

Prying information out of her in such an underhanded manner almost assured he would hear himself described in unflattering tones, but curiosity drove him. "You grew up with him. When he died, didn't you weep?"

She urged her horse to ride ahead. She held her spine and neck poker-stiff, and rode so long without answering that he thought she refused to let the lowly Arnou snoop so intimately into her life.

Finally, she fell back. In a voice so low and calm he had to strain to hear her, she said, "There was so much grief for a while. I was sent into exile alone. My sisters went to a separate location. My father was killed in battle. Grandmamma almost lost control of the country and all of my links to Beaumontagne were severed. The loss of Rainger was...I was sorry, of course. But all my affection for him was old affection, the affection I felt for a playmate. I didn't admire him as a young man and he barely tolerated me. So losing Rainger was just one more blow in a year fraught with agony."

She sounded so composed he scarcely believed any of it. Her father, her country, her isolation seemed nothing more than a test to be endured. Did Sorcha not feel pain?

Then she wiped a tear off her cheek.

Ah, now he remembered. In Beaumontagne, there had been Grandmamma and her interminable rules. She'd strictly trained Sorcha. *A princess does not wail and weep. A princess always maintains her decorum, for a princess never knows who watches her for guidance in proper behavior.* Sorcha might flout some of Grandmamma's strictures, but not all of them. "How did you survive that year?"

"I maintained my dignity, of course, but sometimes I wanted to…to express myself in a…a…a…" She couldn't say it.

So he did. "Loud scream?"

She glanced at him, her eyes wide and almost shocked. "Yes. I suppose I would have liked to…to scream."

An hour ago she was naked in his arms, making demands without a care to her position or to propriety. Now she could scarcely express her desire to show sorrow.

She seemed so open and uncomplicated, but beneath that placid façade, she hid a character forged from the fires of grief and loneliness.

Sorcha fascinated him.

And that could be dangerous, for the last woman who had fascinated him almost killed him.

He was doing the right thing. He was learning all Sorcha's secrets. He was going to take her to his bed. Before long, she'd be nothing but another woman. And, of course, his queen.

"Why don't you scream now?" he suggested.

"Here?" Sorcha looked around as if engaged by the changing scenery. "On the road?"

"Why not? There's no one to hear except me and I won't tell anyone."

"No." She shook her head firmly. "The moment is past."

"Should the moment of bereavement go past without marking it with sorrow?"

She blinked at him as if astonished. "Arnou, that is very wise."

Wise? Yes. Because he knew about despair. He knew about mourning. "Give a loud, long scream of rage and anguish. You'll feel better."

"I feel fine."

Ah. There was Grandmamma's girl! "The ghosts of your departed will rest easier. At least I know *Rainger* will rest easier." He should be ashamed of manipulating her like this, but he wanted—no, needed—to think she had mourned him.

"All right. I could try it." She filled her lungs with air. Tilted her head back. Sat there for a long moment. Then exhaled in a gust. "I can't. I feel foolish. I'll wait for the proper opportunity. Life being what it is, grief will present itself soon enough."

"Yes." Sooner than she realized.

Before he met Sorcha, he had intended to take her back to Beaumontagne, there to marry her, command her army, march into Richarte, and kill Count duBelle.

It had been a sound plan, one that required a deception of Sorcha.

But deception didn't matter. All that mattered was producing a princess to wed so he could take back his country.

Everything depended on him. Men—his best friends—had been dreadfully hurt, had *died* to break him out of that dungeon. He sought to free his people from the dreadful burden of the oppressor. He sought the crown.

He sought revenge.

Sorcha, with her soft lips, nubile body, and wide, innocent eyes, would not stand in his way.

Nor would his weakness toward her.

Her merry voice broke into his reflections. "You have such a grim expression, while I'm so happy. Do you know I've never kissed a man before?"

"I'm glad to hear that." He wouldn't have to kill another man.

"Kissing you was very pleasant."

"Pleasant. Really." She had a unique and marvelous way of insulting a man. "And a raging ocean storm is *cute*."

She thought about that. "You're right. Kissing you was more than pleasant. It was…magnificently overwhelming."

He grunted. He hid a smile. *That's more like it.*

Then the urge to smile faded.

When he was seventeen, he'd believed every ounce of flattery poured into his callow ears. He was a hard man to cajole now—except when the words fell from Sorcha's lips. Then they sounded sincere.

He couldn't keep his hands off her. He accepted that. But a way existed to delude Sorcha, satisfy her grandmother (although not completely, because her grandmother could never be completely satisfied), and permit him marital rights.

He was not going to deflower Sorcha on the ground. Their mating was a matter of state. They had to wed in the official church of Beaumontagne and Richarte, the Church of the Mountain. They had to marry before representatives of their countries, people who would swear the ceremony was performed and was proper in the eyes of God and man. And they had to show sheets stained with the proof of her virginity to prove she'd been with no other man.

Tomorrow morning, they would arrive at the village he sought. The village of exiles.

Tomorrow night, he would hold Sorcha in his arms.

Chapter 16

Sorcha couldn't quite put her finger on what was so unique about this village.

The houses looked different from the other houses in Scotland. Yes, they were humble, but their roofs had a bit of a tilt at the front of the ridge beam. The windows were lower and wider. Silver crosses were tacked up over the front doors—crosses she recognized. Crosses identical to the one she wore around her neck.

Revelation struck Sorcha with the power of a sledgehammer. This was a Beaumontagnian village transplanted to the wilds of Scotland.

"I recognize this place," she said.

"You've been here before?" Arnou lifted a skeptical eyebrow.

"No. Yes." She didn't know what she meant. "It reminds me of my home."

"Isn't that a coincidence?" He didn't sound particularly surprised. "I hear there's a good inn here, and staying there would be a chance for you to clean up before we arrive in Edinburgh."

"Is that really the reason you want to stay at an inn?" She shot him a flirtatious glance.

"Yes."

"Yes." She sighed. Why was the man so stubborn? Why wouldn't he make love to her? Last night they had slept together in a barn, and all night long he'd been ready and willing. When he had held her for warmth, she'd felt his cock pressed against her back.

Still…"Cleaning up is a wonderful idea." To take a bath, a real bath in a real tub, sounded like heaven. Not as much heaven as sleeping naked in Arnou's arms, but she wouldn't mention it again. At least not now. A covert attack might serve her better. She'd bathe and wear the nightgown that the ladies at Madam's had given her. She'd display herself to Arnou and he'd be stricken with craving and give in to her desires….

They turned into the street that led to the town square. There she could see that the buildings were taller and wooden signs hung over the doors—the Red Rock Pub, the Glacier Peak Butcher, the Silver Springs Inn. A cluster of a dozen men and women were gathered around the well in the middle of the square. The women wore small embroidered caps and white aprons. The men wore black breeches and red suspenders. Finally, clinching her suspicion that this was a group of exiles, she saw that the well had a small pointed roof and posts painted blue.

"Look at that!" She pointed.

"It's a well," Arnou said prosaically.

"It's more than a well. The point on the roof deflects any evil from above. The blue blesses the water and keeps away the evil eye. These are traditions in Beaumontagne and in Richarte." To see the reality of it again fed a longing she'd denied for a long time.

"So Beaumontagne and Richarte share the same traditions?" Arnou sounded as if he knew the answer but was humoring her.

"They share a border. They share traditions. They share a language. They share a church. They fight about everything." She grinned, because for Beaumontagnians to complain about Richartians and for Richartians to complain about Beaumontagnians was the most ingrained tradition of all. "Do you know? Are the people here foreign?"

"Foreign?" Arnou directed his *I'm puzzled* glance at her. "Like from another country besides Scotland?"

"Never mind. I'll find out." She urged her horse forward.

A woman with a wealth of wrinkles on her lips, her eyelids, and her earlobes sat on the bench at the well. The village priest in his traditional black cassock and three portly gentlemen stood sampling a wine. Five young women, sisters, Sorcha thought, leaned together watching Sorcha and chuckling as if they found her entertaining. One caressed the bulge of her belly where her baby rested. And two women of perhaps forty-three argued over the well's bucket.

As Sorcha rode into their midst, the people in the square stopped speaking and stared cautiously. She broke into a smile, for the faces had sharp noses, high cheekbones, creamy tan complexions, and every eye color. She'd never seen these people before, but she knew them. They were part of the handsomest nation in the world. She burst out, "Are you Beaumontagnian?"

They drew back as if her enthusiasm alarmed them.

With a grin, Rainger let her go. She wasn't going to get hurt here. The villagers were cautious, but they would find out soon enough who she was. Then they'd understand their good fortune. For now, Sorcha could shower them with her bubbling exuberance and, unless he missed his guess, she'd win them over before they even knew her name.

"Because I'm from Beaumontagne," she called. "Are you exiles from the revolution?"

"Some of us are from Beaumontagne, some from Richarte." Sharp-eyed, thin-lipped, and all bony angles, one older woman abandoned her argument over the bucket and made her way toward Sorcha. "So how do we know you're Beaumontagnian?"

Sorcha dropped into the language of their home. "I'm a long way from home, but at the hearth of my people, I am always welcome."

At the sound of the familiar proverb and Sorcha's sweet and easy rhythm, the woman placed a hand over her heart.

A murmur swept the small group.

"Welcome. Welcome." The woman broke into a smile. "Forgive my caution. We haven't seen anyone arrive from home since we got here. We had to flee the old countries and settled here in New Prospera for safety. Safety isn't always that easy to achieve when some people in Scotland resent the intrusion, and some are frightened of people who speak a different language."

A stout gentleman pushed his way forward to stand by the lady. "I'm Mr. Montaroe, the innkeeper. This is my wife, Tulia. Come in and have some wine. Relax, eat, and tell us what you know about Richarte."

"And Beaumontagne," Talia said.

"I don't know anything. I haven't been home for ten years, but I'm going there now." Sorcha glowed as she spoke.

Rainger wondered if she'd only just realized that, if all went well, she was within weeks of returning.

"What about him?" Mr. Montaroe pointed to Rainger.

"He's from Normandy," Sorcha said.

Tulia scrutinized him. "He looks Beaumontagnian."

"No, he looks as if he's from Richarte," Mr. Montaroe corrected stiffly. "Not every handsome young man is from Beaumontagne."

"They are if they're fortunate," Tulia retorted.

One of the five young women deliberately caught Rainger's gaze. She wasn't more than twenty, pretty and flirtatious. She indicated first the innkeeper, then his wife, and rolled her eyes. At once Rainger realized they fought like all Beaumontagnians and Richartians were prone to do. And as three other young ladies bearing a marked resemblances to Mr. Montaroe and Tulia made their way toward the front, he thought the Montaroes made love with equal fervor.

Sorcha smiled easily. "Actually, this is my traveling companion, Arnou. We were hoping to stay at your reputable inn before we continue on our way to Edinburgh and from there to home."

"Beaumontagne seems safe," Mr. Montaroe said, "but rumor says Richarte is a shambles under Count duBelle's rule."

At the sound of duBelle's name, the old woman spat on the ground and the younger women buzzed like angry bees.

"I will go to Beaumontagne," Sorcha said. "It's time."

Tulia turned to her husband. "I think we should go, too. We could stay with my parents—"

"No," he said. "When the prince comes back and my properties are returned, then we'll return. Not before."

"Prince Rainger? But...he's dead." Sorcha looked from one to the other for confirmation.

"Rumor claims he escaped from Count duBelle's dungeon and is even now gathering an army to take back his country." Mr. Montaroe's hazel eyes glowed green.

Rainger watched as Sorcha's expressions changed from astonishment to pleasure and then, with a glance at him, to dismay.

Sorcha looked from Rainger to Mr. Montaroe. "I can't...can't believe that," she stammered. "Godfrey said Rainger was taken by Count duBelle and killed."

"I don't know who your Godfrey is, but he was wrong. That young man was put in the dungeon for years and by God's grace escaped."

"When?" Sorcha demanded.

"We heard the report almost three years ago." Tulia sounded hopeless. "In an English paper. But they're notorious for lying, trying to build people's hopes."

Three of the girls surrounded their mother. One took her in her arms.

The priest spoke quietly in her ear.

Tulia wiped a tear off her cheek, nodded, and straightened her shoulders.

"So!" Mr. Montaroe slapped his hands together. "How many rooms will you require?"

"One," Rainger said.

Everyone turned to stare at him as if he were a trained bear who had spoken.

"One? What are you talking about?" Sorcha asked. "I thought you said you wouldn't—"

"I'm not leaving you alone." Taking her hand, he pressed it in his. "It's too dangerous."

Under his intense consideration, her lashes fluttered. In her excitement, she'd forgotten to deepen her voice and now, for the discerning eye, she acted like a female with her mate.

The priest noticed, of course. He moved forward to stand before them. A tall, broad-shouldered man, he sternly examined his guests. "Are you married?"

"Married?" Mr. Montaroe harrumphed. "Father Terrance, your eyesight is failing you. These are men."

"That little one's a woman, you oaf." His wife dug her elbow into his side.

"No." But he focused on Sorcha at once, and examined her from every side. In incredulous tones, he said, "No!"

"I saw it at once," Tulia said.

"Woman! You did not." His eyes bulged as he glared at his wife.

"I did. Beaumontagnian women have an instinct about these things," she said loftily.

Rainger listened in amusement as the Montaroes squabbled in an undertone.

The pregnant woman stood near Rainger's boot. She cast him an amused glance and said, "My parents never agree on anything."

Then, in a single voice, the Montaroes said, "You can't stay in the same room unless you're married."

"Except that," the young woman said.

Rainger shot her a grin.

"Young lady, have you remained faithful to our church?" Father Terrance asked.

"Yes," Sorcha said in a small voice.

"You know how strict we are," Tulia said. "We're not like the English and Scots. Lax and immoral people!"

"We have to stay in the same room." Rainger was using the situation to his advantage, but he wasn't saying that for effect. He *wouldn't* leave Sorcha alone. The dozen people had grown to a group of twenty curiosity-seekers, and to them he confided, "She's being hunted by those who wish her dead."

"Arnou." Sorcha glared at him. "You're making a scene!"

"I won't leave you alone," he said.

"You are traveling companions, obviously. You know each other...quite well. If you can tell us you are married, you may stay in the same room." Father Terrance's brown eyes pinned them in place.

Rainger waited to see if Sorcha would lie to the priest.

She tried. "We, um, we are definitely..." She tried very hard. But she was painfully truthful. "That is, if vows of loyalty mean that a union has been formed, then we could say—"

"We're not married," Rainger flatly informed the priest.

Sorcha turned on him and hissed, "Stop that, Arnou!"

"Then we have a conflict," the priest said.

"Father, is there somewhere Sorcha and I can talk alone?" Rainger dismounted and offered his hands to assist her out of her saddle.

"The church is at the end of the main street." Father Terrance pointed the way. "You can talk there."

Sorcha slid into his arms with the ease of a woman comfortable to be there. He held her for a moment, looking down into her eyes, and he was pleased to see her eyelashes flutter and the color climb in her cheeks.

She might not realize it, but once again she gave off signals everyone here recognized. She was his woman.

Keeping his hands on her hips, he said softly, "Do you remember what Madam Pinchon said about the assassins? You vanquished the first one, but there are others waiting for us, and they're smart. They're crafty. They may be here in the crowd right now."

She glanced around. "These are good people."

With his finger on her chin, he brought her face back to his. "Since we left the stone circle, I've been feeling twitchy"—an unfortunate truth—"and I trust my instincts far more than I trust anyone here. Come on." Taking her hand, he led her to the small chapel. It was surrounded by a small cemetery, shaded by a large oak, and painstakingly built to resemble the churches in Beaumontagne and Richarte.

Pushing open the great door, he stepped inside a memory so intense it almost brought him to his knees. He resisted only because of the deceit he must perpetrate on Sorcha. But to him the scent of candles, the wooden altar with its gold-stitched altar cloth, the silver cross, and the statue of the Virgin irresistibly reminded him of all the small village churches in Richarte he'd toured as a young prince.

He hadn't cared for the beauty and serenity then; his visit had been a duty.

Now it was like coming home.

He didn't really understand his own emotions. In the darkness of Count duBelle's dungeon, he'd come to doubt God's grace. He'd prayed so hard in prison—first for vengeance, then for escape, and finally for death. Only when he'd forsworn God had he escaped.

If God had a presence on this earth, Rainger had yet to see proof of it.

He glanced at Sorcha. She had dropped to her knees. Her gaze was fixed to the altar, her lips moved in a prayer, and between her fingers she held the silver cross still connected to a chain around her neck.

The cross Sorcha wore was identical to the ones that her sisters kept around their necks.

That cross was the only object that united Sorcha with Clarice and Amy. He'd heard the longing in her voice when she spoke of her sisters, and if he were a different man, he'd feel guilty about the letters he carried in his saddlebags. The letters written in loving script from Clarice and Amy to their dear sister Sorcha.

Guilt had no place in his plan.

Yet he found a prayer rising from his gut. It wasn't a proper sort of prayer, but it was sincere. *I need Sorcha, Lord. Let me keep her. Don't let her die.*

Because if the assassins killed Sorcha, Rainger's schemes would come to naught.

And if she wasn't there to nag him and tease him and ask him questions better left unspoken, the sunshine would fade, the tides would cease their motion, and he would walk forever in shadow.

But—such sentiment was silly, a temporary weakness caused by too little food and too much apprehension.

Gracefully she came to her feet and smiled at him. "Isn't it wonderful here?"

"Yes. A good place to get married."

"What are you babbling about?" She didn't understand yet. She didn't comprehend his intent—and if all went well, she wouldn't understand why he'd urged this course until it was too late to retreat.

"We must get married in this church because I won't leave you in a room by yourself." Rainger managed to sound prosaic.

"I can't marry you. It's not necessary."

"If they won't let us stay in the same room, it is." Carefully he began his argument. "Besides, it won't count. We're not the same religion."

"No, we're not." She smiled at him fondly. "But dear, foolish Arnou, what does that matter?"

"In the Catholic church"—Rainger picked his words carefully to avoid claiming to be a Catholic—"a marriage isn't legal unless both parties are confirmed. Is it not the same for your church?"

"No. Long ago, both Beaumontagne and Richarte were Catholic. But we're small countries isolated by mountains. The winters are arduous and by the end of the fifteenth century, we had our own cardinal and our own way of doing things. Yet often marriages occurred with Catholics—holdovers from the old religion or visitors to our borders. So in special circumstances such as ours, Father Terrance has dispensation to immediately perform the ceremony for the couple, without a care to their religion, without banns or the other, more proper rituals."

"What special circumstances?" As if Rainger didn't know.

"It appears to the village we've already been sharing the favors of a wedding bed, and now you're insisting we stay in the same room. It seems to them that we have already consummated our relationship." She sighed. "Unfortunately, that's not true."

Wait a few more hours.

"This kind of marriage is officially recognized by the church," she said. "The common people call it 'sliding the banister.'"

He almost laughed. He hadn't heard that for a long time.

"It would be better if we go to a different village and a different inn." But her longing gaze around her belied her humdrum tone. It was clear she wanted to stay with her people.

With a little concentrated effort on his part, he would convince her. "There's not a village or an inn close."

"Then we should find a farmhouse or stay in a field. It's not like we haven't done that before."

"More assassins are waiting, and they're waiting where they know we must go—on the road to Edinburgh. That is what Madam Pinchon told you, isn't it?"

Miserably, she nodded.

"If the money I got off that first assassin is any indication, Count duBelle is paying well."

Sorcha stiffened. "How do *you* know about Count duBelle?"

"Mr. Montaroe mentioned him." Rainger had to be careful. Sorcha was trusting, far too trusting, but she wasn't stupid. He needed to convince her, not make her wary of him. "I will not leave you alone in a room. You know I would never presume more than you let me. I understand my place in your life." Long ago, he would have flinched to tell such lies while standing in a church. Now all that mattered was winning the princess and taking back his country.

"Marriage between us is prohibited for me."

"You said the priest could marry us."

"He could marry us if I weren't a princess...."

Rainger widened his eyes as if confused. "You said your church could marry across faiths."

"The common people can marry across faiths, but we're like the Church of England. Our rulers are the heads of the church and I, as a member of the royal family, have to marry a member of the Church of the Mountain."

"Because you're the head of the church." He shrugged. "We won't tell anyone."

"It's not that simple. If we marry, we can't spend the night together in a single bed. Do you understand?"

He understood far more than she knew. "Because your prince is alive."

She put her finger over his lips. "That's a rumor."

"But maybe it's true."

"Maybe." She sounded unconvinced.

"Wouldn't you be happier if you had to marry him than anyone else?"

"Rainger would probably be the lesser of many evils."

Rainger winced. He'd asked for that.

"But I'm not going to live my life on the chance that report is true. No, Rainger isn't the problem. The problem is—if I go into *my* church and repeat wedding vows which bind me to you, then I dare not consummate that marriage."

He widened his eyes in feigned confusion.

She sighed and tried to explain. "Because there are witnesses who are my people, I'd have to tell Grandmamma and the cardinal and the bishop, and they'll want to perform an annulment to cleanse this ceremony away, and they'll ask me to swear nothing happened between us. I can't swear that if we spend a night together, really together."

"Were you really going to give yourself to me?" For the first time, it occurred to him how little she cared for the trappings of royalty, and he experienced a dangerously warm sense of worth. Sorcha liked him for who he was—a poor, ignorant, simple man.

"Of course I was going to give myself to you."

"But you're a princess."

"Our coming together would harm no one, and it would make me euphoric." She smoothed her finger along his stubbled chin. "I flatter myself it would make you euphoric, too."

"Yes." Stubbornly he returned to his everlasting refrain. "But we aren't going elsewhere, and I won't leave you alone."

"Oh." She lifted her eyes toward the ceiling as if seeking heavenly guidance. "You're impossible!"

"If I deliver you to Beaumontagne alive, I could get a big reward. They won't pay me anything for your dead body."

"Somebody would," she snapped, then bit her lip.

"Killing you wouldn't be much of a challenge, would it?" For the first time, he allowed a crack to form in his doltish façade, and permitted her a glimpse of how dangerous he could be.

She stepped back. "No. No, it wouldn't."

"In these circumstances, Your Highness"—he used her title on purpose to remind her of her importance—"you must take advantage of any stratagem which brings you back to your country alive. Staying alive is what matters."

Sorcha walked away from him. Turned her back on him. Slid her fingers along the polished wood of the pew. In a voice so soft Rainger had to strain to hear it, she said, "Mother Brigette told me almost the same thing." Slowly she nodded. "All right. I'll marry you."

"I promise I'll keep you safe."

"With you, Arnou, I never doubted that." She smiled at him.

Brave, sweet girl. She accepted this small defeat well.

When she discovered the truth, she would undoubtedly acknowledge her rout as graciously.

Chapter 17

Rainger led Sorcha to the door and opened it. Summoned by gossip, the group outside had grown from two dozen to over a hundred. The buzz of their conversations faded as he faced them.

"Heavens." Sorcha peered over his shoulder. "Why are they here?"

"Perhaps they're excited about their first visitor from Beaumontagne." But he didn't believe it, and the crowd made him edgy. "I'll talk to the priest and make the arrangements, but wait here until I'm done." He shut the door in her anxious face and swept the crowd with his gaze, looking for potential attackers.

He saw no one. Everyone here had left their country because they'd been loyal to him or to Sorcha's father and her family, and the hardships they'd endured in a foreign country bonded them together.

But why the excitement? Why the buzz of gossip? Why were they gathered before the church? He sensed an undercurrent, something more than their natural delight in a wedding.

He beckoned the priest in an authoritative gesture that brought the priest's eyebrows up. The crowd parted to allow him to join Rainger, and everyone watched as if their lives depended on this conversation. "What's happened?" Rainger asked.

"A rumor made its way through the village at lightning speed." Father Terrance folded his hands before him and viewed Rainger with a hint of anticipation.

"A rumor? About a female visitor from Beaumontagne dressed as a boy and her bodyguard?" Rainger tried to smile as jovially as Arnou, but the tension wouldn't let him. "It would be a miracle if there wasn't a rumor."

"You called the young lady Sorcha."

A single word. Rainger had destroyed their anonymity with a single word. But he played dumb, spreading his hands in contrived bewilderment. "That's her name."

"Sorcha is a rare name, and the name of Beaumontagne's crown princess."

"Would a princess dress like a boy?" Prevarication, and easily seen through by a priest.

"She would if she was in danger, and you said, *She's being hunted by those who wish her dead.*"

Information given judiciously to pressure her into marriage. How had it rebounded so badly? "Then, Father, it would be better if this rumor was squelched at once," Rainger said softly.

"That might be possible, except that in Richarte, our innkeeper lived near the castle. He frequently saw young Prince Rainger ride by." Father Terrance's sharp gaze searched Rainger's face. "Mr. Montaroe claims you look very much like the prince would look after years...in the dungeon."

Rainger searched the crowd until he saw Mr. Montaroe's round, hopeful face staring at him. It wasn't possible for Montaroe to recognize his prince when Sorcha did not—yet he had. Perhaps the passing glance was more revealing than the careless years of childhood spent together.

The people strained toward him, silent, longing, wanting so badly to be told that their faith had been rewarded.

Earlier, Rainger had thought that guilt had no part in his actions.

But he was wrong.

In his youth, nothing had been more important than sinking his cock into the most accomplished pussy he could find. Because of his folly with Julienne, he'd betrayed his country.

The people here in New Prospera were still paying for his stupid deed.

Until the day he was king and made Richarte a paradise for his people, he would be guilty...and even then, nothing he could do would fix the traditions broken or return the lives lost.

But today, he could help heal the pain. He looked back at the priest. In his native language, he said, "Today you'll perform a royal wedding."

"Praise be to God!" Father Terrance began to fall to his knees in thanksgiving.

"No!" Rainger stopped him. "Listen to me. Sorcha doesn't know who I am. She still thinks I'm dead, and I have my reasons for allowing her to believe that. Please do not betray my confidence."

Clearly Father Terrance wished to ask questions, but Rainger stared him down until the priest bowed his head. "As you wish, sire."

"Call me Arnou. Are there other travelers in the village?"

"None have arrived yet today. None are likely at this time of the year. Travel is difficult."

"Indeed. Sorcha and I are the only travelers on the road to Edinburgh." Carefully, Rainger spelled out the peril. "We are...and Count duBelle's assassins."

The joy on Father Terrance's face faded to a horrible stillness.

"Keeping all this in mind"—taking the heavy pouch from his belt, Rainger pressed it into Father Terrance's hand—"let's celebrate our marriage, but let it be known only to the people of the village. Your discretion, everyone's discretion, is required, for our safety is precarious and everyone's return to Beaumontagne and Richarte depends on it."

"We'll post guards on the road and turn any traveler aside. I'll make sure everyone in the town understands." Father Terrance put his hands on Rainger's shoulders and looked into his eyes. "Trust me, my son. Scotland is beautiful and many people have been kind, but we want to go home." He made his way into the crowd and gathered the leaders in a circle around him.

As Rainger returned to the church, he heard Tulia gasp. Glancing back, he saw her put her hand on her chest and move her lips, but she couldn't speak for emotion. Mr. Montaroe lifted her in a mighty hug. The oldest lady, a woman who could barely stand by herself, performed a festive jig.

Perhaps destiny had directed Rainger here. Perhaps this wedding in this place and at this time was meant to be.

And with the danger that stalked them...perhaps tonight was their only chance to make love.

Rainger had to seize that chance. He couldn't wait any longer.

"All right. It's done. Father Terrance will marry us this afternoon." Arnou entered the church briskly.

Sorcha stared at him. Somehow, against her better judgment, he had managed to convince her to marry him. When had Arnou become so logical—and so stubborn?

Something of her thoughts must have shown in her face, for his expression softened. "What's the matter, sweetheart? Changing your mind?" Before she could answer, he pulled her into his arms. "Let me convince you again."

His body warmed her, easing the tight knot of tension in her neck and shoulders. The kiss he gave her was as light and sweet as meringue, melting on her tongue and making her hum with pleasure.

Drawing back, he smiled into her bemused face. "There. Is that better?"

She nodded.

"Remember, we're doing this for your safety. You can make your grandmother understand that, can't you?"

Sorcha nodded again.

Taking her by the hand, Arnou directed her toward the church door. "Go out to the innkeeper's wife and tell her the good news. We'll be married this afternoon and we want her to prepare the wedding supper."

"Yes. She seems very pleasant." But at the mention of the wedding, the drugging effect of Arnou's kiss dissipated. Sorcha supposed she understood the reasons why they needed to be married, but she could scarcely bear the performance of the ceremony and celebration. It seemed so...deceptive. Her feet dragged as she walked toward the door.

He opened and held it for her.

Stopping, she looked down at the floor and muttered, "Sometimes, Arnou, you're as bossy as Grand-mamma."

"Chin up, Sorcha. I promise everything will turn out right." But he sounded distracted, as if he'd forgotten her and moved on to the practicalities of the wedding.

She shut the church door behind her with a little slam. She looked out at the burgeoning crowd.

Every conversation stopped. Everyone looked at her.

The hush hurt her ears, and the bevy of inquiring eyes made her want to cringe.

She couldn't do this. She had to go back inside and tell Arnou to call off the whole idea.

The square burst into cheers.

She stared at them in horror, but old training held her in place; a princess does not turn away from a tribute.

A row of children with hastily cleaned faces lined up, each holding a spray of dried flowers, and one by one they came forward and presented them to Sorcha. She smiled. She thanked each one. Yet when they had finished, she held an armful of faded scents and a dreadful suspicion. "This is lovely, but I don't understand. Everyone seems so...pleased." In fact, the whole ceremony reminded her of the kind of welcomes she received as a princess.

Had these people somehow recognized her?

But Tulia bustled forward. "We love weddings, and this is your day. Remember, you'll only be a bride once."

Well. Sorcha had no reason to disbelieve Tulia, for she'd never been a bride before. She'd never attended a village wedding. She supposed that people did enjoy the marital celebration.

And really, how could these people recognize her as their crown princess? She'd left Beaumontagne ten years ago. She'd changed.

"Come." Tulia spread her arms wide in a gesture that indicated the path before her. "We'll go to the inn and make you a bride. The men will prepare your bridegroom. Father Terrance will go with them to make sure they don't get too drunk before the ceremony and fall down before it's over"—she shot her husband a glare and tossed her head—"like some bridegrooms I could name."

Mr. Montaroe blushed so red the tips of his ears burned. The crowd hooted.

Sorcha laughed and relaxed. This was easier than a wedding at the cathedral. So much less pageantry. So much more camaraderie. Clutching the flowers, she followed Tulia to the inn, while all around her the women of the village chatted and teased.

The oldest woman removed Sorcha's cap. "Today, we're going to make you a woman again."

With a broad wink, a younger one said, "He's going to make her a woman tonight."

"Roxanne!" Tulia shook her finger at the young woman. "That is not respectful."

"Anyway, it's not like that—" Sorcha began.

But the chorus of reprimands directed at Roxanne drowned out Sorcha's explanation, and then they reached the inn and every female in the village fought to enter and take part in the preparations.

Ruthlessly Tulia directed them to sit on the benches at the tables in the taproom, and such was her force of will that before long, curtains covered the windows, coffee was brewing in a large pot before the fire, water was heating, and everyone was seated and looking attentive.

Tulia stood Sorcha before the massive stone fireplace and Sorcha, ever the properly trained princess, worked frantically to remember everyone's name. Phoenice was the pregnant one. Roxanne was the saucy one. Rhea was logical and always smiling. Salvinia had sad brown eyes. Pia was thin, tall, and pretty.

"The young lady has no wedding gown," Tulia said.

"Call me Sorcha."

The conversation died. Everyone looked uncertainly at her neighbor. Tulia said, "I do not know that that is proper."

"Of course it is. What else would you call me?" Sorcha asked sensibly.

"Yes. What else would I call you?" But while Tulia agreed, she gestured to the table of older ladies as if needing a consensus.

One wrinkled grandmother, twisted with rheumatism, gestured the others close and they consulted each other in trembling old voices. The old lady slowly and with much assistance got to her feet. She proclaimed, "At this place in this time, we are her family. Sorcha she shall be."

The old women nodded. The rest of the room nodded.

"Sorcha, I am Sancia." The ancient one tapped her chest with her warped fingers. "I shall be your nonna, your grandmother."

Again the heads nodded.

Touched, Sorcha said, "I'm honored to have you as my grandmother."

The twisted finger pointed at Tulia. "She is Tulia. She will be your mother."

"I'm honored to have you as my mother," Sorcha said.

"I am the one honored." Tulia wiped her eyes on her apron. "You will bring us good luck."

Grandmother Sancia hobbled over, took Sorcha's cheeks between her palms, and smiled a toothless smile. "We will make this day special to you."

They were so nice and the wedding was not real, and once again Sorcha tried to explain. "I hate to have you go to so much trouble when it's not really going to be a marriage. You see, Arnou is worried about my safety—"

"I know." Grandmother Sancia brought Sorcha's forehead down to rest on hers. "He is a good man."

What was Sorcha to do? No one was listening to her.

Grandmother Sancia and Tulia circled Sorcha, then Grandmother Sancia tugged at Sorcha's cloak. "Take it off."

Sorcha shed the cloak.

Tulia tossed it toward the wall. "Ora, come and stand by Sorcha."

Ora lumbered over. She was approximately Sorcha's age, about Sorcha's height, but she weighed another seven stone.

Sorcha smiled.

Ora dimpled.

Everyone nodded.

"Yes, your wedding costume will fit," Tulia said.

Sorcha eyed Ora's wide waist. She plucked at her own sleeve. "I'm wearing a lot of shirts."

"Yes, we can tell." Grandmother Sancia hugged Ora. "She has gained a little since the twins were born."

Ora dimpled again and hustled away, out the door after her wedding costume.

Oh, well. It wouldn't matter if the costume didn't fit; the marriage wasn't real anyway.

"Bring down the tub," Tulia called.

At that point, it seemed to Sorcha she lost control of her actions—although later she realized she'd lost control the moment she met Arnou.

The women of the village stripped her, washed her, shampooed her hair, dried her, and dressed her in Ora's wedding costume—a long red skirt, a loose black blouse, a vest embroidered with colorful flowers, and a ring of dried flowers for her head. The waist was a little loose, the bosom a little tight, but it fit better than Sorcha expected.

Grandmother Sancia handed her a bouquet of fresh flowers; they were small, winter-stunted, and obviously scavenged from pots around the village, but the ribbon that bound them was silk and the women who looked at her beamed with gratification.

"You look beautiful." Tulia wiped proud tears from her eyes. "Beautiful! Like a princess."

Sorcha looked at her in horror, then decided she meant nothing by her comment.

At sunset, they surrounded her and herded her out of the inn, through the square, and toward the church.

Events rushed at her and reality developed fuzzy edges. Men lined the path, but her sight seemed blurry and they wavered like seaweed in a summer storm. She heard laughter and joking she didn't understand.

She did hear one comment: Tulia exclaimed about "the bride's serenity."

That made Sorcha smile. This wasn't serenity. This was disbelief.

As the women entered the chapel, she clasped her bouquet so solidly she found the hidden rose thorn and bled a little bright red drop of blood. She focused on it, frowning at the pain and worried it would splatter on Ora's costume. Grandmother Sancia placed her at the back of the church facing the altar. Sorcha concentrated her gaze on the flickering branches of candles.

Someone took her arm.

She turned to look; it was Arnou.

He looked...triumphant. The kerchief he wrapped over his eye was clean. *He* was clean, his hair damp, his chin shaved, and he was dressed in someone's best wedding suit. His shoulders strained at the seams. He led her down the aisle as if the fears that challenged her never occurred to him. And knowing Arnou and his simple mind, they probably hadn't.

He kissed her cheek. "Stop frowning. Everything is just as it should be. Trust me."

"I do trust you," she murmured. She needed to remember that. She trusted Arnou more than any man she'd ever met.

He led her toward Father Terrance.

The service started with a mass, and for the first time in years, she participated in the ritual at her own church. Father Terrance spoke English, but even so she immersed herself in the familiar worship.

Then Father Terrance performed the wedding ceremony, and as she recited her vows, the intensity of her feelings for Arnou dazed her; when had he become the man she could swear to love and honor, and mean every word?

And he—when had he learned to speak in such a deep, marvelous voice, to gaze on her as if he needed her above all else, and kiss her lips with such reverent intent? In front of the whole church, he claimed her with his mouth. He tasted clean and warm and intimate, and she lost herself in a world consisting of nothing but Arnou and Sorcha and the memory of yesterday in the fairy circle and tomorrow...

"Hurrah!"

The blast of joy from the people of New Prospera made her jump in surprise. She had forgotten they were there.

Arnou turned her to face the congregation, on their feet and shouting their delight.

Sorcha couldn't help herself—she broke into a smile.

And together they went into the town square.

The villagers seated Sorcha and Arnou at an elevated table. They served them ale and wine, lamb and herbed potatoes. A fiddler and a drummer played while the newlyweds danced. Then everyone joined them.

It was a celebration like none Sorcha had ever attended, without the pomp of the castle or the solemnity of the convent. She thoroughly enjoyed herself—until the moment the women lifted her chair from the table and bore her away to the bridal chamber.

Then she looked back at Arnou.

Hands on his hips, he stood watching her, and he looked not at all like the appealing, puppylike, exasperating Arnou she adored.

He looked like a stranger and a predator.

And he was her husband.

Chapter 18

As they climbed the stairs to the inn's second story, the men, flushed with drink and celebration, shoved Rainger to the front of the group. He winced at the jabs and the sharp elbows, but everyone in the village wanted to say they'd helped him do his duty.

In elaborate pantomime, the men shushed each other, then rapped sharply on the door of the bedchamber.

"Who is it?" a woman inside trilled.

"The bridegroom," Mr. Montaroe boomed.

The door opened. The women were giggling, bright with the pleasure of a celebration and overcome with the honor fate and their prince had allotted them.

"The bride is ready," Tulia pronounced.

With a roar that sounded like a hundred bears, the men shoved Rainger inside the room.

Tall beeswax candles flickered on stands beside the carved wooden bed mounded with blankets. White starched curtains hung by the windows. The fire painted the room with a combination of red light and black shadows.

Sorcha stood by the mattress, clad in that lacy sheer white gown the prostitutes had given her—the gown that had haunted his memory. And he saw the thing he'd imagined, wished for, dreamed of—the shimmer of her unbound hair liberally laced with tiny white blossoms.

His body responded with instant and absolute excitement.

Damn. If a single glimpse of her brought his cock up and his balls tight, how was he going to make it through his seduction? He had a plan—could he carry it out?

But he had to. She was a virgin. She was a princess. She believed their marriage ceremony to be invalid. She knew she needed to marry a prince—and everything he'd done and said had assured her that he was not that prince. Rather, he was the court jester.

"We should undress the groom," the men shouted. "So the bride can see that she has made a marvelous union and we can make sure he's up to performing his marital duties."

"Up to performing his marital duties." Mr. Montaroe, drunk as a lord, fell sideways laughing and tumbled to the floor. "That's rich! *Up* to performing!"

Everyone laughed with ribald excitement, but still with respect and genuine joy. All of them, men and women, saw in this union the end to their exile. All of them wanted for this marriage to bear fruit and secure their future.

Rainger appreciated that, but he was determined they would leave him alone with his bride to conduct his seduction as he wished.

Turning to face the crowd, he blocked the view of Sorcha. He wanted to tell them that when he had retrieved their country, and his, from the evil grasp of Count duBelle, they'd be welcomed with all honors to his capital. But he walked a tightrope—he dared not say too much or Sorcha would realize she'd been duped. And that moment needed to be postponed until the moment he deemed proper. "Thank you, good people, for your kindness and generosity. Sorcha and I will never forget it, or you."

They cheered, overcome with emotion and ale.

"Go and rejoice, and leave us to celebrate in our own way." He grinned a knowing, brash grin, one that made the women giggle and the men grin back. Then he shut the door with a soft, definite click, locked it with a strong movement that made the sound of the latch echo in the corridor, and waited until he'd heard the sound of many feet descending the stairs and the laughter and conversation fade.

Turning back to the room, he found Sorcha had turned her back on him. Her arms were raised, the curves of her body gleaming softly through the sheer material of her nightgown.

She had gathered the glorious fall of her hair and started to make a braid, her fingers moving frantically. "I'm so sorry." Her voice held a chagrined breathlessness that successfully drove out what little sense remained in his head. "I tried to tell the women this wasn't necessary, but they found the nightgown and after that there was no stopping them. They assume we really are married, which of course they would, so they wanted to make you feel desire. But believe me, I didn't want to make you feel desire. Since you told me it's painful for you when you're unsatisfied, I've done everything to make sure I'm not the cause of any pain for you. Have you noticed?"

He grunted, because she was crushing the blossoms as she worked, and a sweet, wild scent filled his head.

Was the scent the flowers…or Sorcha?

"If you'll give me a minute," she said, "maybe turn around to save yourself distress, I'll dress and we can prepare for bed."

Passion and need blasted through him. He found himself beside her. He glimpsed her wide blue eyes sparkling with a sheen of embarrassed tears. Catching her wrists, he removed her hands from her hair. "Don't imagine I don't want to look at you. No matter how much pain I suffer for you, I'll always want to look at you. You were made for me, and right now all I want to do is sink my fingers into your hair." He did, and reveled at the silky sensation as he freed each strand from its incipient prison. "I want to sink my tongue into your mouth." He did, tasting the mint she'd chewed to cleanse her breath and, beneath that, the flavor of bewildered passion…and of Sorcha. "I want to sink my body into yours—" Catching her buttocks in his hands, he brought her close and rolled his hips, putting a pressure against his erection that heightened his passion and did nothing to ease his desire.

A startled gasp escaped her, and he remembered—she had never seen a naked man, must less seen him aroused as a bull.

Too much honesty! Too blunt! This wasn't the way he'd meant to play it!

His fingers trembled and they felt like a stranger's as he forced them, one by one, to release her.

The blood that normally circulated to his brain was elsewhere, so falling to his knees wasn't difficult. Nor was the bowed head, for when looking down he could see her feet, one atop the other as she tried to warm them, and her ankles, slender and graceful. Taking the hem of her nightgown, he lifted it to his lips—he caught a quick glimpse of shapely calves—and said, "Your Highness, I shouldn't have said those things. I should never have touched you. I'm a humble man before you. But your beauty sings to me and I've never wanted a woman…" The words he'd rehearsed poured from him with far too much sincerity. He couldn't seem to help it. He forgot her feet, her ankles, her calves. He forgot that he could artlessly run his eyes up and see through her nightgown to the body beneath.

Instead he lifted his gaze to hers and in all candor, said, "I've never wanted a woman the way I want you, with all my heart and all my soul, and I meant every word of our wedding vows."

Her eyes became a dark blue, the kind of blue that reminded him of a stormy sea and the violent currents that could drown a man. She took a long breath. She straightened her shoulders. Slowly she extended her hand; he had never seen her look more like a princess.

"You have no reason to be humble. You're kind—and so brave. You never hesitated when I told you I was in danger. I know that you made your vows with all sincerity. I felt your emotion, for I feel this way also." Then she covered his eyes with her hand.

Damn. She didn't want him looking at her. She didn't want to tempt him with what she had decided he couldn't have. He would have to go to his next plan of seduction, and in his present desperation he couldn't even remember his next plan.

Then the weight of her nightgown fell onto his wrists.

He didn't understand.

She removed her hand and he, like a fool, looked down at his hands. They clutched the nightgown. The whole nightgown. She stood over him...and she was nude.

He dropped the nightgown as if it burned him.

She stepped back. Stepped out of it.

Did she *mean* for him to look at her? Because he couldn't help it. For the rest of his life, she was all he ever wanted to look at—the long flanks, the gently curved hips, and the fine curly down of fiery red hair between her legs, the tiny waist, the breasts, so perfect, so round, her arms, strong and muscled from gardening and riding, her face...he loved her face. She smiled at him uncertainly, as if she didn't know whether he would enjoy the view. And he needed to reassure her, but his breath was caught somewhere in the vicinity of his chest and he couldn't find his voice.

So he extended a tentative hand, a gesture designed not to frighten her, and lightly stroked the outer curve of her hip.

She sighed, a sigh of simple pleasure.

That was all the encouragement he needed. He ceased vacillating. He rose, slipped his arm around her waist, and kissed her again.

He'd kissed other women, but now he wondered why. With Sorcha in the world, why had he bothered with other women at all?

She broke the kiss, buried her nose in his throat, and took a long breath. "I love the way you smell. I love the way you kiss…. If we could do nothing but kiss, I'd be satisfied."

He winced.

Against his skin, he felt her grin. "For now. I would be satisfied for now. Because it doesn't seem to matter how close I stand to you, I want to stand closer. I want to be closer. I want to be part of you, and I don't know how." Lifting her head, she gazed at him, her blue eyes wide, her black lashes fluttering. "Can you show me how?"

Lifting her in his arms, he placed her on the bed on the clean white goose-down coverlet. She sank into it as if she relished the simple pleasure of its embrace. The scent of flowers rose around them. Totally without consciousness, without fear, she smiled at him.

That smile held such sweet and wanton seductiveness. She'd lived among nuns. She'd been with the prostitutes for less than two hours. Where had she learned such a primal feminine gesture of enticement?

And how could he resist?

As she moved her legs, lifting her knee, wiggling her toes, he caught glimpses of the softest part of her and realized—he couldn't wait.

He needed to take off his clothes. He needed to be as bare and free as she was.

He stripped off his shirt.

She gasped and sat up straight. "Arnou, what happened to your back?"

Damn. He hadn't meant for her to see the stripes that crisscrossed his flesh. "The sea is a rough master." Not a lie, but not pertaining to him, either.

"Come here." She made him sit with his back to her and with light fingers she traced the stripes Count duBelle had placed on him. "This is cruel." She kissed the ridges where white scars met pink skin. "This is wrong."

"There's no pain now." Turning, he took her hands. "It was over long ago. I barely remember it." Amazingly enough, he meant it. Right now he could think about one thing, and one thing only—and it wasn't his back.

She smiled. What a smile she had! Saucy, sexy, taunting, knowledgeable. She managed to look like a woman who knew how to give a man pleasure.

And damned if he didn't believe her.

She stretched her arms over her head.

He removed his shoes and his hose.

She pushed her fingers through her hair, collecting two satin strands, then carefully arranged them to cover her breasts.

His face felt as if were set in stone.

It must have looked that way, too, for teasingly she glanced at him, then glanced again with widened eyes. "You look like my sternest tutor when I played instead of learning my algebra."

Leaning over her, Rainger placed his fists on either side of her shoulders. "Did he spank you for teasing?"

"No." Her lips were wide and moist and pink. "Are *you* going to play a game with me?"

"What kind of game?"

"The kind of game Madame Pinchon's ladies said men like to play. Are you going to pretend to be my tutor and spank me?"

Damn her. Her words brought up the image of her pale body stretched across his lap. His hand would swat her once, but only once, and then the real punishment would begin. He'd sit her up facing away from him and plunge inside her. He'd make her ride him until—

She brought him back to the present with her palm kneading the bulge of his bicep. "I can be very, very bad. So are you going to spank me?"

The surge of blood to his groin almost drove him forward.

He fought the impulse to hold her down and take her. Sweat broke out on his forehead. Because he *would not* take her in a rush. He had her trapped in marriage. Next he must snare her with passion, so that when she discovered the truth, she'd be so head-over-heels in love with him, she'd support him and his goal to regain his kingdom.

Slowly, barely, he conquered the desperation.

Picking the strands of hair off her breasts, he said, "No. I'm going to do this." Placing his lips on her nipple, he sucked strongly, bringing it into his mouth and working it with his tongue.

She gasped. Her hands went to his bare shoulders, and her fingernails dug into the skin.

He exulted in the small pain, knowing it was a sign she had lost herself in passion.

He lightly scraped her with his teeth, then blew on the moisture his mouth had left. Goose bumps covered her skin. Her chest flushed. Her nipple tightened to the size of a berry.

She responded to him so readily, he was both flattered and touched. And it was because she trusted him. She'd said so time and again. She trusted Arnou and, unknowingly, she trusted Rainger. That was all to the good, for Rainger intended to take very good care of her.

He suckled on her other nipple and at the same time his hand descended to rest between her legs. He pressed his palm against her in a slow rhythm that built and built until she writhed and gasped and tried to escape.

He didn't let her. She needed to learn the desperation of unfulfilled passion. That would bring her to his arms again and again. And perhaps he enjoyed tormenting her as he was tormented, with desire so fierce it burned out of control.

But she knew how to torment a man, too. She wrapped her arm around his lower back and caressed his spine, worked down to the edge of his breeches, and slid below. She cupped his buttocks, squeezed them in a slow rhythm that made him pump his hips. With her other hand, she explored his belly, counting his ribs with her fingers and circling his navel before plunging inside.

Everything she did imitated intercourse.

How did she know...? But of course. The ladies of the night had told her. But how did she know *exactly* how to drive a man wild? She was a princess, a convent-bred princess, yet she showed not a shred of self-consciousness as she unbuttoned his breeches and freed his cock from its onerous confinement. She didn't look at it. In fact, she closed her eyes. But only, apparently, to better explore its shape and silkiness. She seemed fascinated with the head. She circled it and traced the teardrop-shaped slit. Finally she wet her fingers and ran them up and down his length.

He wanted to flop on his back and let her service him until he expired from bliss. And when she cupped the sack of his balls, investigated the shape and texture, he found himself on his feet and yanking off his breeches.

They were in the way. They had to be removed.

At last he stretched out beside her. He held her gaze as, time and again, he inserted two fingers inside her. He stretched her until she whimpered in distress, then immediately he erased her memory of the pain with his mouth on her mouth, or on her breast, or between her legs. He made her suffer; he made her come. She accepted his caresses with transparent joy. It was a cycle he taught her, all in preparation for the moment when he possessed her.

When at last he slid inside her, the candles were in their last moments. Their flickering light showed him her exhausted, satisfied face against the pillow. He watched her as he pressed inside, as her face slowly came back to life…as the pain took her…as he swept it away…and when he led her again to climax, then thrust deep and filled her with his seed, he saw her shock as she realized—he had made her his own.

Then the candles guttered out, leaving them in darkness.

Arnou.

Sorcha couldn't believe how much she trusted him.

Arnou.

She didn't understand how a man of his background could be so skilled in the fine art of making love.

Arnou.

He was a Shakespearean sonnet, the very essence of love. He was a fine cognac sipped in a tall easy chair before a warm fire. He was a mighty peak swathed in the first blush of spring green, an airy cake bathed in creamy custard, a perfume created just for her.

Had she believed she had to seek her destiny? What a fool she'd been! Her destiny had found her. He was her destiny.

In his arms, she rediscovered the warmth, the safety, and the magic of the stone circle. The promise of enchantment that had started there had culminated in this—their union.

She was a woman in love.

And she owed Arnou…everything.

"Darling?" She placed her head on his bare chest. She listened to the steady beat of his heart. She caressed his hip.

He wrapped her in his arms. "Yes?"

"You are a prince."

He stiffened.

"What do you mean?" He clipped his words in an almost intimidating manner.

But of course he would. He probably worried she was making fun of him.

"I mean, you're a prince in my heart. *My* prince." Taking a deep breath, she made her objective clear. "I intend to make this a real marriage. I'm not going to lie to Grandmamma about what we did tonight. I'm going to tell her the truth. I'm going to make you my consort."

"Your consort?"

"Yes." Perhaps he didn't understand the term. "A consort is the husband of the queen, the man who stands behind her when she rules, who escorts her and is the father of her children."

His chest expanded in a deep breath.

"Would you like to be the father of my children?"

"I would like nothing more."

"So I will make you my consort. But do you understand what it means? Do you comprehend my deeper meaning?"

"You love me." He relaxed beneath her.

"Yes. I love you. You're my husband in every way possible."

"Good. Good."

The flat satisfaction in his voice surprised her. It was almost as if he expected to hear her declare her adoration, as if some great plan of his had borne fruit.

Then he sat up, tumbled her on her back, leaned over her, and made her forget everything but this marvelous passion between them.

When Rainger finished making love to Sorcha for the second time, she slid immediately into slumber.

He slipped a pillow under her head and gazed at her face in the fading firelight. The coals cast a rosy tint over her sleeping features. Unable to resist, he traced the curve of her cheek, the jut of her chin. He layered a kiss, a single light, sweet kiss on her lips.

She smiled in her sleep.

The cross around her neck glinted blue in the darkness.

She said she would face up to her grandmother to make him her consort.

How much more simple for her when she discovered she loved not Arnou, a one-eyed, unsophisticated sailor from Normandy, but Rainger, her prince and her betrothed.

Seducing her, making her love him—it had been so easy. Of course, he had *hoped* Sorcha would declare her love for Arnou, but he hadn't really *expected* it. Life had taught him to expect a thorny road.

Now he knew—she could be controlled with passion. He could get what he wanted through the skillful application of sex. For the future, this was a lesson he needed to remember.

Well. He shoved that damned rag off his face. He rubbed his eye, the eye he was so tired of pretending was gone.

Think of how thrilled Sorcha would be when she woke to discover it wasn't Arnou she would have to take to her grandmother, but her long-lost fiancé, Rainger.

He couldn't wait to hear her words of joy.

Chapter 19

Sunlight seeped through the windows and into the bridal chamber. Birds perched on the windowsill and cheeped softly. Sorcha shouldn't have been awake; she'd been busy far into the night. But pure joy brought her to consciousness, and she lay with her eyes closed, savoring this blissful shining moment.

She loved Arnou.

Last night she had declared her intention to make him her consort, and the light of day had only strengthened her determination. She hoped her decision didn't cause Grandmamma to collapse and die, although that seemed unlikely. Grandmamma was made of stern stuff, and she'd consider such a death a major defeat. Sorcha could almost guarantee that Grandmamma would stay alive to plague her and nag Arnou.

Poor man. He'd have to learn to act like a prince. But he already had the traits she required: generosity, kindness, and, most of all, honesty.

She opened her eyes. Stretching, she worked the aches from her body. She could wait no longer to gaze on the face of her beloved.

He lay quietly. He must be still asleep.

Gingerly she rolled to face him.

The rag that had covered his eye the whole time she'd known him had disappeared.

Seeing his whole face made him look…different. In fact—she propped herself up on her elbow and stared down at him—his eye looked fine. Not scarred and certainly intact. She thought—no, she knew—he'd said his eye socket was empty.

It most definitely wasn't, because he was awake and looking at her. In fact, the eye was brown and looked as if it functioned quite well. He stared at her with it—with both his eyes—as if he were waiting for something.

Maybe that was because he looked…

She sat all the way up. When she put some distance between them, he looked familiar. Not Arnou-familiar, but out-of-her-past-familiar. But that was impossible. No man of her age out of her past could possibly be—

She gasped so loud the birds, affronted, took wing and flew away.

"No." She snatched the sheet and held it to her chest. No, it couldn't be Rainger. Someone had mentioned him yesterday. Now her mind was playing tricks on her.

Slowly he sat up. "Sorcha?"

It sounded like Rainger. She hadn't noticed that before. How could she not have noticed that before?

"No." Her side of the bed was against the wall, so she scuttled backward toward the foot. The sheet was tucked in; she abandoned it as unnecessary.

"Sorcha, sweetheart." That man extended a hand to coax her back.

She looked at the fingers, the palm; they had far too many calluses for a prince. That had to be the hand of a sailor.

She scrambled naked over the footboard. Her feet touched the cold floor. She lunged for the nearest jacket, threw it over her shoulders.

The arms hung over her hands. The hem hung over her thighs. This wasn't her jacket.

She didn't want his.

That man rose off the bed. He was very tall, very broad-shouldered, with bulging muscles in his arms and thighs—and he sported a long, sleek, thick erection. Last night his overwhelming strength and masculinity had created a rush of anticipation and excitement.

Now he scared her. Enraged her.

Because he didn't *look* like Arnou. He *looked* like Rainger.

But it couldn't be. This man had a scar on his chest. When he leaned over to pick up his breeches, she saw marks on his back. A sailor's life was notorious for brutality and beatings.

So were a prisoner's.

The pain and rage almost made her double up in agony.

It was...dear God, it was true. That man...the man she believed in, the man she'd declared she loved, the man she trusted..."You. You are Rainger!" It was not a compliment.

It was an accusation.

"You recognize me at last." He bowed and smiled, a courtly bow made ludicrous by his nakedness and a smile as intimate as a whisper.

She wanted to slap his smirking face. "Put on your breeches," she hissed.

Her venom seemed to surprise him. "Sorcha, it's all right. We're married."

"No, we're not." In a panic to get out of here, she searched for the clothing the women had left her. "I didn't marry *you.* I married a man who was kind and honorable and protective and generous and trustworthy."

"That was me."

"No. Believe me. It was not." She found the clothing: a fine chemise, an old-fashioned skirt and shirt of
pale blue wool, petticoats, a dark blue ankle-length
cloak, warm black hose, a straw bonnet. Wedding gifts
from the village. The best they could collect from
women honored to bestow their cast-offs.

Beside them was another outfit: black trousers, a
black jacket, a white shirt, underdrawers, a collar, and
cuffs. The villagers had been equally generous with
Rainger.

For the first time, he looked a little irritated. "Don't
pretend you don't understand that Arnou and I are the
same person."

"Of course I understand." She discarded the jacket.
"I understand everything now."

He looked at her naked body. Looked with the begin-
nings of desire and the remnants of passion.

She hated it. Hated him with all the fervor of a
woman betrayed.

As hard as she could, she threw the jacket in his
face.

He caught it, tossed it over a chair, and watched her
as hungrily as a slinking wolf after its dinner.

An apt description for Rainger.

Snatching up the chemise, she pulled it over her
head. She donned the petticoats and tied them around

her waist with such a firm tug she hurt herself. "Despite the huge fool I've made of myself, I am accounted to have a good mind. But I suppose that's compared to other women, isn't it? It certainly isn't as clever as your mind. Or perhaps it would be better if I said—it's not as treacherous as your mind. It's not as sneaky and slimy and...does everyone downstairs know who we are?" Remembering the children yesterday, the flowers, the joy with which the village celebrated their wedding, she realized the absurdity of the question.

"They are very happy for us, their sovereigns." He donned his breeches as if resigned to momentary celibacy.

She scrubbed her hands over her hot cheeks. Mortified. She was so mortified. In the eyes of everyone in this dear little village, she was not their queen. She was a fool.

Get dressed. She had to get dressed and out of here before she lost her temper and leaped at him.

She stepped into the gown. The buttons ran up the back, and she twisted to fasten them. She got the top. The bottom. The middle gaped. She knew it gaped. But she wasn't going to ask *him* to help her.

Because the more she thought about the events that had brought her to this moment, the worse her humiliation. And her anguish. "Dear God, *you're* the one

292 • CHRISTINA DODD

who set the fire at the convent. *You burned my sisters' letters.*"

"It's all right," he said in a soothing tone. "I have others."

"What?" She couldn't have heard him correctly. She stopped chasing the buttons and glared at him. "What did you say?"

"I have letters for you from Clarice and Amy. They're in my saddlebags. Just a minute, let me get them." He started toward his bags.

She launched herself at him. She grabbed at his back, spun him around, and took the front of his shirt in her fists. "My sisters? You've seen my sisters?"

He looked taken aback by her assault. Not hurt, but taken aback. "Yes, and I'm pleased to tell you they're in the bloom of good health. They're married to good men—"

"My sisters are married?" Clarice was married? Amy, her baby sister Amy, was *married?*

"And by now Clarice has a baby."

"Clarice was expecting?" Clarice was a mother. Sorcha was an aunt. And she hadn't been there for the birth. She hadn't held her sister's hand or soothed her pain.

"Clarice married a Scottish nobleman, Robert MacKenzie, earl of Hepburn by name. Amy married an English nobleman, Jermyn Edmondson, marquess of Northcliff by name. I've met them both." Rainger sounded so calm and earnest, as if he thought that would reassure her. "And you may be assured your sisters have made honorable matches."

"Unlike me." She backed away from him.

"You're very angry, much angrier than I expected, but you don't understand." He followed her. "Let me fasten your buttons while I explain—"

"I don't want you to fasten my buttons, and I understand perfectly well. You knew how distraught I was about losing my last contact with Clarice and Amy. In fact, you destroyed that contact." The cloak. She wanted her cloak. She wanted as many layers of clothing between her and Rainger as she could have. She wanted miles between them. Years between them. "But according to you, that was immaterial, for you had in your possession more correspondence, correspondence that could easily be a replacement for the letters which I had read, reread, held close to my heart, and were my most cherished possessions in the loneliness of my exile in a convent?"

"I knew your sorrow was temporary. I knew once I let you discover my identity, I would give them to you."

Right now, scratching his eyes out sounded like good sense to Sorcha. "You *dare*. You let me ride for days through the wilds of Scotland, where I could have frozen or fallen in a gorge or been killed by robbers or assassins, and you say it's acceptable that you didn't give them to me?" She swirled the cape, setting an illusionary boundary he would be smart not to cross. She pulled the collar close across her shoulders. "You were in the dungeon for too long if you can make that logic work for you."

He took a long breath as if trying to gather patience.

He had the guts to act as if *he* needed patience.

"I was in the dungeon for a very long time, but believe me, Sorcha, the hardship there made me a different man. All the things you said about the old Rainger were true. I was feckless, selfish, ungrateful, and unkind. I take full responsibility for the loss of my country and I will do everything to make it up to my people. These people." He waved a hand toward the taproom below.

"Are you trying to tell me you're better now? You have lied to me, deceived me in every way, made me think I saved myself from an assassin..." She paused.

He nodded in confirmation, nodded as if she should appreciate him riding to her aid.

"You encouraged me to think I could take care of myself when I so obviously can't." She pointed a finger at him when a thought occurred to her. "You fixed the horse trading, didn't you? Somehow you made Mac-Murtrae pay the fair price."

"Well, yes." Rainger had the acumen to look slightly abashed at that. *Slightly.* "I couldn't allow him to cheat us."

"You have made a fool of me every step of the way, and in your warped mind I'm supposed to be *grateful* that your hardship in the dungeon made you a different man?" His audacity took her breath away. "It certainly did, and one I do not welcome or want."

He ignored her rejection.

Because he thought ignoring it would make it go away? Perhaps. But more likely because he believed himself to be totally justified in his perfidious charade.

"You insufferable snake. You ghastly hound." This was the problem with living in castles and convents. She didn't know hurtful-enough names. Out of the depths of her mind, she pulled the worst she knew. "You cad!"

The worst she knew wasn't good enough. He did no more than blink at her vocabulary. "I didn't make a fool of you on purpose. The deception was necessary because I didn't know the direction of your mind about returning to Beaumontagne and fulfilling your promise to marry me."

"So you lied to me and kept my sisters' letters a secret?" Shoes. She needed shoes to walk out of here. "How does this make sense?"

"Let me explain."

"Do." She could scarcely grind the word from between her clenched teeth.

"Your grandmother told me I had to find her lost granddaughters and when I married one, she would give me an army to defeat Count duBelle and win back my country. By the time I found first Clarice and then Amy, they had already met their future husbands and in fact were"—he waved a hand at the bed and essayed a smile—"fluffing the sheets with their men."

Did Rainger really think he was funny? Or charming?

"So I knew finding you was my last chance. When I did, I thought it best to assure myself of your affections by—"

"Lying to me?" She snatched up the hose and her boots and sat in a chair.

"By not being the man you despised so heartily."

She paused while pulling on her hose and shot him a scathing glance. "Did it never occur to you that whether or not I despised you, I would still do my duty to my country?"

"I thought it would be easier for you to do that duty if you felt affection for me."

"And you created that affection by pretending to be a simple but noble man." She tied her garters, then had to loosen them for fear she'd cut off the circulation to her feet.

"I'm not simple, I admit that. Arnou is less intelligent than me." He bobbed his head in artful imitation of the role he'd played for so many weeks. "But no one could have guarded you on your trip across Scotland with more dedication."

"I would have to say you are simple. Possibly even moronic." Her poor, worn boots were dry, warm, and polished. She shoved her feet inside and laced them with the same vigor she'd shown for her petticoats and her garters. "You've just told me you deceived me and married me only because I was your last chance to win your kingdom, and you've protected me because if I die, your chance to be king dies with me."

Rainger walked over, looked down at her as if that proved his superior position, and said, "You asked for the truth."

She leaned back, folded her arms over her chest, and looked up at him with as much insolent confidence as she could muster. "Because it makes everything that came before a lie. Arnou protected me and married me for *me*. For the first time in my life, someone was kind, was dedicated, to *me*. Not to my position as princess. Not to what I could do for him. Not to honor tradition or to make a profit. Now I'm the half-wit, for believing that I'm pretty or lovable or worth dying for. You *are* simple for believing I will ever forgive you."

His face grew cold and still and in his lethal gaze she caught a glimpse of his true self—a ruthless prince who would stop at nothing, sacrifice everything, for his vengeance and his position. "Last night you swore you would make me your consort. You swore you'd fight your grandmother and your prime minister for me. You swore you loved me."

"I swore I loved Arnou." She clenched her fist. "Arnou is dead." And she mourned him. God, how she mourned him!

Jumping to her feet, she shoved Rainger aside. She picked up his leather saddlebags, usually so hefty and cumbersome she could scarcely lift them, and shook the contents onto the floor. A coil of rope, a pistol and shot, a corked bottle, and a blanket spilled out onto the floor.

And two sealed letters.

"Don't. Wait. The saddlebags are too heavy." Rainger rushed up her side. "Let me—"

She slammed her elbow into his sternum.

He doubled over with a gasp.

"The ladies at Madam's told me how to do a few other things besides blow the hornpipe—a pleasure you'll never enjoy, at least not from my talented lips." She picked up the letters. She looked at her sisters' dear, familiar handwriting. Her eyes filled with tears, making her realize how precarious was her hold on her poise. "But now that you've trapped me, secured your position and your army, and ensured your crown, I'm sure there'll be other women ready and willing to perform that service. *Don't* let any misplaced loyalty to our wedding vows stop you." She stalked toward the doorway. "But, of course, a vow made for expediency need not be kept. Kings have been proving that for generations. And that, you bastard, is why there are revolutions." She slammed the door behind her.

Rainger rubbed his breastbone and tried to catch his breath. As exit lines went, that was impressive—but he'd sworn he would allow no man to speak to him with such contempt ever again, and certainly not the woman he'd made his wife. Certainly not the wife he'd courted, caressed, and kissed.

She wasn't going to get away with this.

He stalked to the door, flung it open—and heard Sorcha running down the stairs, sobbing as if her heart had broken.

Quietly he shut the door.

He rubbed his eyes. Both his eyes.

That conversation hadn't gone quite as well as he had hoped.

But damn, she did look good in a dress.

Chapter 20

Clutching her precious letters, Sorcha stumbled down the stairs and into the taproom. She glanced around the chamber, which had been so merry last night. She saw men. Men speaking in low, pained voices. Men sitting around the long tables holding wet cloths to their heads. Men with bloodshot eyes and shaking hands.

She contained her sobbing long enough to glare at them. She hated men. All of them. Stupid men. All of them. Horrible, stupid, rude, disgusting, stupid, stupid, stupid...

Whirling, she headed for the kitchen. She hoped it would be empty.

It wasn't. The women were there. Women who looked as hung-over as the men. Women moving slowly about the kitchen. Tulia frying ham and sausages. Grandmother Sancia stirring a pot of oatmeal.

No one was eating.

All eyes turned to Sorcha. Everyone observed her wild hair, her blotchy complexion, her trembling lips.

"Oh, my dear," Tulia said. "Was it that bad?"

The innkeeper's sympathy was the last straw. Sorcha didn't care who saw her, who heard her; she couldn't contain the flood any longer. Letters in hand, she sat down at the table, buried her head in her arms, and once again gave way to a flood of tears. She cried for her father. She cried for her sisters. She cried for the years of loneliness. She cried for herself, because she had believed, truly believed, that people were noble and kind and if she looked for the good in them, she would find it. She cried because the belief had been cruelly betrayed.

When her sobs finally began to dissipate, she felt a hand slip into her empty one. It was a fragile hand with twisted fingers and delicate skin. Lifting her head, she looked into Grandmother Sancia's wise, sad old eyes.

"Stop crying, now," Grandmother Sancia said. "You'll make yourself sick."

"Let me button your gown." Roxanne helped her out of her cloak and fastened the buttons Sorcha had been unable to reach.

Tulia handed Sorcha a large white handkerchief. "Blow your nose, Your Highness."

"The phrases *Blow your nose* and *Your Highness* do not go together." Sorcha blew. "Don't call me *Your Highness*. Not yet. Call me Sorcha. Just Sorcha."

"Every woman cries after her wedding night." Grandmother Sancia squeezed Sorcha's fingers. "It gets better."

Sorcha glanced around. The women, all the women, surrounded the table, nodding.

"At first, it's painful and messy, and he falls asleep immediately afterward, but truly, it does get better." Rhea smiled encouragingly.

"Oh." They were talking about…"Oh."

"Even if it doesn't get better, it only lasts a second or two." Pia sighed hugely.

The women nodded harder.

"Then all you have to worry about is a wet spot on the sheets," Ora said.

"On your side." Roxanne's quip brought a round of laughter. Laughter that quickly died as they watched Sorcha, waiting to see how she would react.

"It's not that." But Sorcha's lips trembled, and she didn't know how to tell them the problem.

She shouldn't complain. They knew who she was. They knew who Rainger was. But like Rainger, they didn't care how she felt about the match. They only cared about themselves.

Sorcha couldn't even blame them. They looked to her and to Rainger for the end of their exile. They wanted her to be happy because they wanted to go home. They would rather believe she hated his love-making than to know she hated *him*.

"He's not too quick. It took hours." She inhaled, her breath still wavering from her bout of tears.

"Yes. A clumsy slow man is worse than a clumsy fast man. Horace, God rest his soul, lived long enough to be both." Grandmother Sancia made a bottoms-up gesture toward Tulia.

Tulia tapped the wine keg, poured a pewter cup full, and slapped it on the table before Sorcha. "Drink. It'll make you feel better."

Sorcha looked at the sealed letters, her sisters' letters, in her hand. She saw how battered they were from their long journey in Rainger's saddlebags. And she drank. She drank all the wine.

Tulia filled Sorcha's cup again.

Grandmother Sancia tapped the table with her finger. Tulia filled a cup for her. Looking around at the other women, she said, "We should all have a drink."

As the cups were filled and passed around, Sorcha tenderly broke the seal on Clarice's letter.

In her elegant script Clarice wrote all the things Sorcha wanted, needed, to say to her. She said she missed Sorcha desperately, that she worried about her constantly. She told Sorcha how she and Amy had survived by selling Grandmamma's cosmetics to anyone who would buy them.

Sorcha read between the lines and recognized the desperation that must have brought them to such a pass.

Gently Clarice broke the news that Amy had run away, but assured her they were in communication and that Amy was all right. She talked about the baby she and Robert would have, and she closed with the prayer that soon they would be together.

Sorcha cried and hugged the paper as if somehow Clarice could feel her affection.

Then, with less care and more eagerness, she tore into Amy's letter. She could almost feel Amy's enthusiasm as she read the sharply slanted script. Amy had had an adventure, one that involved kidnapping a marquess and capturing a villain. She blurred over the details— Sorcha resolved that one day soon she would hear everything about Amy's escapades—but one thing was clear. Amy adored her marquess...and they, too, were going to have a baby.

Sorcha's baby sister was going to have a baby. Sorcha counted the months on her fingers. Amy would have the baby *soon.*

Once more Sorcha put her head down on the table and sobbed.

She'd missed so much of her sisters' lives—lives she now knew had been difficult and vulnerable. She hadn't saved them from starvation or fended off attackers. She hadn't vetted their husbands. She hadn't seen them wed.

Most important, she cried for relief.

Her sisters were alive and well. For the first time in years, she could let go of the frantic worry that they were destitute or hurt or dead. Her joy was so great it was almost heartrending.

She used the huge handkerchief until it was damp. Then Tulia thrust a cold wet towel at her and Sorcha pressed it to her swollen eyes.

The table was covered with cups. Women sat on benches, staring morosely at Sorcha.

Sorcha shrugged, smiled with wobbly reassurance, and worked to completely regain her composure.

"Well, here's the proof there are no good men," Pia said in a lugubrious tone. "If the prince can't make his wife happy, there's no hope for any of us."

"It's not that my husband is quick." Salvinia shoved her cup back and forth in short, forceful gestures. "It's that I don't know when he's put it in."

A burst of nervous laughter followed that pronouncement.

"Is it really so small?" Roxanne was wide-eyed.

"Like a new potato," Salvinia assured them. No wonder her brown eyes were sad.

Sorcha sniffed into the handkerchief. "That's not Rainger's problem. In fact, one of the prostitutes at Madam Pinchon's said he was well endowed."

"He's already visiting whores?" Tulia asked in horror.

"No, I was visiting them." Sorcha cradled the wine between her palms, stared into its depths, and wished she could get Rainger's bare face out of her mind. "He came to tell me it was time to go and Eveleen looked him over and told me he had a large cock."

All the women in the kitchen took a drink of their wine. Tulia blotted her upper lip and murmured, "Hot flash."

"It's that, from the moment he had me cast out of the convent—"

The women gasped in horror.

That gasp gave Sorcha a great deal of satisfaction. "It's true. He's a villain. He set fire to my cell so I had to leave or face putting the convent in danger."

"That's rather clever," Rhea said thoughtfully.

Grandmother Sancia coughed and, with a jerk of her head, indicated Sorcha.

"For a man, I mean," Rhea added hastily.

"But Your Highness, I don't understand." Looking puzzled and mutinous, Roxanne said, "If it's not too small and he's willing to take the time and the noises you were making last night weren't complaints—"

Ora thrust a plump elbow in Roxanne's skinny ribs.

"I just want to know what's wrong with him!" Roxanne insisted. "Sorcha, why are you so mad at him?"

"I'm trying to tell you," Sorcha said impatiently. "He chased me out of the convent. He tricked me into letting him travel with me all the way across Scotland. He lied to me about who he was and what he wanted. Worse than all that, when he burned my cell he burned my sisters' letters, too."

"The other princesses?" Grandmother Sancia drew back in horror. "He burned Prince Clarice and Princess Amy's letters?"

"Yes." Sorcha relished blackening Rainger's character. "I didn't know if Clarice and Amy were alive or dead." She saw the women's anxious expressions and assured them, "They are alive."

In thanksgiving, the women looked to the cross that hung above the table.

"I thought my last link to my sisters had turned to ashes. I cried about those letters. He *saw* me cry." Sorcha sniffed at the memory of her tears barely withheld. "And do you know what?"

Every woman in the kitchen shook her head.

"He had new letters in his saddlebags the whole journey and until this morning, he never, ever let me know they were there." Sorcha indicated the letters on the table, leaned back, and waited.

"Men!" Grandmother Sancia shook her bony fist toward the taproom.

"Well-endowed or not, he deserves to be strung up," Salvinia said with some regret.

"He's as spoiled a prince as everyone back in Richarte claimed." Tulia filled Sorcha's cup to the brim.

"He's a…a reprobate." Sorcha stared into the depths of her ruby wine with such heat the liquid should have simmered. "He's a…a wretch. He's a miscreant. He's—"

"A whoreson," Roxanne said.

Tulia shushed her.

But that was exactly the term Sorcha had been searching for. "Yes. A whoreson! A filthy, slimy whoreson. A disgusting lousy—"

"Dilberry," Ora said.

"Yes. A dilberry." Sorcha didn't know what it meant, but it sounded awful. "He's a ghastly, repellent dilberry."

"Devil's dung," Grandmother Sancia said.

"Certainly he's devil's dung." Sorcha relished the phrase. "A steaming, stinking pile of devil's dung."

"A gravy-eyed frig pig," Phoenice said.

"Yes, he is the worst, most horrible gravy-eyed frig pig I've ever seen." Sorcha made her pronouncement with a great deal of zest.

Roxanne put down her cup. "Actually, I think he's rather handsome and important-looking."

Every woman in the kitchen turned and glared at her.

"Gravy-eyed and a frig pig," Roxanne said hastily. "I don't know how I missed it."

"I don't know how you did, either." Sorcha showed them Clarice's letter. "Clarice is married to Robert, Lord Hepburn, of MacKenzie Manor here in Scotland. Do you know where that is?"

"MacKenzie Manor sits just outside the town of Freya Crags." Tulia turned to Ora. "Your husband rides down that direction when he buys mutton. How far would you say it is?"

"From New Prospera to Freya Crags is only a day's ride on a good horse," Ora answered.

Sorcha stood. "You mean if I leave now, I could see Clarice tonight?"

"Yes, but Your Highness, you can't go by yourself." Phoenice's alarm transmitted itself to the other women, who shook their heads. "Prince Rainger may be a gravy-eyed frig pig, but he's right. Count duBelle's assassins—"

Grandmother Sancia spit on the floor.

Tulia rushed to clean it up.

Phoenice continued, "Count duBelle's assassins would find you an easy target. We're not going to lose you now."

"No, you're not," Sorcha assured her. "I don't intend to get myself killed, so give me a well-armed escort. I ride to Freya Crags immediately."

As soon as Rainger finished dressing in his new garments—and he was very thankful to wear clothes that fit him—he hurried down to the taproom.

There he found the men gathered in small, worried groups. Father Terrance. Montaroe the innkeeper. Vernon the butcher. Chauncery the tailor. Alroy, Savill, Paul, Octavius. Two dozen men packed the room and all of them were glancing at the kitchen, then up the stairs, and when Rainger stopped in the doorway, Montaroe said with false heartiness, "Please, Your Highness, come in."

"Where's Sorcha?" Rainger wanted to get this issue of her unhappiness settled right now.

"She's in the kitchen with the women."

Rainger started after her.

Father Terrance stopped him with a forceful hand on his arm. "She'll be all right. They'll take care of her."

"I need to explain a few things to her." More than a few things, apparently.

"No. No, you really don't," Montaroe said.

"We need to explain a few things to you." Alroy took Rainger's other arm. "Sit down over here."

Alroy was the blacksmith. His chest was the size of a bull's and his shirt bulged with muscle. When Alroy guided, a man moved.

So Rainger found himself seated by the fire. It was the fanciest, most comfortable chair in the taproom, but Father Terrance pulled up a footstool and sat on one side of him while Alroy guarded the other side, and from the way Alroy crossed his hands over his chest, Rainger knew he wasn't going anywhere.

Montaroe shoved a tankard of ale in Rainger's one hand and a rasher of bacon on toast in the other.

Rainger looked at the food and drink, then glanced around at the men, all standing stern-faced with their arms crossed. "What's all this about?"

"Drink up, Your Highness, you're not leaving until we've finished our talk." Father Terrance waited until Rainger took a bite and a drink. He moved his footstool to face him. "In the normal manner of things, you'd be married with your family there to celebrate with you."

"Yes." Rainger waited tensely.

"The wedding celebration would take days. There'd be dinners and plenty of chances to meet your new relatives and converse with your bride, and perhaps you'd be allowed a chance to sneak a kiss." Father Terrance accepted his own mug from Montaroe, drained it, and wiped his mouth on his hand. "On the morning of the ceremony, your father and your uncles would take you aside and give you good advice on the proper handling of your bride during the wedding night."

Rainger couldn't believe he was hearing this. "I know how to handle a woman."

"Yes, Your Highness, but the women you've handled in the past haven't been princesses. Possibly they weren't virgins." Father Terrance's voice rose to a low shout. "Certainly they didn't come downstairs afterward crying as if they'd been torn from stem to stern."

Montaroe hastily interceded. "What Father Terrance is trying to tell you is—with a princess as delicate as your bride, you need to be a little gentler."

"I made her happy!" Rainger snapped.

"Of course." Father Terrance's voice dripped with sarcasm. "I've never seen a happier-looking bride than Princess Sorcha when she ran in here, glared at us like we were beasts, and ran out."

"Eventually she'll get used to it. Then you can ride her like a mare rather than a filly." Alroy's voice rumbled in his massive chest. "It just takes some patience."

Rainger started to tell them all to go to hell.

Then Vernon said, "Even if she doesn't get used to it, it only lasts a few seconds."

Rainger stopped, stunned, and realized his mouth was hanging open.

"Lots of patience," Alroy repeated. Standing, he headed for the bar and poured his own ale.

All the men poured themselves an ale.

Chauncery leaned against the bar and said, "My wife says my organ is tiny, but even the biggest pipe organ seems small when it's playing in a cathedral."

Rainger ate his bread and bacon and finished his tankard. If they were going to keep talking like this, he needed sustenance. When he'd finished, he declared, "I didn't hurt her."

The men turned to look at him.

"I took my time." Half the night in fact. "As sweetly as she sang, I feared you would hear her throughout the inn."

"We did," Montaroe admitted. "But when we saw her this morning, we thought—"

"*That's* not why she was crying." Montaroe offered another ale, but Rainger thought better of it. He and Sorcha should leave as soon as possible and he needed his wits about him. "She's angry because she says I made a fool of her."

"Ah, is that it?" Father Terrance stroked his chin. "She's right. I never did understand why you didn't tell her who you are."

"Or why you wore that scarf across your eye," Chauncery said.

"I had my reasons." Rainger did not have to explain himself to these men. For as much good as it had done him, he shouldn't have explained himself to Sorcha.

"Well, whatever they are, they're unlikely to impress her," Father Terrance said. "Have you never been made a fool of? It's a painful experience."

Rainger *had* been made a fool of. Julienne had made a fool of him and even now the memory of his naked defense of her made him wince.

Father Terrance watched him with wise eyes. "Yes, forgiveness might take a bit of time."

All right. Rainger would accept she felt the sting of mortification. But her reaction to the other issue was extreme and absurd. "She actually seemed more aggrieved that I burned her sisters' letters." He expected the men to laugh.

"You burned her sisters' letters?" The length, strength, and unity of the outcry surprised Rainger.

"Yes." He debated telling them the rest of it, but it seemed they knew something he didn't. "And I had some new letters and kept them from her."

The collective sighing and head-shaking was prolonged and unnerving.

"Not that my wife and her sisters get along, mind you, but I made the mistake of stepping between them when they were fighting." Alroy swallowed and his eyes widened with remembered fear. "I still have the scars to prove it."

"They turned on you?" Rainger wanted to laugh at the absurdity of women attacking this strong man.

"Like a pack of wolves," Alroy said. "They don't like each other—"

Octavius interrupted, "Except when they do." He tapped his chest. "I'm Alroy's brother-in-law."

Alroy nodded. "But a wise man never interferes where sisters are involved."

Rainger rubbed his forehead. His head ached. Not from too much drinking, but from counsel that baffled and confused him.

"So the little princesses are alive?" Vernon's eyes were alight.

"Very much so," Rainger confirmed

The men clapped each other on the back, offering congratulations as if they were new-made fathers.

Their happiness warmed Rainger and told him how much Sorcha had touched their hearts. "Amy lives in southern England. Clarice is married and lives not far from here."

"Uh-oh," Montaroe said.

The men shook their heads at him.

Rainger was getting tired of this silent communication they shared.

"Princess Sorcha is going to want to visit her sister," Vernon told him.

"She can't." Rainger had already thought of this and he'd made his decision. "We need to get to Edinburgh and on a ship as quickly as we can. When the kingdoms are safe, her sisters can come to visit, but until then—"

Alroy snorted. "If you think Her Highness is going to let a little detail like assassins stop her from going to her sister after years of separation, you're more naïve than I can even imagine."

"You must be patient, my son," Father Terrance told Alroy. "He lived in a dungeon for eight years."

"That's the only way a man manages to remain so ignorant of women." Alroy snorted again. "Well, that and living in a monastery."

Rainger rose to his feet and stood toe to toe with the much larger, much stronger Alroy. "You're disrespectful."

"Before you came down, Father Terrance said we were to be your family. Well, I'm talking the same good sense to you I would tell my brother. Princess Sorcha is furious at you. Admit it's your fault, beg her pardon, take her to see her sister, and crawl until she forgives you."

"That's ridiculous. I've never heard such nonsense." More than that, when he'd escaped that dungeon, he'd sworn two vows—that he would go back, kill Count duBelle, and rescue his kingdom, and that he would never crawl again.

Certainly he had no intention of playing the penitent to his own wife.

"Sooner or later you're going to want back in her bed, and an ice queen is a cold bedmate," Alroy said.

"She's not cold." Of all the facts Rainger knew to be true, this was infallible. "I made sure of that."

"Tell me that tomorrow morning, Your Highness." Quick grins flashed around the room, and Alroy repeated, "Tell me that tomorrow morning."

Chapter 21

Rainger leaned against the door of the bridal chamber and watched Sorcha placing a bottle of wine and brown paper packages in her saddlebags. "What are you doing?"

"I'm packing."

So her fit of temper hadn't faded yet.

"That's a good idea. We need to get to Edinburgh before the assassins discover where we are."

"I'm not going to Edinburgh. At least not yet."

He straightened. "What do you mean?"

"I mean I'm going to see my sister. Remember? Clarice, the one who married the Scottish earl? The earl whose estate is only a day's ride from Edinburgh?" Sorcha's voice rose. "Did you think I would get so close to Clarice and not go to see her?" Her voice dropped back into the normal range. "Besides, once I get there, Robert will send an escort with me to catch the ship to France."

"If you can get there safely," Rainger injected, whipping scorn into his voice.

"I can get to Freya Crags as safely as I can get to Edinburgh. More safely, since I'll be going in the opposite direction the assassins expect."

She was right. Rainger didn't like it, but in this she was right. "Did you imagine you were going alone?"

She faced him, hands on hips. "No, I'm pretty sure I can command a guard from this village. Oh!" She feigned surprise. "I suppose you'll want to come along, too, to protect your investment. After all, you went through a lot of trouble to find the one princess who wasn't *fluffing the sheets* with another man."

He had come up here determined to make things right with Sorcha. To follow the men's advice and apologize even though he was right. To convince her to see matters his way.

But when she stood there like that, so cocky and smart-mouthed, she sent his temper soaring. Where had his merry traveling companion gone? When had she turned into a shrew?

The men were wrong. Rainger needed to trust his own instincts. Last night, he'd made her his woman. Last night, he'd proved she could be softened with sex.

Now, using all the considerable intimidation he had at his disposal, he strode toward her.

She didn't back up.

He loomed over her.

She maintained the same belligerent stance.

Wrapping his arms around her waist, he lifted her onto her toes and kissed her. Kissed her with all the skill at his disposal and the passion she roused in him.

At first she didn't answer. She hung loosely, her hands dangling at her sides, her lips firmly sealed and unresponsive.

Gradually she came to life. Her fingers clutched his forearms, then slid up his biceps and pulled him tighter into her. Her lips softened under the probe of his tongue. She allowed him into the sweet cavern of her mouth, met his tender search, and, as if curiosity could no longer be denied, she even explored his mouth.

The sensation of her feminine form made his body leap to life. He remembered all the tender, passionate moments of the night before. He imagined all the fiery, exhilarating love bouts they would have in the future. He wanted her now so urgently he might never have had her. She had become his obsession. He started to back her toward the bed...

An alarm blasted through his brain.

They had to leave now.

But she was reacting to his desire.

They had to escape Scotland.

But she kissed him so sweetly.

The vultures were gathering and he and Sorcha had only a little time to save themselves and their countries.

For the first time in his life, he damned his duty and damned his country. He need an eternity to love Sorcha properly.

He didn't have eternity, so sternly he brought to mind why he'd started this—to thoroughly remind her how much she loved him. He had done that. Yes, he had done that very well.

In stages he drew back. Then kissed her eyelids, her forehead. Then drew back again.

At last she stood on her own two feet.

She swayed for a moment, then straightened her bodice, smoothed her skirt.

He had made an important and inescapable point— she couldn't resist him.

But when she looked up, her face was still and set. "If you're done slobbering on me, I'd suggest you get packed. I'm leaving within the hour and I'm not waiting for you."

He hoped he didn't look as stunned as he felt. He groped for his lost authority. "We're going to Edinburgh."

"*I'm* going to see my sister. You can go to Freya Crags, you can go to Edinburgh—or you can go to hell."

The winding road to Freya Crags was better than any road Rainger had yet traveled in Scotland, but that didn't improve his temper worth a damn. For one thing, there were inns where assassins could stay in comfort and watch for them. There were places assassins could prepare an ambush: barns, rocky outcroppings, lonely stretches. He'd been watching for danger for so long, he felt taut and stretched, and despite the fact every male villager from New Prospera who owned a horse rode with them, he felt as if disaster was poised to descend.

The men would tell him it already had in the person of his bride, one Princess Sorcha.

Rainger eyed her. She rode boldly astride, her breeches beneath her fluttering skirts. Their escorts surrounded her, not only to keep her safe but so they could bask in her attention.

The men, of course, were exhausted after celebrating the wedding far into the night, but they valiantly followed her wherever she led. She enchanted them, she urged them forward with smiles and bribes of sweetly sung songs, and they would do anything for her.

She didn't bother to extend her enchantment to Rainger. She didn't bother to look at him. And he found himself jealous of the other men.

The other men—old Montaroe, blushing young Adrian, stout Chauncery, girlish Savill, hulking Alroy, his brother-in-law Vernon, and six other men. It didn't matter that none of them were a match for Rainger in youth and strength of character, or a match for her in position and nobility. Every smile she sent their way, every virtue of theirs she extolled, every song she sang for them infuriated Rainger.

At last, after three hours, he could bear it no more. The horses needed a breather. The men needed a rest. And he needed to recapture Sorcha's attention in any way he could.

Before them loomed a gorge where the road wound through low cliffs, and before they entered, he needed to know what these men could do.

Or so he told himself.

"Halt!"

The men pulled up and faced him inquiringly.

She shot him a glare that clearly told him her opinion of his character.

Sadly he considered that better than being excluded.

But he ignored her malice and pointed at the road. To the troop, he said, "This place reminds me of Speranza Gorge in Richarte."

The older men looked it over and nodded.

"A lot of robberies and murders happened in Speranza Gorge," Montaroe said.

"Exactly," Rainger said. "Before we go in, I'd like to see what you can do with your weapons." If these men were like the rest of the men in Richarte, they were deadly shots, especially with the crossbow. In Beaumontagne and Richarte, on the edge of the mountain wilderness, a man learned to protect his family and property.

Grinning, the men drew their armaments—their pistols, their muskets, their crossbows—from their saddle holsters.

A slab of rock stretched long in the meadow. A lightning-struck tree stood nearby.

"You men with the muskets, shoot at the center of the rock. You men with the crossbows, shoot at the center of the trunk." Rainger pulled his own crossbow. "I'll pay five guineas to the man who hits closest dead center."

"Who's going to decide the winner, Your Highness?" Alroy asked.

Rainger grinned. "I am."

The men looked at the crossbow in Rainger's hand. They groaned and laughed.

Rainger laughed with them.

They lined up to shoot anyway. These men shot for the pleasure of the game, not for the prize.

"Keep a lookout," Rainger told Sorcha. That should put her in her place.

She didn't look as if she were in her place. She looked impatient. "How long is this going to take? Because I want to reach MacKenzie Manor *tonight*. I want to see Clarice *tonight*."

"This is for your own safety," Rainger said.

"I thought it was so you could boast about your shooting abilities," she answered.

"I am the prince. I do not need to *boast*." Although perhaps that she would be impressed with his mastery had crossed his mind.

Certainly it had crossed the minds of the villagers, for as they shot they taunted each other.

"Give it up, Montaroe. You're so old and shaky you'll aim at the tree and hit the rock."

"Hey, Octavius. The day you shoot dead center is the day you're aiming at your mother-in-law."

"Duck, everyone, duck! Savill holds a loaded musket in his hand!"

But the shots were good and true, and Rainger would have trouble deciding which of the men should have the prize.

But first he had his chance to shoot. He moved his horse up to the line. He lifted his crossbow.

"Rainger." Sorcha's voice was low and urgent.

Now that he ignored her, she wanted his attention.

"In a minute." He squinted and aimed.

"Rainger, there are men coming down the rocks."

He whipped his head around just as a bullet whistled past his ear.

In less than a second, he assessed the situation. As he feared, the enemy had been waiting for them. It would have been best for their foes to remain in the gorge, but when they heard the shots they imagined someone else had attacked their prey. Now they descended toward the villagers, moving with stealth and precision, slipping from one cover to another, trying to make every shot count. They were professionals, mercenaries hired for one purpose—to kill Sorcha, or Rainger, or both.

But the men of New Prospera responded immediately, wheeling their horses with a ululating cry and riding in a circle around Sorcha.

She, smart girl, bent down over her horse's neck and rode in the circle in the opposite direction. Some of the enemy shots might hit a target, but not easily and not the target intended.

Rainger's men used their shots wisely, bringing first one mercenary, then another tumbling down the rocks.

"Ride, Highnesses," Montaroe shouted, "ride for Edinburgh. We'll keep them off your tail."

Rainger saw Sorcha's rebellious glare, but when he indicated that she lead the way, she rode as commanded.

"It's us they want," he shouted. "When we're gone they'll be trying to follow us and our men can pick them off."

She nodded and kept riding as hard as she could back up the road toward Edinburgh. They passed through a village, then out onto the flats.

Before them, Rainger saw a barn on one side of the road, a grove of trees on the other, and when he saw movement in the trees he recognized the place they'd find a second ambush.

He loosened his pistol in his belt. He kept the cross-bow in his hands.

Two horsemen charged from the barn side, one from the grove.

"Head for the trees," he shouted at Sorcha.

But she'd anticipated his command. She raced into the grove, deftly dodging branches, using the trees as cover.

One of the horsemen chased after her.

Two rode at Rainger, one from the left, one from the right.

He squeezed off his arrow. He didn't watch to see it land, but he heard the scream, abruptly cut off. He bent low in the saddle and off to that side. A pistol shot roared close at hand. He felt the heat as the bullet creased his horse's neck.

Alanjay flinched and danced in a rearing, furious circle.

"Gently, boy, gently!" Rainger said, and held on.

How many shots did the mercenary carry?

"Gently, boy. Good boy!" He regained control—and out of the corner of his eye, he saw a flash of gunpowder in the trees.

As another shot whipped past him, he used his reins, his knees, and the gelding's affection for him to turn him toward the grove. "Sorcha!"

"Sorcha. To me!"

At the sound of her name and the words called in her own language, Sorcha automatically checked. But although she recognized the voice, it wasn't Rainger's deep rumble.

Who was it?

The trees rushed past her. She dodged branches, cutting in and out, making herself a difficult target to hit. Leaves whipped at her face. Her breath burned in her lungs. But her hands on the reins were sure, and Conquest responded beautifully, twisting and cutting without slipping at all. They were still alive, but they were coming to the end of the grove.

Her pursuer was herding her into the meadow. There she would be an easy target.

She had to stay alive.

"Sorcha!" the stranger's voice called again. "Let me help you."

Who was it?

"Let me help you again."

She broke out of the trees. She heard the thrashing behind her as the rider broke free, too.

Stay alive.

And that required bold action. Using all her skill, she turned Conquest in a sharp circle and galloped right at her pursuer.

She saw a huge bald man on a gigantic horse. His features were battered. His pale eyes were narrowed. He wore a sword and a dagger.

"Godfrey!" She recognized him now.

Godfrey was Grandmamma's trusted emissary and bodyguard, the man who'd taken Sorcha from her sanctuary in England to the convent in Scotland, the man she thought protected her from harm—and he pointed his pistol at her.

"Whoreson!" she shrieked in fury. She stared with narrowed eyes right at him. How dare he? How dare he point that at her? How dare he threaten her with harm?

His pistol wavered. He fired. He missed.

She whipped past him at close range and back into the trees. She could see someone racing straight at her. Two somebodies.

Rainger, galloping with all his might. And another whoreson right on his tail.

At the sight of her careening toward him, the second whoreson grinned a black-toothed grin. He lifted his musket, aimed at her—

And Rainger turned in his saddle and blasted him with a shot from his pistol.

Blood blossomed in his chest and he blew backward off his horse.

Once again Rainger turned forward. But too late.

Godfrey dashed toward him, sword upraised.

Just in time, Rainger caught a glimpse of the steel. He leaped out of the saddle. He hit the ground on his back.

Godfrey's blow whistled in the air where Rainger had been.

Alanjay galloped away.

Godfrey turned his horse back toward Rainger, intent on his prey, riding as hard as he could.

Rainger was motionless. Winded? Or dead?

Not dead. Please, not dead.

Godfrey's gaze never wavered from Rainger's body.

She saw the outstretched branch.

Godfrey did not.

She shrieked his name. "Godfrey!"

At the sound of her voice, he turned—and the fat branch knocked him out of the saddle.

The branch cracked under the impact. She gasped with relief and prayed that Rainger would rise.

Even on the ground, Godfrey was formidable, but she still had Conquest beneath her, and for Rainger, Sorcha and her horse wouldn't hesitate to stomp Godfrey into the ground.

Then, thank God, Rainger stirred. He was alive. He shook his head, rolled to his feet. With a glance he assessed the situation, and while Godfrey gasped for breath, he charged. He leaped on him. He slammed a fist under his chin.

Godfrey's head snapped back. He twisted like a dervish.

Sorcha saw the glint of a knife in his hand. "Look, Rainger!" Foolish to yell a warning—but she already knew she was a fool.

Rainger grabbed Godfrey's arm. The men wrestled, straining, muscles bulging.

Grandmamma had chosen Godfrey for his strength. He was hulking, so much larger than Rainger.

Sorcha couldn't sit here on Conquest and watch the struggle. She looked around for a weapon.

The branch. She grabbed the end, leaned with all her weight, and broke it free. She rode toward the grappling men, lifted the branch over Godfrey's head—and the men rolled.

Rainger was on top.

Sorcha could do nothing.

Without warning, the knife disappeared. She heard a bubbling gasp and realized—one of the men had been stabbed.

Bounding out of the saddle, she ran toward them.

Rainger staggered to his feet, blood on his hands and shirt. He looked down at Godfrey.

The knife blade was buried in Godfrey's chest.

She stopped, her relief so great she swayed. Rainger was alive. That was all that mattered. Rainger was alive.

He glanced at her. "All right?"

"Yes. Just…yes."

Kneeling beside the thrashing Godfrey, Rainger leaned over him. "Did Count duBelle hire you?"

Godfrey laughed, a gasping sound. "Years ago."

"Why?" Sorcha rushed to his side. "Why would you betray Grandmamma?"

"For money. Isn't that always the reason, Godfrey?" Rainger stood and whistled, calling in Alanjay and Conquest.

"He said…he said…why would I work for a woman when I could work for him?" Godfrey spasmed with pain.

Sorcha touched his shoulder. "No man is tougher than my grandmother."

"Not me." Godfrey's breath rattled in his lungs.

Rainger looped the reins of their two horses over a branch. He looked around alertly, and she knew he stood ready to snatch her up and run at a moment's notice.

But she hated to leave even Godfrey alone to die.

"You…you princesses were such sweet girls, pretty and soft," he murmured. "Nice to me."

"Yes." Sorcha and her sisters *had* been nice to Godfrey. They felt sorry for him because he had to work for Grandmamma.

"I couldn't bear to kill you." Godfrey tried to inhale, but he coughed instead. "So I sent you away...where no one could find you. And *he* found out—"

Rainger glanced around at the mayhem in the small grove. "Godfrey!" he said in a loud voice. "How many more assassins are there?"

Godfrey didn't seem to hear him. His eyes had turned glassy and he stared at Sorcha as if he couldn't look away. "When I shot at you, you were angry."

"But your pistol wavered."

"After all these years...still couldn't kill you." Blood trickled from Godfrey's lips. "When you're angry, you look...like your grandmother."

The thunder of hooves shook the ground.

Rainger looked up the road, then said urgently, "Godfrey! How big is the reward to kill us?"

Godfrey was drifting into another world, and only Sorcha kept his attention. "When he found out you... were alive, he gave me one...last chance. He thought since you knew me I could get you...but I still couldn't do it."

Rainger reached for Sorcha to bring her to her feet and take her away. Then they heard the shout. He relaxed. "It's the men from New Prospera. We'll be safe...for now. We'll ride for Edinburgh and home as quickly as possible."

Still in that dreamy voice, Godfrey said, "No matter how much it cost me, I couldn't...kill you. But I could have killed *him*." His gaze slid to Rainger. Abruptly, reason returned to his clouded blue eyes. "The reward is a thousand gold guineas, Your Highness. You figure out how many men are after you."

Running toward the road, Rainger flagged down the villagers.

Godfrey whispered, "Tell Queen Claudia...in the end, I didn't betray her."

Chapter 22

Sorcha stood on the deck of the *Luella Josephine* as it cut through the water toward Southern France. The voyage would take less than two days and, she hoped, leave their assassins in the dust.

Yet Godfrey was dead.

Alroy was wounded.

On the road to Edinburgh, the men of New Prospera had had to fight off three more attacks. They had ridden through the night, and when at last the party reached the ship, the villagers had taken Alanjay and Conquest and promised Sorcha they would be well loved.

Then Rainger and Sorcha had boarded and waited, nerves stretched thin, until the ship sailed on the tide.

But at last she was on her way home—on her way home with a man she knew so well, yet barely knew.

She ignored the prickling sensation at the base of her neck. She wanted to watch the shoreline of Scotland disappear over the horizon into the morning mist, and she did. Yet all the while, she was aware that Rainger stood on the deck above, dressed in black, scrutinizing her with his dark gaze.

Who did he see standing by the rail? She wasn't the same girl she'd been when she'd been forced from Beaumontagne. She wasn't even the same woman who'd left the convent. But yesterday, when she saw Rainger on the ground and believed him unconscious and possibly dead, she had learned something very important.

It didn't matter that he'd made a fool of her or that he'd burned her sisters' letters. Arnou or Rainger, she still loved him—which made her a bigger fool than ever.

But she needed to talk to him. Really talk to him, and explain how she felt and who she was.

He would want that, too. For their marriage to survive, he would have to understand her pride as she understood his.

And at last she responded to his unspoken demand, turned and looked up at him. He leaned against the rail, his hands folded before him, his dark gaze fixed on her. It seemed as if he summoned her across space, demanding she submit to him.

That was wrong. She was a princess—and not just any princess, the crown princess, a woman destined to be a queen. She did not submit, not to him, not to anyone. Yet they could have a marriage of mutual partnership. She would tell him, and he would listen. He was a reasonable man. Or at least—Arnou had been a reasonable man.

All she could see now was open water. The wind blew the sails full and whipped her straw bonnet off her head. Only the ribbons tied around her chin kept it from blowing away. Catching the brim, she moved toward the cabin, knowing full well Rainger would follow and follow soon, for like flint and spark they ignited each other.

Their cramped cabin held a narrow bed with a straw mattress, a small round table with two chairs and a lit lantern swinging on a hook. Rainger had paid dearly for this booking, and for that reason the captain had ignored the fact that they had no chest, no clothes, no linens, and he had provided bedclothes and blankets to keep them warm.

Removing her battered bonnet and cloak, she hung them on hooks against the wall. She hesitated with her hand on the breeches she wore beneath her skirt. She'd grown used to wearing them. She liked them. No—she loved them. No wonder men wore them. They provided a protection skirts and petticoats never could. For her, they bestowed freedom of a sort she'd never imagined. Clad in her breeches, she'd sung in a tavern, she'd visited ladies of the night, she'd bartered with a horse trader, and she'd loved every minute of it.

But she had to return to being a woman and a princess, and that meant discarding the trappings of a boy.

So she did. She removed her shoes and her breeches. Yet...in light of Rainger's brooding gaze, she wondered if she'd made a wise decision....

She changed her mind. Standing, she grabbed her breeches, lifted her skirt, stepped one foot in the leg—and the door opened.

"While you're at it, take off everything."

At the sound of Rainger's rough command, she stumbled backward and fell into the seat.

He shut and locked the door behind him. His menacing gaze had not lightened.

She smiled at him anyway. "I was putting them on."

"Why?"

Because you're looking at me as if you're a wolf and I'm a tasty rabbit. And she didn't like being a rabbit.

Carefully she freed her foot. Agreeably she said, "If there's one thing I learned today, it's that we need to talk, and although we've been married only a day, I already know we won't talk if I take off all my clothes."

"That's funny." He leaned against the door and removed his boots. "If there's one thing I've learned since I met you, it's that talking is overrated." Unbuttoning his trousers, he dropped them and his underdrawers in a single motion.

"It's easy to tell what your purpose is." With his cock at full attention, how could she doubt it? Standing, she brushed her hands at her gown. "But before things spin out of control, Rainger, I'd like to say that what happened today was—"

Without finesse, without warning, he stepped over to her, shoved her skirt up, and lifted her off her feet. He wrapped her legs around his hips and held her with his arm under her bottom.

Their bare parts met and she jumped from shock. He burned her with his heat and when she looked into his eyes, she saw why. He was furious. He was tense. He was anguished.

Anguished? But why?

"Today I thought you were dead."

"Since I'm the last princess left to you, I can see that would be upsetting." She held her breath, waiting for him to deny it.

"When I saw that shot in the grove, I imagined…the worst." His chest heaved. He backed her toward the wall.

The wood was hard and chilly through her clothes. "I thought you were dead, too." She shivered as she remembered the sight of his body landing hard on the ground, the horse galloping away, and Godfrey charging.

"Yes. We both came too close. Never again." Rainger's fingers clenched her thighs. "I am never going to fear like that again."

Talking. Yes, they were talking. Unfortunately, he was also rubbing himself against her. She shifted, trying to get away, and discovered the friction felt good in any spot.

"When Godfrey was on the ground, you should have run away," Rainger said.

"You're not making sense. I was safer close to you." She was wide open and vulnerable to him and he was making her ache with need. "Safer there than chasing down the road and running into the next group of assassins."

"You should have hidden."

"But I couldn't allow Godfrey to kill you."

"I can take care of myself."

Rainger spoke so abruptly, so harshly, she flinched. That sounded as if he was rejecting her. Rejecting her help.

Yet over and over, he ground his erection into her sensitive tissues, pinning her between him and the wall, pinning her between desire and the yearning to communicate. Her words came in tiny gasps. She could scarcely speak in sentences. "I almost saw you...killed today, too, and that's why I say we need to...talk." Her breasts were tightening to the point of painfulness. Her loins were warming and growing moist. "Oh, please, Rainger, talk to me."

"I have a better idea." His voice was guttural. With his hand under her bottom, he adjusted himself, found the entrance to her body, and worked his way inside.

The sensation caught her by surprise. This was not the long, drawn-out, tender possession of their wedding night. Tonight he seemed larger, stretching her, moving on her, making her whimper in frightened anticipation. This was hot and desperate and needy, an act to be done in a hurry. He was on fire and the blaze communicated itself to her.

She tried to move, to meet his plunges, to grab her satisfaction, because suddenly, urgently, she needed to come *now*.

But he held her pinned, pumping his hips in deliberate, sweeping thrusts. Each time he pushed in, the pressure was like hot needles of anticipation. She gritted her teeth, no longer a woman in pursuit of anything but sex, and more sex, and more sex, until all the thoughts and memories had been dissolved by a primal rhythm and a reckless mating.

His face grew dark red. The cords and veins of his neck strained with the effort. He gazed down at her as if trying to possess her mind as he possessed her body. It was almost as if he wanted to take her again for the first time, or imprint on her what it meant to be his.

The heat between them grew.

Her hands clutched his shoulders, not because she feared he would drop her, but because she didn't know where she was going. She was drowning in rapture, powerless to fight against the current, but wanting... wanting...

The spasms, when they struck, were overwhelming, a tidal wave of climax that caught her, carried her along, and slammed her onto shore.

And he rode the wave with her, groaning out his greed for her.

When the motion slowed, when it stopped, he stood gasping, pressing her against the wood.

She was trembling, covered with perspiration, unable to comprehend something so violent and so savage.

With a primitive grunt, he lifted her away from the wall and carried her to the bed.

With his erection still embedded inside her, he carefully laid her across the mattress. It was wet between them, proving he had come, yet still he was hard. Still he filled her body and filled her passions.

She had reached satiation.

Yet if he wanted to take her again, she would let him. More than that, she would delight in him.

Bending over her, he opened her bodice. Picking up her cross, he held it in his palm. He closed his eyes, and a tremor shuddered through him.

"What is it?" she asked. "Are you in pain?"

"In pain? God, yes. Sorcha, listen to me." He caught her face in his hands. "I have instructions for you."

"What are you talking about?" Why was he using that tone? He was pulling her out of her blissful respite and dragging her back to the real world. Not the real world where they saved each other's lives and afterward talked together, but the real world where he'd made a fool of her and burned her sisters' letters.

"I'm talking about you. You're never again to dress in boy's clothes. You're never again to go to a whorehouse or a low tavern."

She tried to struggle up on her elbow.

He subdued her with a thrust of his cock, then another, then another. When her hips rose toward him, when she clutched him with her knees, he spoke again. "You're never again to smile at another man. You are never again to trade horses for any reason."

She didn't understand him. She didn't know why he lectured her when they could be just...just talking. Communicating. Together. "Why are you so angry? I don't understand."

"You're never to put yourself at risk again. Never. Never. Never." He punctuated each word with a movement of his hips.

No matter how much she wanted to argue, the friction he created inside her made her writhe with pleasure. She forgot what she wanted to say, why he made her so angry...

Until he said, "Tell me you love me."

"I love you."

"That's what I wanted to hear."

And although she waited for him to answer in kind, that didn't happen. Instead she discovered that Rainger could make love without stopping and that he could drive her beautifully crazy.

And, in the cold light of morning, she realized that once again he had manipulated her.

Chapter 23

Queen Claudia, the dowager queen of Beau montagne, sat huddled in a blanket in her bedchamber, watching the snow whip across the courtyard below. She hated winter. She hated the wind, the snow, the cold, the icicles hanging off the eaves, the starving deer, the dead flowers.... When she had finally finished her task here and turned the kingdom over to her granddaughter, she was going to move somewhere warm. Italy, perhaps, or Spain. She would sit on a veranda in the middle of winter. She would smell the roses and watch the peasants beg for money. If they impressed her with their story, she might even give them a coin or two.

She was an excellent judge of a good story well told. Since the rumors started whirling that Rainger and

Sorcha had been married and were returning, the imposters had been scuttling out of the woodwork to tell their tales. She had heard more melodrama and nonsense in the past two months than any normal woman heard in a lifetime.

And why did she listen to them?

Because it was winter, it was cold, and nothing could heat her old bones except a good bout of laughter.

There. Outside at the gate. There was another young couple. They spoke to the guard and, as usual, the guard looked up at her for direction.

And, as usual, she indicated that the guard should allow the couple to cross the courtyard and enter the palace.

The strange man took the woman's arm and pointed out where Queen Claudia sat.

The woman jerked her arm away from him and stalked along the shoveled walks.

Interesting. Either they were playing a different version of "Rainger and Sorcha are Reunited" or the female was fed up with the male.

Queen Claudia certainly understood that sentiment. A queen surrounded by males spent most of her time quashing grand male pretensions and petty male vanities.

But about the couple…she could judge nothing about them and their looks, for they were covered from head to toe in capes and hats and gloves.

The woman headed not for the grand and formal double doors that led into the foyer, but for the family entrance, a smaller door on the side of the terrace. A pretty bit of authenticity, and Queen Claudia was impressed enough to come to her feet, gather her cane, and hobble—these days, she always hobbled for a few minutes before she worked the kinks out—toward the door in her sitting room. It took more time than she liked. That infuriated her and made her rap on the wood harder than normal.

The door was opened at once by a young footman, still quaking from the last time she'd given him a tongue-lashing. He'd had the audacity to try and assist her when she had one of her spells. She had informed him that footmen did not touch the queen without permission.

Then she'd made him help her into her bed, thus assuring he would never lay a hand on her again.

She ought to have a bevy of ladies-in-waiting attending her, but she'd outlived them all and she didn't have time to train new ones who were her age.

Besides, there was no one left who was her age.

Her gait was loosening now. By the time she got to the throne room, she'd be the freakishly healthy old

crone feared and respected across Beaumontagne, Richarte, and beyond.

The footmen stationed at every door froze at attention as she passed. Peter opened the throne room for
her and bowed as she entered. "Give me ten minutes,
then show them in," she told him.

He bowed again and shut the door behind her.

She eyed the throne and the steps leading up to it
with virulent hatred. What short, insecure milquetoast
of a king had designed those steps? And in marble. If
Rainger and Sorcha didn't appear pretty soon, Queen
Claudia was going to fall down and break her neck. And
then her grandchildren would have trouble, for she'd
haunt them with a virulence that made her previous
stringency seem like kindness.

Taking a breath and using her cane, she climbed the
two steps, groaning from the pain in her hips, and lowered herself onto the throne.

Damn thing. It was covered with gold paint and
colder than sitting on an ice sculpture. But it looked
impressive, and when Peter opened the doors for the
imposters, that was all that mattered.

The female stalked in first, head high, fists clenched,
chin outthrust. She walked like the epitome of offended
royalty—and Sorcha, dear, kind Sorcha, would never
walk like that.

Queen Claudia's heart sank. It always sank when she realized it wasn't Sorcha, for no matter how much she denied it to herself, she always hoped that it was.

"Grandmamma—"

The girl's voice was very good. Noble, clear, and she had a bit of an accent like someone who had lived in England too long and picked up bad habits.

"Did you really send that dilberry to find and marry me?" She pointed back toward the door, toward the rumble of two men's voices.

"You sound like the princess Sorcha," Queen Claudia said in a cold, clear voice. "You've only made one mistake. Sorcha would never burst into the throne room and speak to me in such a manner."

"She would if she'd been through what I've been through." The female removed her hat.

She sported hair the same color Queen Claudia's had once been, and for a moment, a wave of memory dragged Queen Claudia back to the past.

"Darling, your hair...I must paint you, naked and glorious, with your hair draped around you. It is the color of sunrise."

The pain bit deep into Queen Claudia's shoulder, pulling her back to the present.

What a hell of a time for the old body to betray her.

She breathed deeply, waiting for the spell to subside and staring at the girl's stormy face. When she could, she slowly rose to her feet. The female's complexion was chapped with cold, her blue eyes were furious, and she wore the expression of a woman who had fought many battles—and won at least a few.

This was not the Sorcha Queen Claudia expected to return.

But she was definitely Sorcha.

Thank God. Thank God.

In a voice that revealed none of her exultation, Queen Claudia said, "Yes, I did send a dilberry to retrieve you."

As she spoke, Rainger stepped inside, and he groaned. "Already?"

With a lightning glance, Queen Claudia checked him out. Yes, it was definitely Rainger. "I sent a princely dilberry. I'm sorry, but he was the only one available."

"Obviously." Sorcha removed her gloves and cloak and cast them on a side table.

Queen Claudia hadn't expected to enjoy her granddaughter. Sorcha had always acted as if she feared the south wind. Now she looked ready to embrace the north wind himself. "Come, greet me properly."

Sorcha strode up the stairs to Queen Claudia, pressed her lips to each of the queen's wrinkled cheeks, and offered her arm.

"I ordered refreshments to be laid in the upper drawing room." Rainger stood with his hands behind his back and watched the two women descend the steps.

"Don't be ridiculous," Sorcha said. "Can't you see she can't climb the stairs to the upper drawing room?"

He looked at Sorcha as if he wanted to strike her.

No, wait.

That wasn't fury. That was hunger.

How fascinating.

"Rainger always was a snotty little scion of a noble family." Queen Claudia gave him a toothy grin." So tell me, what has he done now?"

"He's married me." Sorcha glared at him. "And I want an annulment."

Chapter 24

Springtime came to Beaumontagne in a rush of color. The flowers bloomed, the birds fluttered and sang, the crops sprang from the ground—and the maps of war lay flat on the tables in the throne room while Rainger and his advisors talked about the strategy for invading Richarte. The discussion made Sorcha glad to sneak away from her ladies-in-waiting and into the garden just outside the castle walls. There she could sit alone and not hear the words "cavalry" "tactics" or "cannon." Nor did she have to hear, "duty" "diplomat" or her least favorite remark, "With child?"

She walked the paths she had walked as a girl, breathed the air perfumed with familiar scents, and hoped that Rainger didn't remember her favorite haunt.

Because if he did, he would come to find her soon. He always did, insisting she stay at his side throughout the conferences of war, while the learned economists explained the workings of the treasury, and especially when the people came to welcome them back or plead a case for justice. He trusted her to tell him the truth, and needed her to learn while he learned so she could govern while he was gone.

To war, he meant, and especially if he didn't return, she needed to know how to be queen.

The idea should have given her pleasure—she hated the man and, to the dismay of their courtiers, she didn't bother to disguise her disdain. At the same time, at the thought that he would die on some lonely field fighting for his country...she almost died, too. It wasn't fair, the way she felt about him, for he wanted her for three things—her country, her body, and the child he would receive from her womb.

After all, he'd made it clear enough that he needed to marry one of the Lost Princesses and she was the only one left. The words echoed in her mind and every night he made her realize anew how very much he meant it. Every night he—

"Your Highness!"

She pretended she didn't hear the voice that called and continued down the gravel path.

"Your Highness, please, I want to talk to you and I can't keep up."

Marlon. Of course. Rainger's companion from the dungeons, one of the men who entered with him—and the only one who returned alive.

Sorcha turned as if surprised and said, "Marlon! How good to see you. A lovely day for a walk, isn't it?"

"It's more of a hobble for me."

She winced.

"It was a joke. It's all right to laugh." Marlon hadn't died in the dungeon, but he had paid a price to get Rainger released. Marlon walked with two canes; his legs had been crushed and the constant pain drove deep grooves around his mouth and between his brows. Yet he bore his tribulations stoically and proved himself to be one of the brightest minds in their government.

He also made Sorcha uncomfortable. Not because of his disability, but because he made no secret of his deep admiration for Rainger, and because he had, more than once, hinted that he would gladly fill her in about the missing years of Rainger's life.

She didn't want to hear it. She didn't want anything to disturb the even tenor of her acrimony.

"Can we perhaps sit down?" Marlon asked. "Over there? I believe I heard Rainger say it's one of your favorite places in the castle."

"He remembers everything," she said with irritation.

"He makes a point to remember what's important to you." Marlon took her arm.

Together they slowly made their way to the bench just outside the castle wall overlooking the valley. An arbor surrounded the bench and from here she could look down to the base of the hill where the village of Prospera looked like a cluster of toy houses. Beyond that, antlike farmers plowed their fields. And beyond that, the whole kingdom blushed with the pleasure of spring.

"Ah." Marlon lowered himself onto the bench. "I see why you like it so much—but what I don't see is why you dislike Rainger so much."

Don't interfere. But no matter how much she wanted to snap at him, the dreadful disability he suffered kept her civil. Or at least—relatively civil. "That's a wife's prerogative."

"But if you knew about the dungeon—"

"I don't want to hear about the dungeon."

Marlon ignored her protest. "In the dungeon, things were done to him. And he did things…things that made me despise him."

She laughed bitterly. "That doesn't surprise me." But it did surprise her that Marlon admitted it.

"And things were done to him that made me...cry for him."

"I don't care." She fervently did not.

Marlon continued as if she hadn't spoken. "And things happened that...that made me worship him."

"I just said I didn't want to hear about the dungeon," she said impatiently. "So why are you telling me this?"

"Because I can't stand to watch you bring him such pain."

"Bring him pain? I doubt that." Every night Rainger tortured her with kisses on every part of her body. Every night she struggled to remain true to herself, and every night he broke her resistance, then brought her to climax. He did it deliberately, and no matter how much she struggled, afterward when she cried, he held her to witness his triumph. Damned if she would feel sorry for Rainger.

But she couldn't tell Marlon that. She couldn't tell anyone, so she smiled, a scornful twist of the lips. "I don't intend to listen to you, so let me send someone to help you back to the palace and I'll continue my solitary rambles." She stood.

"Would you deliberately walk away from a man who can't chase you down to make you listen?"

She paused.

"That seems unnecessarily cruel for a woman who has a reputation among her people as a most gentle princess."

Marlon knew how to maneuver Sorcha, but she set her mind against him even as she returned to sit beside him. "So, speak, but please don't be overlong about it. My duties fill my hours and I find little enough time to walk in the gardens...alone."

Stoically, Marlon started his story again. "I don't know what Prince Rainger has told you about his captivity."

"He doesn't talk about it." And she didn't ask.

"Because he's ashamed."

Now Marlon had piqued her interest.

"He was a vain young man who put his friends and his country at risk for the love of a woman."

Digging deep into her memory, Sorcha remembered the gossip from long ago. "Countess duBelle."

Marlon nodded. "The lovely Julienne, the most treacherous female the devil ever created. She betrayed him and all his friends and laughed as she did it."

Sorcha remembered the woman. She had been so beautiful, so graceful, so sensuous, that while in her presence, Sorcha had felt like a clumsy peasant.

"While in prison," Marlon said, "Rainger was beaten once a year."

"The scars." She swallowed as she remembered how they felt beneath her fingertips. "They are…brutal." Then, ungraciously, she added, "And they taught him nothing but brutality."

"He has *hit* you?" Marlon couldn't have been more astonished.

"No." She owed Marlon no explanation. Indeed, she suffered humiliation every night. She would never tell anyone the details.

Marlon searched her face, then sighed. "Something happened to him in that dungeon. I've never understood it, but let me tell you the story. He had five companions—Cezar, Hector, Emilio, Hardouin, and me. We were raised at his side and trained to always protect and defend him. As we grew, we accompanied him on his journeys and his…" He hesitated.

"His liaisons," Sorcha said.

Marlon bowed his head in agreement. "When Count duBelle's guards took His Highness, we fought. Hardouin and Emilio were killed. The rest of us were dragged through the streets and thrown into the dungeon. Rainger was kept in a tiny cell by himself. The rest of us were together. But before we were thrown in, Count duBelle hung Rainger up with chains and beat him with a cane. He made us watch. It was a brutal beating, but His Highness never made a sound. We were horrified. We were proud." Marlon's hand shook as he clasped the edge of the bench. "We were next. Count duBelle told us this was our punishment for failing to join him in his bid to topple Richarte's royal family, and when he was done, he joked about the aching in his arm."

She had known Count duBelle was a villain. More than once, he'd tried to have her killed. But to complain that beating four men had wearied him—that was sarcasm most cruel.

"The first year, we didn't understand. We waited for rescue. We thought we could appeal to the noble nature of the guards and they would help us escape. Prince Rainger commanded them as their sovereign to release us." Marlon laughed at his own naïveté. "The guards didn't have a noble nature. They lived in the dark and they liked it. They liked cruelty. They cared not at all if we were hungry or thirsty. Illness and death meant nothing to them—they saw it every day. Hector was the first one of us who realized we had no hope. When they took us out of the cells after the first year to beat us, he was gone. Dead of a fever."

She bled for Marlon's sorrow—and for Rainger's. "He was your friend."

"Yes. The second year we learned to communicate with His Highness by tapping on the grilles. We never talked about it, but I spent every day desperately wanting my mother. And I was so afraid of the beating. I was no longer a man. But no matter how I fought the passage of time, the day came. The guards threw blankets over our heads. They pulled us out of the cell. During the beating, His Highness cried from pain, but he never begged. Neither did Cezar. Neither did I. Then it was back into our cells for another year."

She couldn't imagine. She didn't dare try.

"After that, we started digging. Cezar had found a weak chink in the floor. The prison was far below the castle. The castle was on a cliff. No one ever escaped, but we had never been imprisoned there before and we didn't know that. It was grueling work, but at first we were relieved that we were doing something to help our prince. The rats nibbled on us—and if we were lucky, we nibbled on the rats. Yet the digging took so long. We used our shoes. We used spoons. We used our fingers." Marlon held up his hands. His middle fingers had no fingernails. "And all the time the prince was alone. He had no idea what we were doing. He had no hope. And again Count duBelle had the guards throw a blanket over our heads, drag us out, and beat us."

"Did he complain about his arm?"

"After the first year, he had the guards beat Cezar and me. We weren't important enough for him to weary himself. But he still beat Rainger. He enjoyed beating Rainger." Marlon shifted uncomfortably in his chair. His gaze dropped. He took a long breath. "The last year, Rainger…Rainger couldn't…he wasn't able to…"

"He wasn't able to…" And she realized what Marlon meant. "He begged."

"It had been seven years. He'd been alone in the dark. His cell was small. Almost a coffin. He hadn't talked to anyone."

Terror branded her. What would she do if she lived in a cell for seven years, alone in the dark with only the promise of pain to look forward to? "I would have broken much sooner," she whispered.

Marlon nodded. "But what you must know is— Count duBelle listened to him. Encouraged him. Made him admit his fear to us. To his friends. We were embarrassed for him. We felt as if we'd been loyal to a prince who deserved no loyalty. We went back to our cell. We still dug, but although we didn't admit it to each other, it was for ourselves now." Marlon closed his eyes to hide his tears, but one escaped and trickled down his cheek.

He was in pain. He was in pain, but he bore that pain to tell the tale of his prince. He had laid his life down for Rainger. He had sacrificed his health, and now he sacrificed his pride, too.

She didn't want to hear. She didn't want to feel Marlon's pain or understand Rainger's character, because she didn't want to give up her sense of grievance and her anger.

But how could she not listen when Marlon suffered so in the telling?

"Cezar and I dug with all our strength and we began to smell fresh air. We knew we were close. We didn't know where we would come out. But it didn't matter. For the first time in seven years, we had hope." Marlon opened his eyes and gazed into hers with such intensity, she couldn't look away. "Except that our prince had stopped tapping. He wasn't dead. We knew that. We could see through the grilles on the door and we hadn't seen the body go past. Yet he wouldn't answer us and we feared…madness. And something did happen in the dark, for the next year, when the guards covered His Highness with the blanket and dragged him out of his cell, he was different. He didn't fight. His fear was gone."

With an insight that proved she knew Rainger far better than she wished to, she said, "When he begged for his life, the worst had happened."

"Exactly. His Highness had reached the bottom." Marlon's face grew hard and twisted. "That day, Count duBelle taunted Rainger with the cane, then with a whip. Rainger did nothing. Said nothing. He simply looked at him and the expression on his face—sometime in the last year, he had become a king. Nobility shone from him. Count duBelle went berserk. He beat the clothes off His Highness. He beat his back until the blood ran and we couldn't see the skin. He beat his buttocks. He beat his legs. Cezar and I were fighting our chains, begging duBelle to stop, then trying to stop him. The guards were muttering—it was even too much for them. We knew all Rainger had to do was beg or cry and Count duBelle would have quit. But Rainger wouldn't say a word." Anguish tumbled from Marlon. "And he was conscious. His eyes were open, but...he just didn't care."

Sorcha held her hand in front of her mouth, sick with the horror.

"When Count duBelle started on Rainger's chest, the countess stepped in. She offered water to the count. She offered wine. Like a whore, she offered herself, taking Rainger's blood on her finger, licking it, and smiling. It was disgusting, but Count duBelle attacked her like an animal and while he was taking her there on the stone floor, the guards hustled Rainger back to his cell and us back to ours." Marlon gasped for breath as if the effort of speaking exhausted him.

"But Rainger…didn't he need someone to help him?" Oh, God, why did she care?

"Of course he did. But the guards were afraid of Count duBelle. Wouldn't you have been? When they brought our food, we begged them to let us help him. Finally, they did. After three days, they carried him in to us, told us it was too late, that he was dying." Marlon's eyes were bleak as he remembered that awful time. "He was. He was so weak. He couldn't eat. He couldn't drink. But he could talk. He thanked us for our loyal service to him. He begged our pardon for the youthful vanity which had landed us in there. He asked that we remember him fondly."

"Was he running a fever?"

"No. We thought…I still think he had willed himself to die. We tried to keep him. We told him about digging the hole, how close we were to getting out." Marlon smiled. "He was so happy—for us! He said that relieved his last worry, that he'd be leaving us rotting in prison. He begged that we take our freedom and use it wisely. And while I held him…he died."

"What?" Shock held her immobile.

"He died." Marlon squeezed her arm. "I swear he did. It was dark. It was close. I heard that slow dripping of the water. And I felt the life go from his body."

The air was foul. The indifferent stones closed in around her. No voice disturbed the silence. No hand reached out to bind her wounds or cure her pain. The bones of rats were her bed and the long drape of cobwebs her blanket.

She was buried alive.

And she didn't care. Somewhere close, water seeped into a pool, and the slow drip which had once driven her mad now contributed to her indifference. Her world was sorrow and loneliness. She was dying, and she welcomed the end of desolation, of grief, of anguish.

Her fingertips touched the skeletal hand of Death...

Sorcha shuddered. *She had been there.* In a dream, she had been there. "What happened?"

"He was gone. He was cold. I was in shock. Cezar was sobbing. And all of a sudden—Rainger convulsed. It was as if something smacked him in the chest. His heart started again. He took a gasping breath. And he was back with us." Marlon groped for the cross that hung around his neck. "It was a miracle."

She didn't want to believe it. Not about Rainger, with his intelligence and his will and his horrible, ridiculous belief that he could force her to love him by using his intense sexuality.

"He came back filled with purpose. He wanted to escape, to get his revenge on Count duBelle for the rape of his kingdom, to marry and have children and live forever through them. He remembered what we'd said about the hole, and he told us which way to dig to get to safety. And he was right. If we'd kept going the way we were, we would have ended right on the main path out of the castle. We'd have been spotted immediately and recaptured. Instead, he set us to the narrow path that led to the long-abandoned postern gate."

She didn't want to believe this. "What about the guards? Didn't they want to bury Rainger?"

"We told them he was slipping away, but that he had great and hidden strength. After he'd survived the beating, they believed that and they didn't want anything to do with him. Odd as it sounds, I think they were afraid of him. They thought he had special powers, that the hand of God had been laid upon him." Marlon bent his head and sighed. "I thought so, too. His purpose was of the purest and highest and his recovery astonished us. When we broke out two days later, he crawled through the hole and walked down the hill. When they discovered our escape, he went in a separate direction than Cezar and I, leading the guards after him."

Marlon wasn't telling her everything. "What did you do?"

"What do you mean?"

"Rainger is still here. Cezar is gone. You've been crippled. How is that possible?" She had to know the end of the story. "What did you do?"

"He was our prince. We'd doubted him once, but after he came back to life, we couldn't doubt him again. So we attracted the guards' attention and led them after us. Cezar was killed. I was trampled by their horses." Marlon indicated his legs. "But Rainger got away, and that was all we cared about. It's well worth it to sit here and know he's going to take Richarte back from that fiend."

In the convent, she'd been taught to believe in nobility. Then time, experience, and bitterness had eroded her belief.

Now Marlon proved that nobility existed.

Was what Rainger had done and been worth inspiring this nobility?

Marlon thought he was. And Rainger was going to war soon. Very soon.

"He'll march into Richarte," she said. "Our sources say Count duBelle has bankrupted the treasury. The people hate him. The army is in disarray. Victory is virtually assured."

"Rainger will survive," Marlon reassured her. "He didn't survive the dungeon to die on the battlefield."

"I'm sure you're right." She had to believe Rainger would not die.

"But while I'm happy, he is not. He deserves more than success. He deserves happiness—and Your Highness, you can give it to him."

The familiar resentment welled up in her. "He could have had happiness, but through his suspicion and his deception, he threw happiness away."

"He spent eight years in a dungeon. His friends were killed. He was hunted. He died. He has reasons for being suspicious...of everyone."

Marlon's explanation did not touch her. "We traveled for days together. He knew who and what I was. Yet still he deceived me. I am not an evil usurper. I am not a woman given to flights of fancy. I lived in a convent and tended a garden while patiently waiting to be called to do my duty. And he...and Rainger made a fool of me." She realized—she wasn't angry anymore. She was hurt. Hurt that he'd accepted her love, yet offered nothing but tenderness and an overwhelming sexuality in return.

He didn't love her, and she wouldn't allow it any longer.

Marlon opened his mouth, closed it, and thought, then said, "Perhaps it isn't even that he was suspicious or that he should be a better judge of character. Maybe he made a mistake, a grievous mistake, and since he's only a man, he doesn't know how to apologize."

370 • CHRISTINA DODD

"That's ridiculous." *So* ridiculous. "He's an adult. All adults know how to apologize."

"I beg to disagree, Your Highness. Only half of the adults know how to apologize. The other half are men, and speaking for my gender, I assure you a man will move heaven and earth rather than say, *I'm sorry.*"

She wanted to argue more, except the truth of what Marlon proposed seemed suddenly self-evident. She'd never heard a man admit he was wrong. Never heard a man say he was sorry. True, she had had little experience with men in the last years, but this made Rainger's insistence on holding her while she cried a little more in keeping with his character.

In his mind, he wasn't enjoying his triumph. He was giving her comfort. In a tone of discovery, she said, "He's a jackass."

"I fear that may be true," Marlon said.

"I'm going to go talk to him right now." Standing, she shook out her skirts.

Out of respect for his queen, Marlon came to his feet.

"He's going to hear my mind on the matter," she said, "and when I'm done with him, he'll apologize just to…to make me stop speaking my mind."

"A sound plan, Your Highness." Marlon leaned on his canes.

She started down the path toward the palace, then returned to Marlon. "Thank you." His eyes were agleam with contentment, but she allowed him that. "Thank you."

She walked away again, and when she reached the hedge near the postern door, two men stepped out. One was handsome and vigorous, the other older, seasoned, and battle-worn. And tall. The older man was tall, with fists like hams.

"Excuse me, gentlemen." She tried to walk around them. She needed to speak to Rainger now.

The older man bowed. "Your Highness, Princess Sorcha?"

Had Grandmamma sent for her now? *Now?* Her grandmamma had a dreadful sense of timing. "Yes, but my husband, Prince Rainger, has expressed his wish to see me, and—"

A third man approached from one side, a fourth from the other, and when she glanced around, she saw two more moving in to close the trap.

A trap.

These weren't Grandmamma's men.

"Who are you?" she asked sharply.

"If you'll come with us," the older man said, "you'll not be hurt."

His young companion rested his hand on the hilt of his sword and jiggled his foot as if danger made him edgy. The other men divided their attention between her and their surroundings.

Of course, they should be nervous. Their plan was bold. They had come to capture the princess on the palace grounds.

"Who are you?" she demanded again. Her gaze fell on the young man's jerkin, almost covered by his cape. There she saw it. A small symbol, a brown coiled snake against a scarlet background.

Count duBelle. These were his men.

Without warning, she threw back her head and screamed as loudly as she could.

A rough hand across her mouth cut her off in mid-shriek. The six men closed in, surrounding her, hustling her along the hedge toward waiting horses.

She struggled, flinging herself about, but with no chance against their combined strength. But she managed to turn to look back toward Marlon.

The branches were moving where he had stood.

Rather than face Count duBelle and his dungeon again, Marlon had fled. She was on her own.

Chapter 25

The footman cleared his throat in apparent agony as he opened the grand gilt doors of the throne room for Rainger to enter.

Absentmindedly, Rainger glanced up from the map he held. "Peter, you'd better do something about that cough. It sounds awful."

Then he stopped short.

Grandmamma sat in the throne on the dais. White-haired, thin, elegant, carrying a cane she used as a weapon. The old woman was cold as the winter when the river froze over.

No wonder Peter had made such a dire noise. He'd been trying to warn Rainger of the awful fate that awaited him, and Rainger had been too involved in his war plans to take note.

As usual, Grandmamma's expression boded ill for anyone who dared come before her. It certainly boded ill for Rainger.

Show no panic, he told himself. *Like a hostile dog, she senses fear and attacks.*

The trouble with Grandmamma was that she attacked regardless of her victim's terror. Probably she couldn't sense fear because *everyone* was afraid of her.

"What a pleasant surprise." He bowed with the respect due the tough old woman. "How may I assist Your Highness?"

"By making my granddaughter happy." Her eyes sparkled with hostility. "I would have thought that was obvious."

Peter shut the door, abandoning his prince without conscience.

Yes. Grandmamma always attacked, and without warning or posturing.

But Rainger was master here now, and he answered to no one. "What's obvious is that you should mind your business and allow us to mind ours," he said coolly.

"An heir to the throne is my business, and Sorcha can't breed if she rejects the stallion that covers her."

"She is not a breeding horse!" As a belated afterthought, he added, "Neither am I."

"Then act like a man!" Grandmamma smacked the arm of the throne. "You've made some grievous mistake or she wouldn't treat you like a bug to be scraped off the bottom of her shoe. Apologize to her."

"I apologize to her every night. She doesn't—" He wanted to say *listen*, but he hadn't actually verbalized his remorse. He demonstrated it.

"Apparently that's not enough." Using her cane, Grandmamma rose to her feet. "Women like gifts. Have you given her gifts?"

"I've been a little busy with the running of the country." The country by day, Sorcha every night, and he didn't know which challenged him more.

"Give me your arm, boy."

He climbed the stairs and helped her down. He hadn't realized it, but Grandmamma hobbled now.

"Prioritize, Rainger! Didn't I teach you to prioritize? Besides, how long will it take you to ask me for the crown jewels?"

"The crown jewels of Beaumontagne?" The old lady astonished him. She delighted him. "Do you have them?"

"If I didn't, they would have vanished during the revolution."

"I thought they *had* vanished."

"You give me too little credit." Her thin lips crooked upward in what could have passed as a smile. "When my son went to war, I took them into my possession."

"Of course you did." She was a wily old woman who understood human nature all too well. She never would have trusted anyone else with custody of the priceless diamonds, sapphires, and pearls.

"I have them still." She sank her nails into his arm. "But I'll give them to *you*, so ask me."

He hated being manipulated, but capitulating now saved him time better preserved for planning war—and making love to Sorcha. "Please may I have the crown jewels to give to Sorcha?"

"I'll send for them immediately."

"And thank you for your quick and clever thinking." Normally it would have hurt him to toady to Grandmamma, but he'd do anything to turn the subject away from his wooing of Sorcha.

He should have known better.

"You're welcome. How will you give them to her?" Grandmamma shot the question at him like a bullet.

"I hadn't thought about it." How could he? He'd just found out about them—not that Grandmamma would accept that as an excuse.

"I can't believe I'm advising you on this matter. I'm the least romantic person in the world. But obviously you're the second least, and you need help. So listen to me. You will present the crown jewels to Sorcha tomorrow night at the ball celebrating your return." Grandmamma had planned his courtship down to the last minute and motion.

"She'll like that." He'd like it—she would have to smile at him and maybe, for once, she'd mean it.

"It's a grand gesture, one that needs to be made, but she won't like being the center of attention. Don't you know anything about her at all?" Grandmamma seemed to consider this a rhetorical question. "Sorcha is the kind of woman who would rather you picked her a bouquet of flowers. So pick her a bouquet of flowers. It won't work if you have the gardener send flowers. That will make her unhappy."

"I know that," Rainger said with irritation, all the while wondering, *Why?* Rainger didn't know anything about flowers. He didn't know which colors to put together. He didn't know which ones had thorns. He didn't know how to arrange them. Why *wouldn't* Sorcha like the gardener's bouquet? The gardener was paid to do a better job with flowers than the king.

"She's a soft little thing. She'd like it if you took her for a walk after dinner in the garden." Grandmamma tapped her wrinkled lips. "In the moonlight. The moon is almost full. Tonight would be a good night."

"The French ambassador is due to dine with us tonight," Rainger said sarcastically. "Won't he think it odd that I carry off my wife rather than remain to speak with him?"

"He's French. He'll think it's odd if you don't."

Rainger spread the maps across the table and weighed down the corners. Anything to avoid looking Grandmamma in the eye. If he did, he'd probably confess that he'd written a letter informing Clarice and Amy of Sorcha's return and begging that they come to visit as soon as possible. Because of all the things he'd done in Scotland, the thing Sorcha seemed maddest about was when he'd burned her letters. And second maddest about—having more letters and not letting her know. And third maddest—not letting her visit Clarice.

It wasn't even his fault they hadn't gotten to visit Clarice.

Sorcha didn't care. She blamed him for being suspicious and distrustful, so she might as well blame him for the assassins that had turned them back from her sister.

Truthfully, he hadn't comprehended the strength of the bond between the sisters or realized how desperately Sorcha worried about them, and perhaps—just perhaps—he'd made a mistake by not reassuring her as soon as he'd ascertained her character. Certainly he saw no reason not to beg Clarice and Amy to visit, and he was desperately relieved that they had written back to say they would be here soon.

Maybe that would melt Sorcha's heart.

"Look, boy"—Grandmamma had a way of reducing him to infancy—"you don't understand. I raised that girl you married. I met her when she was but a babe, and from that day, I feared for her. She is sweet, she's kind, she's vulnerable—the kind of woman men like you would use without any appreciation for the gem they've been handed."

"Men like me?" What the hell did she mean by *men like you?*

"But Sorcha has changed. She's not that lovable, vulnerable woman anymore. I can catch glimpses of the old Sorcha, but something fired her resentment and changed her completely, and—don't lie to me—that something is *you.*" Grandmamma's cold blue eyes drilled holes into his pride. "So unless you want to live your life holding the chain of a woman straining to get away, you'll listen to me."

He stared at the map of Beaumontagne and Richarte and tried to remember why he'd thought them so important. "Why should I listen to you about my wife?"

"Because I'm putting all my hopes in the fact that you've changed, too."

Grandmamma was right. Damn her, she was right. He had to do something about Sorcha—or rather, something else about Sorcha, because his plan to force her to freely give her love to him was failing miserably.

Even as he held her in his arms every night, even as he brought her to unwilling climax, he felt her slip further and further away. And all the time he spent with generals and ambassadors and maps, he was aware of his own low-level misery that threatened at any moment to explode into fury and anguish.

He had felt like that in the dungeon. He didn't want to feel like that anymore.

"Rainger, pity an old woman and prove you're not the same spoiled lad you were before you were taken." Grandmamma sounded more tired than cranky, and that in itself was frightening.

In a low voice, he asked, "What should I do?"

"Jewels, flowers, a walk"—Grandmamma shook her crooked finger in his face—"during which you tell her you're a fool for doing whatever it was you did to her and that you'll never do it again."

That was exactly what he'd been trying to avoid. "When I escaped the dungeon, I swore a vow that I would never kneel before another soul, I would never crawl, I would never beg. It was a *vow*."

"Then I'll stop planning your formal wedding and crowning in the cathedral, and instead I'll get this marriage annulled," Grandmamma said coolly.

"What?" he roared.

"I'm not going to have Sorcha live in misery because you're stubborn." Grandmamma's eyes were glacial chips of blue. "You were married in a foreign country. I can bribe the witnesses, make the proof vanish, and find her another prince who can make her happy."

"You'll do no such thing." His hands curled. He would never strike a woman, certainly not an old woman, but if he was ever tempted, Grandmamma would be his first choice. "Sorcha's mine. She'll always be mine. I secured her because I wanted to win back my country, but I'll keep her because…"

Grandmamma leaned forward. "Because why?"

Because he loved her.

He loved her, yet he'd made her miserable.

He'd stripped her of her pride in herself as surely as Count duBelle had stripped him of his.

Why had it taken him so long to see that?

"Rainger!" Marlon called from the doorway.

At the interruption, Grandmamma groaned like an old horse and propped herself against the table.

Leaning on his canes, his face pale and streaked with sweat, Marlon hurried toward them trailing anxious guards and statesmen in his wake. "For God's sake, Rainger, listen, and quickly!"

"What's wrong?" Rainger sprang to help him.

"They have her," Marlon said. "Count duBelle's men."

Grandmamma grabbed her arm as if she were in pain.

"They've taken the princess. Count duBelle left this ransom note." Marlon fumbled in his pocket and brought out a paper stabbed through with a knife. "He has set a date and a time for you to come and get her."

Rainger snatched the paper and read the message.

"In a fortnight, not far from his castle where we were imprisoned. Your Highness," Marlon said, "he wants *you*."

"Me he can have." Rainger threw down the paper and strode toward the door. "But Sorcha he will not keep."

Chapter 26

A fortnight later, men clothed in black slipped through the darkness of the hushed forest, searching for the spot where tomorrow's drama would play out.

One horse rode with them, and from atop that horse, Marlon called softly, "Your Highness, they've found it."

Rainger recognized the tone in Marlon's voice, and his heart sank. He followed Marlon to a spot overlooking a meadow full of grass that waved in the breeze.

Marlon pointed.

In the light of the half-moon, Rainger saw the trap duBelle had set for him. "Hell," he said, and it was more of a description than an expletive.

"Perhaps there's another way," Marlon said. "Someone who can dress up to look like you—"

"No." Rainger would win this battle with himself.

"We could catch Her Highness as they bring her here and rescue her before—"

"No." Rainger comprehended Marlon's worry only too well. "I won't fail you this time."

Marlon gazed down at Rainger and his voice rang with sincerity. "I have faith in you."

"And I in you. Here's what we're going to do." When he'd given his instructions and Marlon had gone off to direct the men, Rainger looked again at the trap.

Of course. It had to be this.

The one thing he dared not face.

Yet he had to. For his people. And for Sorcha.

"Your Highness." Hubert held the door, but took care not to cross the threshold into Sorcha's cell. "The court's going hunting and they beg your presence."

"Beg? Do they?" Sorcha didn't turn to face Hubert. Instead she kept her gaze on the panorama visible from the castle tower. The black mountain peaks pierced the blue sky. The verdant green forests crept up the slopes. The distant fields awaited the first growth. "Richarte is a beautiful country—from a distance."

"Please, Your Highness, I must deliver you to the great hall."

"Yet the closer I look, the more apparent Count duBelle's failure becomes."

"Please don't make me come in and get you."

She didn't doubt for a moment Hubert sincerely wanted no trouble. He'd been one of the castle guards under Rainger's father.

Yet still she continued, "Behind the castle walls, holes gape in the thatch of the kitchen and the stable. Weeds choke the herb garden. The paths are untended."

"Your Highness, please."

She turned to face Hubert. "The castle was once beautiful and is now decayed. The servants wander about, stoop-shouldered and dispirited. Everyone hates Count duBelle."

"Shhh!" Hubert glanced behind him in alarm. Count duBelle always sent Hubert to deliver his messages to her, and Sorcha knew why. Hubert could be trusted to speak and not touch. He was the man who followed Count duBelle's instructions and planned the daring kidnapping right in the heart of Beaumontagne. He was older, battle-worn, and gray, and he never overstepped his bounds.

"Why don't you rise against him?" Sorcha asked. "If everyone in the castle joined together—"

Hubert lowered his voice. "We can't. I can't. Do you know why I am head of the guard?"

She shook her head.

"The others in the guard...some of them died fighting for the king." Hubert glanced behind him again and inched into the room. "Some of them died fighting Count duBelle's little wars. Every year, another war.... Last year some of them attempted rebellion. They wanted me to join them, but I've got a mother. She's old. And two daughters. They're young. I can't take a chance—"

"I know," Sorcha said gently. She did know. Every night she'd lain awake, waiting for some man to open the door and drag her into the darkness. Every day she'd listened for footsteps in the corridor and grown faint with fear when they stopped before her door. Yet nothing had happened to her...yet. Icy anticipation held her in its inescapable grip.

"When the rebellion failed, those guards disappeared...into the dungeons." Hubert wet his lips. "Count duBelle's dungeon is dark and deep. He's famous for the tortures. The beatings. Sometimes he goes down to make sure they're being carried out as he commands. Sometimes the countess goes with him, and when she returns, her eyes...they're bright like new-minted coins. Every few months there'll be a new head hanging on a pike at the crossroads. I try not to look, but sometimes I can't help it. Sometimes I recognize a face, and even if I don't, I recognize the expression."

"Terror," she said.

"No. Relief. Every one of them wanted to die." Intensely he whispered, "What has to be done to a strong, healthy man to make him welcome death?"

She shivered. Was that what had happened to Rainger?

"Please, Your Highness, please come with me," Hubert said. "If you don't, I'll have to force you."

"Of course I'll come with you." She smiled at the hulking guard. "We don't want to give them the pleasure of seeing me forcibly subdued, do we?"

"Not yet," he muttered.

"What?"

He cleared his throat. He opened his hands, palm out. "I'm to tie your wrists."

"Is the great Count duBelle afraid of a mere princess?" She spoke mildly, but her rage soared.

"I'm to tie your wrists," Hubert repeated. "Please."

He was so miserable she extended her hands without argument.

Taking the length of rope from his belt, he tied her wrists together. In a low voice, he said, "There's a rumor that Prince Rainger escaped from Count duBelle's dungeon. Is that true?"

"Of course it's true. You know Count duBelle would never have released him."

Hubert took a deep breath. A slight smile lifted his lips. "Then there is hope."

"There's always hope."

"No. Not for a long time." He stepped back. "Is that too tight?"

"It's fine." Actually, it was so loose she held it on with her fingers. She had no doubt he knew it, too.

He walked before her down the steep, winding stairs, telling her to avoid the loose boards, catching her when she stumbled. It was a strange, grim walk toward God knows what kind of dreadful fate, yet she was almost glad the waiting was over at last.

From the soaring arch ahead, she heard loud voices and shrill laughter.

"They're at breakfast," Hubert told her.

"A little late for a hunt, aren't they?" she asked.

He hunched his shoulders, took her arm, and led her into the great hall.

The room where Count and Countess duBelle dined glowed with a thousand candles and glittered with the sparkle of gold: on the plates, the tapestries, the jewelry, even the thread on the uniforms of the serving staff. Yet beneath the scent of expensive perfume, a pervasive odor tinted the air, an odor like decaying teeth, like rat-infested walls, like rampant, rotting ambition.

The count and countess glittered, too—the countess wore rings so grand they weighed down her slender fingers. The count wore a gold chain with an ornate pendant and a large sapphire of such fire it glittered in the candlelight. They certainly had the looks and lineage to be royal, yet like the castle, they reeked of hidden rot.

Richarte's nobility hadn't joined them in their coup, and that left the count and countess to consort with people of low origins, overweening ambition, and—Grandmamma would say worst of all—poor manners. The count and countess had sunk to the level of their associates.

As Sorcha entered, the countess called, "Here she is. Our little sacrifice." Julienne laughed as she spoke, a small trilling giggle like a schoolgirl enjoying a guilty pleasure.

Far more than the words, the sound of her merriment drove terror into Sorcha's heart.

This was no ordinary hunt. Something was planned. Something horrible.

Count duBelle caught sight of her, waved her forward, and called, "Princess Sorcha, I trust you've enjoyed your stay at our castle."

"It's not what I'm used to." She lifted her tied hands and showed them. Better to pretend indignation about the knots than to have them checked by another guard.

"It's necessary. For your own safety." At the ripple of laughter, Count duBelle shot a knowing smile around the room. "You see, we're going hunting...for a prince."

Oh, God. Oh, God. Her heart thumped with increasing speed and vigor. Her chest rose and fell as she tried to get her breath. "And my role is?"

"Why, Your Highness." His smile chilled to the temperature of a glacial stream. "You're the bait."

"He's going to try to rescue me and you're going to capture him," she said.

"I count the first time I captured him as the crowning moment of my life. It's not often a man has two such"—Count duBelle ran his tongue around his red lips—"climactic experiences."

She wouldn't give him the satisfaction of fainting. She would not. But as the blood ebbed from her brain, she looked around her with sharpened focus.

There. At the table. That man. He watched her with avid eyes like a weasel smelling blood.

That woman. As she laughed, it seemed her teeth lengthened and sharpened.

Another man. He watched her as if she were a fox and he a hound.

And the countess...she leaned back in her high-backed chair, toyed with her silverware, and smiled so happily she might have been a child offered a treat. Her blond hair was styled in a fashionable swirl. Her riding costume wrapped her lush figure in glorious blue velvet. Only her avid sapphire eyes showed a knowledge of what would happen to Sorcha. And to Rainger, her former lover.

Sorcha had fallen into a den of beasts and none of the other horrors she faced on the road—not the mean-spirited MacLaren, not the sly MacMurtrae, not the treacherous Godfrey—could ever hope to match these people and their corruption.

"Are you fond of him, your prince?" Count duBelle leaned forward and avidly watched her. "Do you like the scars on his back? I put them there. Did you know he's afraid of the dark? I taught him that. I made him the sniveling coward he is today."

"If Prince Rainger is such a coward," she asked in a clear voice, "then why do you think he'll take the bait and rescue me?"

Hubert took her arm and almost jerked her off her feet. "Come on!"

"Where are you taking her, Captain?" Count duBelle's voice snapped like a whip.

"To the stables, Yer Lordship," Hubert said, "to wait for yer pleasure."

A great many of the men snapped their fingers in encouragement.

"Hey, hey, hey, Egidio, she's going to wait for your pleasure!" one of the men at the high table called. "She's a pretty tidbit. Your pleasure would be great."

"His pleasure could be shared." Julienne flushed a mottled red and the hand that gripped her cup curled into a claw. "Then we'd see how pretty she is."

Sorcha cast a glance around the room. Handsome men. Pretty women. Vacant eyes. Lascivious smirks.

She looked at Count duBelle. At his sculpted face, his athletic body, his bloodshot eyes filled with the soulless desperate need to prove his domination.

She met the countess's gaze and saw in her the lethal venom of a woman whose beauty had unfolded as an exotic blossom and now, day by day, withered into the humiliation of old age. In this lawless land ruled by one ruthless man, Julienne would do anything to retain her position as his lover, including flinging Sorcha to the pack.

Hubert jerked her again. "Move," he growled.

She moved, taking care not to run, not to incite them to give chase.

Outside the great hall, she shuddered.

Hubert took a long breath. "She's a rabid bitch, that one is."

Sorcha hurried now, putting distance between herself and the court. "What awful people. They wallow in beauty and don't know the difference between a palace and a pigpen."

"I'm sorry, Your Highness. I'd help you if I could." Hubert sounded wretched.

She touched him on the arm. "You did help me. You got me out of there in one piece. I'm grateful."

"Ye don't know what they're going to do to ye." Hubert's feet dragged more than hers.

"I have an idea. But don't worry. My husband will come for me."

"That's what he's supposed to do, and they're going to—"

"I know, but you don't understand. He's a different man than he was when he was your prince. He won't let anything happen to me." That she did not doubt. It didn't matter that Rainger had tricked her or that she despised him or that he used her for her body to bring his heir into the world. Against all logic or hope, she knew Rainger would come to rescue her. *Would* rescue her. "Rainger will save me."

"I know he will, Your Highness." But Hubert's bleak tone belied his hopeful words.

The stable was a madhouse of activity as the grooms and hostlers saddled the horses. Dust and cursing rose in the air, and Sorcha supposed her equippage would be chosen to ridicule her and her station.

She was right. The rough, humble cart resembled the tumbrel that carried French aristocrats to the guillotine. The horse that pulled it had huge hooves, sturdy legs, and a swayed back—an old, worn-out farm horse.

Nine swordsmen surrounded it, their costumes as elaborate as any cavalier's and with Count duBelle's family arms sewn into their sleeves. Two were older men, seasoned and stoic, but the other seven were young and proud, fingering their swords and looking at her with thinly disguised scorn.

"Gentlemen," she said.

They ignored her. The hunter does not converse with the fox.

She petted the poor horse's head and told Hubert, "I'm surprised it's not an ox."

"That'd take too long, and they need to get ye up there in time for—"

"Hubert, you forget yourself!" one of the swords-men snapped. He had an aristocratic accent, a fashion-able haircut, and a superior sneer.

But Hubert held the senior rank, and he snapped back, "What do ye think she's going to do, young mas-ter? Escape and defeat Count duBelle? She's naught but a woman, and a skinny one at that. I think I can safely say that we ten men can control her."

The two older guardsmen laughed.

"You really are insolent, my man." The young man put his hand on his sword.

The other young men followed suit.

He continued, "When I am master of the guard—"

"What's your name?" Sorcha infused all Grand-mamma's haughtiness into the question.

The young man jumped. He looked down at her as if seeing her for the first time and his gaze faltered under her gimlet stare. "Baptiste. Baptiste Chapele, son of Comte d'Aubert."

"You are never going to be master of the guard. When Prince Rainger hears of your impertinence to your leader, he'll send you home to your father with a note chiding him for raising such a spoiled brat."

Flushed with mortification, Baptiste said, "Prince Rainger is not in command here."

"He will be."

"He'll be dead," Baptiste said.

"Are you a betting man?" Sorcha asked. "Because I'll take that wager."

The young men exchanged glances, uncertain for the first time.

"Before the year is out, Prince Rainger will be crowned king of Richarte in the cathedral in Bellagrande. I will be crowned queen of Beaumontagne in the cathedral in Beauvallee. And we are married and will be king and queen for each other's country, also." She smiled. "Dear foolish lad, you've made a serious mistake."

Hubert made a sound, the slightest wincing noise. Her arrogance alarmed him. But she knew Baptiste's type: brash, ignorant, and easily swayed.

"Prince Rainger has no chance." Yet his tone was uncertain.

"Prince Rainger is intelligent, ruthless, and has the power of Beaumontagne's military at his disposal," she answered.

"But he's so soft, he doesn't want to fight his own people." Baptiste looked around at his friends for support.

To a man, they nodded.

"How many of the old nobility in Richarte will fight for Count duBelle? How many of the commoners will take up arms for Count duBelle?" Sorcha climbed into the cart and sank down on the straw, her spine braced against the board at the front. "Rainger won't have to fight them. The people of Richarte will open the gates to him."

One of the horses shied, and one of the other young men sputtered, "Th-that's what Father said, Baptiste!"

Ah. Baptiste's brother. Speaking to him, she added, "Taking me to be bait for a trap is the last act of a desperate man."

"Father said that, too, Baptiste!" The brother was wide-eyed and nervous.

His bewilderment infected the other youths and they glanced uneasily at each other.

"Ye ought to listen to yer father." Hubert gathered the reins of her horse. "He's a wise one."

Baptiste stared angrily at Hubert. "Oh, shut up."

"Temper, temper," Sorcha chided. The whole country was turned inside out. Discipline was needed and Rainger, with his steely gaze and unwavering resolution, was just the man to provide it.

With a jerk, the cart started, rumbling down rutted roads. Five men rode in front, five in back, keeping their hands on their swords. Obviously they'd been warned to watch for a rescue attempt and Sorcha, too, constantly swept the forest with her gaze. The cart turned off onto a track that led up the mountain behind the palace. The fir trees joined branches overhead, providing green dappled shade. Shrubs brushed against the side of the cart. The horse labored, its sides heaving on the uphill trek.

And once she thought she saw…something. She sat straighter and stared hard. A man. It looked like a man dressed in black looking back at her.

In the distance, she heard the blare of hunting horns and the sound of galloping hooves and raucous laughter.

And the illusion faded. No one was there.

"C'mon, lad," Hubert said to the horse. "Count duBelle wants everything in place when he gets there, and that means we'd best finish the climb. He's not one to spare the whip and ye're not one who can bear it."

Heavens, no. The poor horse didn't need the whip to be miserable. It was already miserable enough.

Sorcha rested her arms on her upraised knees. She clenched her fists. She wished…she wished this was over. She wished she knew the best thing to do to help Rainger.

She wished she hadn't been so unyielding with him. Yes, he'd tricked her and, more to the point, made a fool of her. But he'd had his reasons, and if she thought those reasons were fatuous—well, she was right.

But when he decided on his deception, he didn't *know* her. He didn't know she was meek, obedient, and dutiful.

Indeed, some of her behavior on their trip through Scotland may have given him the impression she had a mind of her own.

But that was simply because the adversity they encountered required ingenuity and intelligence to counter…All right, Rainger had reason to worry about her intentions for the future. She had enjoyed that trip through Scotland more than she'd ever enjoyed anything in her life. The cold, the rain, the mud, the hunger had been nothing compared to the pleasure of meeting challenges and succeeding against all odds. She'd never enjoyed such unimaginable freedom—and she never would again.

She was the crown princess now, with a princess's duties and a princess's authority. And using the skills and the wit she'd learned on the roads of Scotland, today she would prove herself worthy to be queen.

Again she flicked a glance around the cart. She had to be alert. She had to be ready to help Rainger. Because, God help her, she still loved him—and if he was killed rescuing her, she would die, too.

"Here we are, Your Highness." Hubert pulled the horse to a halt. "Please, if ye'd descend from the cart and step over to that tree. Baptiste, help Her Highness out of the cart." As the court rode nearer, Hubert moved briskly and without any apparent regard for Sorcha.

Baptiste did as he was told; he helped her out of the cart and led her to a stout pine. "Stand there and I'll get the rope."

The grove where they'd stopped was perfect for an ambush. The trees stood close together around the edge, then thinned enough to allow a clear view of her from the meadow below—and to allow the court a clear view of the trap. The guards had affixed a net and a blanket in the branches and when Rainger approached from below, they would drop the snare on his head and knock him to the ground. Then, while he struggled, the guards would wrap him up and Count duBelle would order them to take him back to the dungeon, there to rot forever.

Rainger's plan was undoubtedly different.

Again Sorcha scanned the area, looking for help, but all she saw was the court, riding into the clearing. All she heard was their vapid laughter and endless chatter.

Baptiste headed her way with his coil of rope, but Julienne dismounted not far away and called him to her side. As she walked her fingers up his buttons, the young man looked embarrassed and panicked, and his desperate glances toward Count duBelle clearly said he feared reprisal. He lifted the rope, obviously using it as an excuse, and started toward Sorcha.

And Rainger stepped out onto the meadow.

Chapter 27

"There he is." Count duBelle stood behind Sorcha, his breath warm on her neck. "Your handsome young hero. Does he know about the snare set for him, do you think?"

"I don't know," she said.

Rainger looked wary as he strode toward them, glancing from side to side as if expecting an ambush.

"Perhaps not. There's a rule of hunting that is a universal truth, and that is that prey never looks up." Count duBelle ran his finger down her arm.

Her skin crawled at his touch.

"But even if he knows, I wager he'll walk into the trap for your sake. He is such a gentleman. Such a prince." Count duBelle's deep, rasping voice mocked the concept of nobility. "He probably has some hare-brained plan for rescuing you, for all the good it will do him. I constantly remind the people of Richarte what an awful leader he was and that they don't want him back. And in case they forget, I've got hired mercenaries and members of the guard who are as loyal to me as they are to their families."

So Count duBelle deliberately picked people like Hubert. People with responsibilities. People he could threaten.

"He's getting closer...closer..." Carelessly, as if he didn't realize what he was doing, Count duBelle kissed her shoulder.

She wanted to wipe off the stench of his breath.

And Rainger had seen it, for he broke into a run.

She wanted to shout for him to go back, but she knew how foolish that would be.

Count duBelle chuckled in delight.

Sorcha looked around in desperation.

Julienne stood not far away, her attention divided between Rainger's approach and her husband's attentions to Sorcha.

Baptiste had dropped the coil of rope and retrieved his musket. Hubert held one, also. So did Baptiste's brother and all the members of the guard.

Sorcha's blood froze. She tried to dive down the hill. Later she didn't know why, but it wasn't a plan, it was an instinct.

Count duBelle caught her arm, twisting it painfully. Just as Rainger reached the center of the net, the Count shouted, "Now."

The blanket and net covered Rainger. He struggled frantically.

The court watched. They laughed.

"He hates being confined in small spaces," Count duBelle called to them. "It reminds him of his old home in my dungeon."

"Rainger, please, Rainger." Sorcha squeezed her fingers together, trying to pass some of her strength through the air. To him.

But to no avail. In but a moment, his struggles failed.

She had to *do* something.

"That's always the problem with our Prince Rainger. He provides no great sport, for he gives up so easily." Count duBelle shrugged as if disappointed.

She had to provide a diversion. What was it Madame said would distract any man's attention anywhere? It wasn't sex, it was…

"Ah, well," Count duBelle said. "Shoot him and be done with it."

"Shoot him?" Sorcha couldn't believe it. "You're going to take him to the dungeon."

Count duBelle's eyes grew lethal. "Not this time, my dear. I'm done with this prince. He's going to die."

The guards lifted their rifles.

Madam Pinchon had claimed that men like to watch women fight.

Sorcha freed her wrists from her bonds. Shrieking, "Whore!" she leaped toward the countess. With both hands, she grabbed Julienne's blond hair and yanked. The hair held for one moment—then Sorcha staggered backward, holding an artfully arranged wig and its attaching pins.

Julienne stood revealed—her short, thin hair was a salt-and-pepper gray. Reaching up, she felt her head. She screamed from pain and rage.

Sorcha experienced one moment of intense satisfaction. She had succeeded. No shots had been fired. All eyes were on her and Julienne.

Then Julienne launched herself at Sorcha, shrieking, "Bitch, I'll kill you for this!"

Her weight knocked Sorcha flat on her back. She hit Sorcha hard enough to make her ears ring.

Sorcha slammed her elbow into Julienne's chest.

Julienne doubled over, gagging.

"You betrayed Rainger!" Grabbing her around the neck, Sorcha rolled her over, sat on her, and smacked her. Her own latent bubbling fury astonished her. "You destroyed his trust. You watched while they beat him. You harpy! You traitor!"

Julienne flailed beneath her, slapping at her, but Sorcha's anger gave her strength. Dimly she could hear the crowd clapping, urging them on as if they attended a catfight.

She didn't care. Nothing could dim her satisfaction.

Julienne *deserved* this.

In midflail, someone grabbed Sorcha by the arms and pulled her up.

Two of the guards.

Wild with rage, Sorcha fought them.

Julienne came to her feet. She landed a blow to Sorcha's face. "Mongrel!" She raised her fist to strike again.

Count duBelle grabbed her around the waist.

Sorcha heard a man's pleading voice in her ear. "I beg ye, Yer Highness…please, Yer Highness…"

It was Hubert, restraining her, trying to keep her from harming herself.

All around them, the men and women of the court laughed and cheered.

Mud caked Julienne's spiky hair. Grass stains marred the pristine velvet of her riding costume. Blood dribbled out of one nostril. She cried in gasping, furious sobs, and the tears tracked through the dirt on her face.

She looked like hell, and Sorcha was glad. Glad, proud, and still in a rage. She thought she probably looked as bad as the countess, but she didn't care. It was about time someone taught Julienne a lesson, and she was pleased to be the one.

From the surreptitious grins and thumbs-ups being sent her way, she suspected everyone felt the same way.

"Princess Sorcha, that was very impressive," Count duBelle drawled.

"What?" Julienne asked violently. "How dare you praise her!"

"But it won't save your husband." Count duBelle's blue eyes gleamed with cold amusement. With a flick of his wrist, he pointed to the guards. "Fire on Prince Rainger."

"No!" Sorcha flung herself at one of the riflemen.

As the rifles roared, Hubert pulled her back.

"No!"

Holes blasted through the wool cover and the net. The material smoked.

The crowd gasped, stilled....

Sorcha heard a single shocked whisper. "The king...."

Petrified and in agony, Sorcha stared around her. Men stood with their mouths open. Women held their hands before their mouths, tears in their eyes. Julienne stood with her hand over her heart.

Even these dissipated courtiers harbored doubts about killing their rightful ruler.

Then Count duBelle laughed. Laughed loud and long.

Sorcha's hands curled into claws. She wanted to kill him. She wanted to sob. She wanted to die.

"At last. At last. Throw back the net." Count duBelle grinned hugely. "Let's see the body."

Sorcha wanted to cover her eyes. But she couldn't *not* look. More than anything, she wanted not to see Rainger's corpse.

She got her wish.

The guards threw back the net.

A straw dummy lay there, its arms arranged in a rude, yet significant gesture.

From his place in the shadow of the trees, Rainger watched the rush of furious color to Count duBelle's face. He listened to Julienne's loud gasp and observed the way she shrank back against Count duBelle. He heard the murmur of amazement and alarm from the courtiers. All that gave him incredible satisfaction.

But more important, Sorcha stared at the dummy—and smiled with joy. Eyes alight, she looked around as if seeking him, and it was all he could do not to go to her and wrap her in his arms.

But the battle was not yet over.

Count duBelle made an abrupt gesture at his guards. One of the young, arrogant fools leaped down the slope onto the meadow and pushed the dummy and the loose leaves aside. He revealed the wooden planks beneath that. With his polished boot he nudged one of the planks away—and there it was. The trench through which Rainger had escaped.

Count duBelle's ruddy color turned choleric. He took steps toward his worthless trap, then violently swung back toward his wife. "This is your fault."

And Rainger stepped out of the shadows, his hand on his sword, gaze fixed on Count duBelle. "Surely you can't be surprised at this turn of events. The one thing we all know you taught me was how to excavate."

Count duBelle lifted a shaking finger. "Shoot him now!"

"Rifles down!" one guardsman shouted.

Rainger recognized him—Hubert. He'd been in the guard during his father's reign. Somehow he had survived through to this day. But the past eleven years had etched age and cynicism into every line of the old boy's face, and now those lines were set in determination.

"The man who aims at our prince answers to me," Hubert shouted.

Grabbing the nearest pistol, Count duBelle aimed and shot in one smooth motion.

All around the courtiers, Rainger's men materialized, rifles aimed, swords drawn.

But Count duBelle didn't shoot at Rainger. He shot Hubert right in the chest.

The burly guard teetered, surprise on his face, then plunged over like a great felled tree.

Sorcha screamed. She dropped to her knees beside him.

The courtiers shrieked and tried to stampede like a herd of cornered deer.

Rainger's grim-faced men stopped them.

Rainger walked farther into the light. "Beaumontagne's army waits not five miles down the road, watching for the signal to march in and take Richarte by force. But there's an easier way, Count duBelle. You and I...we'll fight and the winner takes the country."

"And the loser?" Count duBelle asked.

"The loser dies." Rainger knew what he risked. Count duBelle had a fascination with weapons and a deadly fear of assassination. He practiced with firearms, with swords, with knives and his fists. He was older than Rainger, but he was also strong, healthy, and ruthless. Most important, like an indestructible demon, he walked in Rainger's nightmares.

Count duBelle knew it, too. He smiled, that slow, cruel smile Rainger had seen so many times before. Had seen every year as the guards dragged him out of his cell. As he whimpered and cried and begged for mercy from a man who was merciless.

"Yes. The loser dies." Count duBelle's cold voice tasted the words with satisfaction.

The tone. That expression. Rainger could almost feel the skin on his back shrinking toward his bones, trying to avoid the blows he'd been trained to expect.

He needed to remember—remember that Count duBelle had killed Rainger's father, imprisoned his friends, ravaged his country. Count duBelle had kidnapped Rainger's wife and, given the chance, he would beat her, rape her, kill her. Everything depended on Rainger's winning this fight. He must focus on only one thing—overcoming Count duBelle. Nothing else mattered.

The two men moved to the center of the clearing.

Count duBelle glanced at the raw young leader of his guard. "Baptiste, you know what to do."

The youth was staring at Hubert's body, at Sorcha crouched over it, at the blood on her hands and the tears in her eyes. And he nodded. "I know what to do." He unbuckled his sheathed sword and placed it on the ground.

Count duBelle turned on him with a hiss. "Are you insane?"

"No, my lord. I'm quite sane." The youth's voice shook, but he crossed his arms over his chest, lifted his chin, and held Count duBelle's gaze. "You shouldn't have killed Hubert, my lord. My father says he is a...he was a good man."

"Your *father.*" Count duBelle sneered. "To whom do you owe your loyalty?"

Rainger allowed his gaze to touch Sorcha. Slowly, she stood, Hubert's body at her feet. She stared at Baptiste, a steady, clear-eyed stare.

Baptiste looked back at her, then cleared his throat. "I don't know, my lord. I don't know."

Violently, Count duBelle turned to another of his young guards.

That youth's hand trembled so much he could scarcely unbuckle his scabbard, but he, too, placed his sword on the ground. Together the young men moved to Hubert. One took off his jacket and laid it over Hubert's face. They lifted him and placed him on the cart.

"It appears your men believe our fight should be fair." Rainger lowered the tip of his sword.

Swift as a striking snake, Count duBelle lunged. "Too bad."

Rainger snapped his sword upward, but his blade struck too late. He deflected Count duBelle's death blow, but the point pierced his shoulder, striking bone.

Count duBelle leaped back—and laughed.

The pain, the laughter, slapped Rainger like a gauntlet, sharpening his wits, wiping fear from his mind.

The worst had happened. Count duBelle had drawn first blood.

So what?

All that mattered was who drew last blood.

He heard the murmurs of disapproval from the crowd. No doubt Count duBelle heard them, too. So Rainger smiled, a slight lift of the lips.

Count duBelle's eyes widened for one betraying second of shock, then slid almost shut as he tried to hide his blast of enmity.

He hated Rainger, hated him beyond all reason. Hated him for surviving. Hated him for being. And feared him for his legitimate claim to the throne.

Rainger allowed his smile to widen. Enmity and fear. Good signs. Even better that Count duBelle couldn't hide his feelings. That showed a loss of control.

Blood trickled down Rainger's arm. He noted a numbing in his fingers. He tossed the sword to his other hand. "Come, my man. While you've been practicing your swordsmanship, I've been wandering the world in search of my princess. And...something else. What was it I was doing? Ah, that's right. Being beaten with your cane and rotting in your dungeon."

"You'll rot in your grave when I'm done with you."

Sorcha flinched at Count duBelle's cruel words, then flinched again as, without warning, his sword rippled toward Rainger.

But Rainger skillfully parried. He grinned and said, "You're right, of course. *En garde* is such an old-fashioned turn of phrase."

She should have been glad he had the wit and confidence to jest...but she wanted him to stop talking and *fight*. He had to win. Not because of their wretched countries and their thrones and their crowns, but because beneath the tangled knot of her resentment and distrust lay a bedrock of love so intense she could scarcely stand to watch—yet couldn't turn her gaze away.

As the swords flashed in the dappled sunlight, she winced, faltered, recoiled with each stroke. Her breath quickened as if she were fighting. Inside her chest her heart ached with its frantic beating.

"You can't keep this up." Count duBelle panted as he spoke. "You're losing blood."

"True," Rainger agreed.

In a move so swift Sorcha's gaze couldn't follow, Rainger slipped past Count duBelle's guard—and slashed his cheek to the corner of his mouth.

The men muttered, the women whimpered. Julienne screamed as the skin sagged to show the white of his teeth.

Sorcha grinned with savage satisfaction. She felt no pity for Count duBelle. For the pain and death he'd caused, if she could, she would kill him herself.

"There. Now you're losing blood, too." Rainger held his sword at the ready while with his fingers Count duBelle explored the injury.

"You worthless royal whelp!" Count duBelle's voice sounded odd, as if he couldn't articulate well. "You've mutilated me."

The swords clashed again.

Again Rainger's sword flashed.

Count duBelle parried, but blood blossomed on his other cheek. He stumbled backward.

Again Rainger stopped and stood waiting. "There. That must improve your mood. Both sides match."

Count duBelle turned to glance at his wife. At the sight of his face, now a death's head, Julienne's beautiful big eyes grew large and horrified. She clapped her hand to her mouth, turned away, and vomited.

When Count duBelle turned back to Rainger, his gaze was lethal. He leaped into the fight with a searing array of strokes so swift his steel blazed with fury.

Rainger might have learned to fight like that once, but it had been so long. Since then, he'd been wandering the world in search of…Sorcha.

Yet Rainger's sword leaped to answer Count duBelle's challenge.

Beside her, someone lightly touched Sorcha's arm. In a low, warm voice, a woman said, "Rainger's probably not as good a swordsman as Count duBelle, but he's showing a remarkable ability to shake him."

Sorcha remembered one of Grandmamma's axioms. "The prisoner comes to know his jailer's fears as well as the jailer knows his prisoner's anguish."

On her other side, Sorcha felt another light touch. "Rainger is pacing himself quite well. He's not allowing Count duBelle to push him into rapid swordplay."

"Now you can see the difference between youth and experience," the first voice said. "Count duBelle is sweating like the pig he is."

The voices seemed vaguely familiar, but right now Sorcha didn't care. She couldn't look at these women. She needed to keep all of her concentration on Rainger.

She couldn't blink. She wanted somehow to *help*, yet she was only a spectator.

One of the women at her side slid her hand through Sorcha's arm. "Rainger won't lose. He's fighting for you."

The assurance simply annoyed Sorcha. The distraction made her want to shriek. Couldn't these women see what was happening? See the silver swords flashing through the air, the sunlight glinting on the points, the blood oozing from Rainger's wound, the death's-head horror that was Count duBelle? The clash of steel against steel filled Sorcha's mind. Didn't these women realize Rainger could *die*? Sharply, she said, "He's fighting for his *life*."

On her other side, the second woman hugged her. In a soothing tone, she said, "Yes, of course he is. His life, his country, and his love."

"His love will give him strength," the first woman said.

He didn't love Sorcha, but if love would give him strength, then she had enough for the both of them.

She took her first unrestricted breath and accepted the two women's comfort.

And before her, Count duBelle's sword work took on a new intensity.

Rainger had begun to falter.

Rainger's chest heaved with the effort, and time and time again he barely brought up the sword to defend himself.

Count duBelle showed the technique he had honed through years of practice. His pale eyes flashed with malevolence as he drove Rainger ever backward.

Sorcha heard the calls start—calls for Count duBelle to finish the job, and quieter calls for Rainger to hold on, to win. She wanted to call to Rainger, also, but her mouth was too dry, her anguish too violent.

Count duBelle drove Rainger toward the barren edge of rock, toward the drop into the meadow, toward the trap he'd prepared for him. Count duBelle panted, but still he smiled as he said, "You are going to die where I tell you."

Rainger's foot slipped out from underneath him. He went down on one knee.

Count duBelle lifted his sword for the deathblow.

And in a move so quick Sorcha's eye couldn't follow, Rainger brought the point of his sword up under Count duBelle's guard. Under his rib cage and into his chest.

Count duBelle teetered, hanging on Rainger's sword, a ludicrous expression of surprise on his face.

"No," Rainger said to him, "I'm not." Jerking his blade free, he swept his arm under Count duBelle's knees and toppled him into the grave.

Chapter 28

Slowly, painfully, Rainger stood, turned. He looked down the slope at the body of his enemy.

All around the clearing, no one moved, no one breathed.

For years, in darkness and in light, he'd imagined, anticipated this moment. He had planned each move, each thrust, each parry. He'd thought he would experience glee.

Instead he felt nothing but the satisfaction of a job well done. A job long overdue.

One fellow shouted, "He did it!"

As if those words were the trigger, pandemonium broke forth. Women shrieked, men yelled.

Rainger faced the crowd.

Some of Count duBelle's well-dressed, overfed supporters slipped backward into the crowd. Rainger nodded to his men to let them go.

Yet genuine joy lit more faces than he had imagined. More than one supporter, more than one of Count duBelle's guard, had genuinely hated him.

Rainger had planned a thousand stirring speeches to the cheering multitude.

Instead he wanted to speak only a few heartfelt words to one woman.

He searched for her face, needing to see that she was healthy, see if she was pleased that he had vanquished Count duBelle. Pleased that he was alive.

He found her at once, her beloved face pale, her glorious eyes wide, her expression deceptively still.

What did she think? What did she feel?

He hadn't known her since the day she'd discovered his deception, since the day he'd told her his plans, given her his mandate, and demanded her cooperation. Since that day, she'd given him just what he required—and nothing of what he wanted.

He knew what he had to do.

As he strode toward her, Sorcha wanted to run to him. To scream her joy. To throw herself at him, to hug him, to kiss him.

But he wanted a queen, not a wife.

So she held herself still, waited for him to reach her. When he was close enough, she held out her hand and said, "Well done, my lord." Her voice trembled in a most unqueenly manner, and carefully she corrected it. "I never doubted you would triumph."

But he…he didn't act like a king at all.

He acted like a man.

He caught her in his arms, embracing her as if she were his dearest possession. As if he were desperate to hold her. In a voice choked with emotion, he whispered, "Dear God, I was so afraid the bastard had killed you. Hurt you. Did he?"

Shocked by his tempestuous outburst, she shook her head.

"When I saw you standing here, all my prayers were answered and I knew…I *knew* I would prevail. For you. Because I had to live for you. With you." He took one step away. He caught her face in his hands. He looked down at her, his dark eyes alight with something that looked like…if she were a fanciful woman, she would say it was…

"I love you." Before she could catch her breath, he knelt gracefully before her. "When I crawled out of that dungeon, I swore two solemn vows. I swore I'd come back and kill Count duBelle, and I swore I'd never again kneel before another soul. But some vows are made for good reason, and some are made for pride. Thank God, you showed me the difference."

"Rainger…" Her hands shook in his. She should stop him *now*.

He was wounded. He was bleeding. He should be cared for.

More important, a man who would be king should never humble himself at the moment of his triumph. Not in front of all these people. Grandmamma would be appalled at him—and appalled at Sorcha for not stopping him.

Yet Sorcha couldn't bring herself to do the right thing. She wanted to see Rainger humble—before her. She wanted to hear him beg—for her forgiveness. She wanted to hear him say it again—*I love you.*

Had she imagined it? Would he…would he tell her again?

"For eight years, I lived in darkness. The only light I had was the memory of your face. I remembered the way you pouted when I teased you, the sound of your laughter when I joked. I reviewed every glance from your eyes, the sway of your walk, the way you grew from child to woman."

"You thought of me while you were in prison?"

"Every day." His dark eyes glowed as he told her the truth at last. "So on the day we wed, I swore another stupid vow. I swore I'd never tell you."

"Why?" She wiped her thumb across the smudge on his cheek.

"Because what I feel for you is so strong, I feared you'd *force* me to kneel before you."

Her thumb hovered above his skin. "I would never do that."

"I know." He didn't take his gaze from her. "But I've known women who would."

Julienne. He was speaking of Julienne.

"I am not one of those women." And she did *not* appreciate the comparison.

"I know you aren't. I knew it then, but I...I was afraid." He was pale. Sweat beaded his forehead.

She *had* to stop him before he fainted from loss of blood.

But he must have read her mind, for he squeezed her hands. "Let me. You need this. If something happens to me, you'll be queen and everyone must know where you stand in my regard."

The glowing ember of her hope cooled. "You're doing this to guard my position in case your wound kills you?"

"In part."

"Perhaps you shouldn't worry that your wound will kill you." Her words were cordial. Her tone was not.

He laughed. Not laughed, really. It was more of a painful chortle, and he shook his head. "No, you misunderstand. I would protect you in case of my death, yes. But I could accomplish that easily enough without the effort—the agony—of prostrating myself before you. I'm doing this because…because you need to know. Because just once I need to tell you…I can't live without you. When I discovered you'd been taken, I realized you didn't know the most important thing about me." He glanced around. Slowly he came to his feet. "Can we walk a little?"

"Of course." As he took her arm, curiosity prodded her. He'd said so much in front of so many. What did he wish to keep private?

He led her away from the crowd, walking slowly and leaning on her as if he needed the support—as if he knew he could depend on her to support him. He stopped by the trees and in a low voice, he said, "I need to tell you about what happened in Count duBelle's dungeon."

She didn't know if Rainger would consider the fact that they'd discussed him as a betrayal, but she confessed, "Marlon told me."

"Good. But Marlon didn't tell you the most important part. He didn't know. No one knows except me—and you."

"Me?" Rainger was being cryptic and that was quite unlike him. "What do you mean?"

"For eight years, I lived in dark and the cold and the damp, and the seventh year, I broke. I begged and I pleaded that Count duBelle give me my life and my health and my freedom. Worthless. Useless. Of course." Rainger's mouth curled bitterly. "Marlon despised me, but it was nothing compared to the way I despised myself. For the year after, I hated myself with such virulence I didn't care if I lived or died. I had betrayed my family, my father—you!"

"Not me."

"Only because I'd been so spoiled and ineffectual you had no expectations of me. But in my mind, I had betrayed you. I lay in the darkness and gradually I reached a place beyond fear. When I was taken and beaten the next year, Count duBelle couldn't break me. He tried. He tried to kill me, and when the guards put me back in my cell, I knew he had succeeded. The life oozed from me—from wounds on my back, but from also my spirit and my heart."

Rainger spoke in such a solemn tone, watched her so intently, that the hair rose on the back of her neck.

"When there was no hope that I would live, the guards carried me into the other cell to expire with my friends around me." His voice dropped to a whisper. "In the dark, it was easy to welcome death."

"So you did die." She knew he had. She knew this story.

"I definitely did. I remember everything about it. The air was foul. The indifferent stones closed in around me. No voices disturbed the silence. No hand could bind my wounds or cure my pain." Softly, he asked, "Do you remember, Sorcha?"

Yes. She remembered. She remembered the dream as vividly as the night she'd dreamt it. "The bones of rats were my bed and the long drape of cobwebs my blanket," she murmured.

He took up the tale again. "Somewhere close, water seeped into a pool, and the slow drip which had once driven me mad now meant nothing. My world was sorrow and loneliness. I knew I was dying, and I welcomed the end of desolation, of grief, of anguish. I reached out and touched the skeletal hand of Death—and I slipped beyond."

Sorcha's eyes swam with tears. She could barely stand to hear the story, relive the story with him.

Rainger grasped both of her hands. He looked into her eyes. "I saw a cross. It gleamed like a blue coal. I couldn't resist. I had to touch it. When I did, it burned me. I realized it hung around a woman's neck—and with a gasp, I returned to excruciating, painful life."

Sorcha saw in him the memory they shared. She said, "And the first light of dawn shone in my cell, and the first seabird called its high, sweet call outside my window."

"It *was* you, my darling." He smiled, a slow, sweet, powerful smile. He kissed her fingers. "I knew it was you."

"Yes. It was me." Bringing the cross out from beneath her neckline, she showed it to him.

"I haven't believed in God for years. Why should I honor God with my worship when He treated me so cruelly? But now I have the evidence of God's grace. I have you and I have your love, and all I can do is love you in return." He showed her the mark burned into the palm of his hand. "I don't know if that's enough, but I hope it is."

She put her fingers over his lips. "I don't know if it is, either. But if you love me forever, I think it might be."

As if he couldn't bear not to, he kissed her. "My darling Sorcha, no matter what happens, you have more help than you can imagine. Have you not noticed who stands behind us?"

She wrenched her attention away from Rainger, to the two women who had steadied her during the fight.

Blond. Petite. Curvaceous.

Brunette. A surprising height. Slender.

Both dressed in a modified soldier's gear. They were familiar. So familiar.

"Clarice? Amy?" Sorcha woke from the long dream of loneliness and unspoken fear.

"Sorcha." They spoke together. They rushed at her.

She laughed and she cried as they embraced fervently and spoke in broken sentences, trying to explain ten years in a moment.

Clarice told her news. Amy told hers.

"A boy?" Sorcha said to Amy. "A girl!" She said to Clarice.

Glancing up, she saw Rainger standing with two other men, watching with a gleam of satisfaction.

"Excuse me." She kissed her sisters. "Excuse me."

She returned to Rainger. She took his hand. "Did you bring them here for me?"

"As soon as we got to Beaumontagne, I sent a special courier and invited them. They had to wait until spring, but—"

"You are so good to me! So smart and wonderful! How can I ever repay you?"

She found herself in his arms before she could react. He bent her back and kissed her. No art. No finesse. Just glorious passion and burning excitement.

He swept her along, feeding her heat and love and need.

And she wrapped her hands around his head and answered him, tasting him, relishing him, giving him everything in her soul—because she had to. Because they were one.

Chapter 29

"In my day, babies did not toddle all over the throne room. They were kept in their nursery by their nursemaids, as was proper." Queen Claudia tapped her cane on the marble floor and glared at her great-granddaughter. In her day, the world was not a jumble of anarchists, children knew their places, and the crowning of a king and queen was treated as a ceremony worthy of respect, not a circus where maids ran with hairpins in their mouths, great piles of petticoats littered the throne room, and all three of her granddaughters spent most of their time doubled over with laughter, apparently at her.

Baby Sorcha promptly grinned, showing five perfect white teeth, and toddled in Queen Claudia's direction.

"Get that child before she drools on my silk gown!" she commanded.

Clarice snatched up her baby and in soft baby talk she asked, "Is baby Sorcha going to drool on Grandmamma's silk gown? Is she? Is she?"

"Clarice, she's going to drool on your silk gown, too," Amy observed. "Watch out. There she goes!"

As a long string of spit dangled from the baby's mouth, all three of Queen Claudia's granddaughters laughed in delight. They acted as if the child had done something clever. Queen Claudia didn't understand how she'd managed to raise three such hobbledehoy granddaughters.

But at least they were good breeders. Clarice had this little one, Amy had a boy baby who actually was asleep in a cradle upstairs, and although Sorcha had confessed to nothing, Queen Claudia hadn't lived this long without knowing what that glow meant. Sorcha was three months into the performance of her dynastic duty. Sometime in the winter, she would provide the two kingdoms with an heir.

But first she had to be crowned. The ceremony started in less than two hours, and none of the princesses were ready except for Clarice—who now had drool on her shoulder.

"How much longer will you be?" Queen Claudia asked hopelessly.

"All of us have our hair pinned up, Clarice is dressed, and all I have to do is put on my gown. And Sorcha's behind the screen complaining that her corset is too tight." Amy winked at Queen Claudia in a quite hoydenish way.

Queen Claudia wavered between reprimanding her and calling her over to confirm Sorcha's pregnancy.

Then Clarice put the baby down and once again she toddled toward Queen Claudia.

"Isn't she walking early?" Queen Claudia asked.

"Very early," Clarice confirmed. "But Robert's sister Millicent said he walked early, too."

With freezing formality, Queen Claudia said, "I'm sure whatever precociousness this child has, she received from our side of the family."

The girls laughed again.

"Yes, Grandmamma." Clarice caught baby Sorcha and swung her in a circle.

"At least tell me you're sending the baby to the nursery for the crowning," Grandmamma said.

"Yes, Grandmamma, at least for that." In all seriousness, Clarice said, "We wouldn't want you to get upset."

"Oh—blast that!" Queen Claudia snapped.

Sorcha stepped out from behind the screen. Clarice and Amy stared at her. All three of her granddaughters looked shocked.

"Grandmamma! Are you feeling quite yourself?" Amy sounded genuinely concerned.

Ever since Sorcha had been kidnapped by that ruffian Count duBelle and Queen Claudia had suffered a pain in her chest so severe it sent her to bed for a week, the whole family hovered anxiously, waiting—probably hoping—for her to turn up her toes. Well, it wasn't going to happen. Not until this visit was over. Not until the heir was born. Not until she went to Italy and warmed her old bones.

Pointing a crooked finger at Sorcha, Queen Claudia said, "If she can say *cock*, then I can say *blast*."

The girls looked scandalized for another second, then they broke into laughter.

"Yes, Grandmamma, you can say whatever you like." Clarice looked lovely, a lock of her blond hair curling on her shoulder, her bright amber eyes sparkling with joy, her silk gown a lovely blue and only slightly damp.

"Don't mention anybody's cock today, all right, Sorcha?" As always, Amy had a hint of mischief about her, but marriage and a child had calmed her more than

Queen Claudia had ever hoped. With her black hair and green eyes, she had grown into a striking woman.

"I only do it to tease Rainger." Sorcha lifted her arms to allow her maid to drop her gown over her. When her head peeked out, she added, "Since we got married, he's so stodgy. He'll hardly ever let me sneak down to the—" She broke off and sent a guilty glance toward her grandmother.

Queen Claudia sighed. "Down to the tavern, where you drink heaven knows what kind of wine and sing vulgar songs?"

"Yes. He doesn't want me to do that anymore." Sorcha's gown was white satin, trimmed with gold braid and covered with every decoration her family ever earned. She wore a huge rope of pearls and pearl earrings. With her red hair swirled high on her head, diamond hairpins sparkling in every curl, and her blue eyes calm and clear, she was the epitome of royal dignity.

Which was why it pained Queen Claudia to hear her talk about taverns.

"Men are like old tomcats," Clarice observed. "When they get married, they stop roaming and spend all their time curled up before the fire."

With naughty amusement, Amy said, "Yes, and every once in a while, they look at you as if to say, *Isn't there something we're supposed to do?*"

The girls were laughing again, laughing so hard no one heard the knock at the doors.

With a hand over his eyes, Rainger stuck his head in. "Is everyone dressed? We need to go to the cathedral now."

"You can look. Everyone is dressed. And they're not going to start the ceremony without us," Sorcha said tartly.

"True, but if we're too late getting back, Cook will ruin dinner." Rainger grinned. "I've known you princesses your whole lives, and you love a good dinner."

"He's right, we've got to go." Sorcha clapped her hands and organized the family. "Rainger, you take Grandmamma. Clarice, give the baby a kiss and give her to her nursemaid. Amy, somebody's got to help me with this monstrous train."

Rainger came and helped Queen Claudia to her feet and toward the door. There, against all the rules, he turned to look at the girls. His gaze swept Clarice, Amy, and at last lingered on Sorcha. In a soft tone, he said, "Look, Grandmamma. The Lost Princesses. They're found, they're together, they're happy, and they're wonderful."

Queen Claudia turned, too, and there they were— her granddaughters. They had their arms around each other, their heads together, and they were smiling at each other. Blond, brunette, and redhead, they were a dynasty of which she could be proud.

Rainger squeezed her arm. "You did a good job, old girl. You did a good job."

"Yes," Queen Claudia said with satisfaction. "Yes, I did."

And they would all, by God, live happily ever after— or they'd answer to her.

ABOUT THE AUTHOR

CHRISTINA DODD's novels have been translated into ten languages, have won Romance Writers of America's prestigious Golden Heart and RITA® Awards, and have been called the year's best by *Library Journal*. Dodd is a regular on the *USA Today*, *Publishers Weekly*, and *New York Times* bestseller lists. *The Prince Kidnaps a Bride is* the third book in her classic new series, The Lost Princesses, following her enormously popular novels *Some Enchanted Evening* and *The Barefoot Princess*. Christina loves to hear from fans. Visit her website at *www.christinadodd.com*.

Visit www.AuthorTracker.com for exclusive information on your favorite HarperCollins author.